THEY THOUGHT HE WAS SAFE

ALSO BY THIS AUTHOR

Cowritten with D. D. VanDyke
California Corwin P. I. Mystery Series
The Girl in the Morgue

Stand Alone Suspense Novels
Looking Over Your Shoulder
Lion Within
Pursued by the Past
In the Tick of Time
Loose the Dogs

YOUNG ADULT FICTION:

Medical Kidnap Files:
Mito
EDS
Proxy
Toxo

These and much more at pdworkman.com

THEY THOUGHT HE WAS SAFE

ZACHARY GOLDMAN MYSTERIES

P.D. WORKMAN

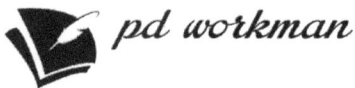

ISBN: 9781989415139

For those who are lost or invisible.

CHAPTER ONE

T HE LITTLE FAMILY GATHERED around the dining room table was about as far from a traditional nuclear family as one could get. Lorne Peterson had been Zachary's foster father for a few weeks when he was young, following the house fire that had been the last straw in the break-up of his biological family. But Zachary and Mr. Peterson had kept in touch, connected in part by a love of photography and his former foster father's darkroom facilities.

Mr. Peterson—Zachary tried, but could rarely bring himself to call him Lorne—had gone through his own family dissolution a few years later, when his wife had become aware of his alternative relationships. They had lost their certification to foster, and separation and divorce followed soon after.

Zachary remembered the initial shock when he had stopped in to visit Mr. Peterson and get some film developed and he realized that Pat, the other man in the apartment, was not a neighbor who had stopped in for coffee, but Mr. Peterson's partner. He had known that Mr. Peterson was seeing someone named Pat, but had mistakenly assumed that Pat was a woman. More than twenty years later, Lorne and Pat were still together, and society had changed enough that they were able to live together openly in the mainstream rather than keeping their relationship quiet.

Pat was between Zachary and Mr. Peterson in age, still muscular and vital, though he was definitely looking more distinguished than he had in his twenties, gray creeping in at his temples and fine lines mapping his face. Mr. Peterson's deeper wrinkles all pointed up, ready to burst into a sunrise when he smiled. He was losing his hair, and the fringe that was left was almost pure white. But even as his body got older, he remained energetic and young at heart.

They had been a constant in Zachary's life for two decades and, despite the fact that Mr. Peterson had only been his foster parent for a few weeks and Pat never had been, they were the closest thing to family that Zachary had. He hadn't kept in touch with any of his other foster siblings or parents, and much of his adolescence had been spent in youth centers and group homes. With his severe ADHD and PTSD, he hadn't been an easy kid to parent.

Tyrrell's face at the table was a new one. In spite of the fact that he was Zachary's biological brother, they had not seen each other from the time that Tyrrell was six until he and Zachary had been reunited on Christmas Eve.

As Christmas Eve was the anniversary of the fire that had destroyed their family more than thirty years previously, it was always a dark time for Zachary. Some years he had almost not made it through the holiday. Being reunited with his brother had been the fulfillment of what he had thought was an impossible dream. He had been sure that he would never see any of his biological siblings again. Even being a private investigator, he had never looked for them, never daring to interfere with what might be happy lives to remind them of the horrible thing he had done in causing that fire.

Tyrrell's facial features were similar enough to Zachary's to recognize a family resemblance, though Zachary's face was still gaunt, not yet filled out following his pre-Christmas depression. Tyrrell's hair was dark like Zachary's, but longer and shaggier. He was clean-shaven. It was his eyes that Zachary found startling. In spite of the hard life that Tyrrell had been through, they were still the shining blue eyes of the six-year-old brother he remembered.

They gathered around the table to exchange stories of Zachary's and Tyrrell's separate lives, comparing notes and getting to know each other again. Zachary needed an environment where he felt safe to share in spite of any flashbacks or surges of emotion brought up by the retellings. A restaurant or bar would just not have worked. Some of their experiences were similar, and others were not. Tyrrell had been younger at the time of the family's dissolution, and therefore less damaged than Zachary, and he had been able to stay with the two younger kids for most of his childhood, so he'd had that constant in his life. Zachary had been alone, bounced from one family to another so quickly that he'd been known to return to the wrong family after school, forgetting where he was supposed to be.

But in spite of the smiles around the table, Zachary knew there was something wrong.

At first, Zachary hadn't been able to put his finger on it. He thought that maybe Mr. Peterson and Pat were just awkward having a new 'son' at the dining room table. They were used to Zachary and his quirks, but Tyrrell was a recent addition and they didn't know enough about his past to know what might trigger him, or about his interests to know what questions to ask to encourage his participation in the conversation.

But it was more than that.

There were a number of looks exchanged between Lorne and Pat that didn't seem to follow the rhythm of Tyrrell's participation in the conversation. Mr. Peterson put his hand over Pat's as they ate, something Zachary had rarely seen him do at the table. Their natural cheer was diminished, as if there were something pulling them away from the conversation to think sad thoughts. Like someone who had recently lost a loved one but was trying to act unaffected.

He watched the two of them more closely, but didn't call them out in front of Tyrrell. Obviously, whatever was going on was something they didn't want to share with Tyrrell. Maybe not with Zachary either.

Tyrrell didn't know Pat and Lorne like Zachary did, and didn't seem to notice anything amiss. He tried to catch Zachary's eye.

"Do you remember that?"

Zachary hadn't realized how distracted he had become from Tyrrell's story. He licked his lips. "Uh… sorry… I missed that."

Tyrrell looked at him for a minute, nonplussed. He shook his head. "About time to top up your Ritalin?"

"Uh… not taking any ADHD meds right now," Zachary admitted. "Sorry."

"I didn't mean…" Tyrrell flushed pink. "I wasn't serious. It was just supposed to be a joke. Because you were distracted."

Zachary flashed a look toward Mr. Peterson and Pat, noting that their hands were again touching, and Mr. Peterson was giving Pat a questioning look as he thought Zachary was occupied by a separate conversation. Zachary swallowed.

"I try to only take them if I really need to focus on something. I don't like to have to take them all the time, and they can interfere with other meds. So I just take them when I really need to."

"I didn't mean you to take it seriously…"

"What were you talking about? That I missed?"

Tyrrell looked like he didn't want to cover the same ground again. Mr. Peterson put down his fork and jumped in.

"It was about your sister Jocelyn. I gather she was sort of a second mother to you guys?"

Zachary nodded, glad to segue to something in the past rather than focusing on the issues he still battled. "Yeah, she was really bossy. I resented it, because… well, who do you think got most of that bossiness? It wasn't the little guys; she was pretty patient with them. But me… she figured I was old enough that I should have figured out how to behave myself. We were supposed to pay attention to her and fly straight, but… I was always going off-script."

Tyrrell chuckled. "Is that what you call it?"

Zachary felt his own face get warm. "I tried, but… I wasn't any better at following her rules than I was anyone else's." He included Mr. Peterson and Pat in his broad shrug. They had either experienced or heard the stories of some of his more disastrous choices.

"Joss was a little bossy," Tyrrell admitted. "But she really helped me to figure out what I was supposed to do. I really wished that we'd been able to stay together when we went into foster care. She would have been able to help me to figure out the rules when I was in a new home. I often heard her little voice in my head, telling me how to behave properly, when I was trying to sort it out."

Zachary often had too many little voices in his head, and they all told him different things. But it wasn't usually until *after* he'd impulsively done something that he actually heard them. The voices of Joss, his parents, his social worker, or some other authority in his life, telling him that once again, he'd done something exceptionally stupid and that there were going to be consequences.

Zachary shrugged and looked down at his plate. He ate a couple of bites, forcing himself to eat despite the bubble of anxiety in his stomach from trying to figure out what Mr. Peterson and Pat were so worried about. As he'd told Tyrrell, he was off of his ADHD meds, so he actually had an appetite, and Pat was a good cook, but the unspoken tension in the room was getting to him.

"Have you had any contact with her?" Mr. Peterson asked with interest.

"A little," Tyrrell said. "Mostly just email or social media, you know. We haven't gotten together face-to-face. I think… she's got her own life and isn't that interested in reconnecting. It can be hard… stirring up old memories. She's got her own family now."

"You guys should have a reunion, get everyone together. It sounds like you know where everyone is now."

Tyrrell nodded slowly. He glanced sideways at Zachary. "I have ways to contact everyone now. But I'm not sure if everyone wants to get together. They're all living their own lives."

"But you grew up with the younger ones. You guys must have a pretty good relationship."

"We were together until I was fourteen or something, so yeah, we have a lot of shared memories, but then we didn't have anything to do with each other because we were in different homes until we were adults. It's a real hodgepodge of relationships."

"I can't imagine what it must be like not to know where your siblings are," Pat contributed. "I just have one sister, and we've always been in contact, even if she didn't particularly approve of my 'lifestyle choices.' It would be hard, not even knowing where they were."

There was a suspicious crack in Pat's voice that set alarm bells ringing for Zachary. Pat didn't usually get emotional about his family. He laughed about their attitudes, mentioned them now and then, but even when his father had died, he hadn't cried about it. Not in front of Zachary, anyway. With the number of times that Zachary had broken down around Pat, Pat certainly shouldn't have felt awkward about shedding a few tears in front of Zachary.

Zachary studied Pat closely, and then Mr. Peterson. Lorne apparently caught the significance of the look. He made an infinitesimal shake of his head, which might have even been unconscious, and Zachary knew it wasn't the time to ask what was going on.

"I guess it's a different experience," Tyrrell agreed, "but I've never known anything else, so for me, that's just the way families are. You spend a few years together, and then you don't have any contact for a decade or more. Now with the internet, you have these opportunities to touch base again and find out what people have been occupying themselves with. We're all adults now, so it isn't like we're looking to live together as a family again."

"I'm glad you reached out to Zachary," Mr. Peterson said. "It's been really good for him to have contact with someone from his family again."

Zachary nodded reflexively.

"I think everyone needs to know that they have somewhere they belong," Mr. Peterson went on. "Not just somewhere like this," he spread his hands to indicate his home, where Zachary was a welcome part of the family any time, "but biologically, too. I've heard that a lot of people who are foster or adopted kids really miss that biological connection, even if they never met their biological family before. There's just a hole where they feel like they don't belong or aren't a part of the family who raised them."

Zachary let his eyes linger on Mr. Peterson for a few moments. It was only natural that, as a foster parent, he would be aware of the needs of foster kids to find some kind of genetic connection. But he didn't want Mr. Peterson to feel like he hadn't been a good enough parent or friend to Zachary.

Tyrrell gave a shrug. "I guess so. I always knew I had biological siblings out there. Even parents, if I wanted to look for them. But I was more interested in building a family of my own. Getting married, having kids. I guess that was my way of having a genetic connection with someone. My own kids."

Zachary felt a pang. He hadn't told Tyrrell his own history with his ex, Bridget, and the issues that she'd had with having children. Zachary had always thought that he would have a family, a house full of kids to remind Zachary of the family that he'd lost. To make up for the pain that he'd caused.

Even though Bridget had said from the start that she didn't want kids, he'd thought that she would change her mind. That biological clock would start ticking, she would see what a great father Zachary would make, and she would decide it was time.

He'd been sadly mistaken and things had not ended well.

Mr. Peterson flashed a look at Zachary, knowing the history. Maybe that too was part of what he had read. How kids with no biological heritage longed for children of their own. Maybe it was an established pathological desire.

CHAPTER TWO

THEY GOT THROUGH THE evening. Zachary found the time went much more slowly than usual as he watched Mr. Peterson and Pat, waiting for a flash of insight into what was going on with them. He was intuitive, skilled at reading body language and facial expression, and he knew Lorne and Pat well, but he couldn't quite put his finger on what was going on.

After saying his goodbyes, he walked out to his car, and waited until Tyrrell got into his and drove away. Then he returned to the house.

Pat opened the door, looking at Zachary with surprise. "Forget something?" he asked, looking behind himself to see if Zachary had left a book or bag.

Zachary shook his head. He hesitated. "I just wanted to see if there was something I could do…"

Pat looked at him for a minute, then stepped back. "Come in."

Mr. Peterson came around the corner. "Oh, Zachary. What's up? I thought you were on your way."

Pat looked at him, communicating something by his manner. Mr. Peterson nodded slowly. "I guess I should know better than to try to get anything past you." He led the way to the living room and they sat down. Mr. Peterson normally liked his easy chair, and Pat was usually back and forth, preparing coffee or checking something in the kitchen, playing the part of the diligent host. But they both sat down together on the couch, holding hands again.

Mr. Peterson looked at Pat. "You want to start?"

Pat blinked, looked down, then nodded. "Sure." He cleared his throat. He looked at Zachary, gaze steady. "A friend of mine is missing."

"Oh." Zachary thought about that. "I'm sorry. How long has he been missing? Have you talked to the police?"

"I talked to the police… they weren't really that interested. They said that they would look into it, but as far as I can see, they haven't done much. They said they would get back to us if they found anything, but…"

"You haven't heard anything back from them," Zachary finished. "They can keep their investigations pretty close to the chest, sometimes. If you're not the next of kin, they don't have any requirement to report back to you. They haven't said anything?"

"They don't think there's any foul play. They think that he just... left town."

Zachary nodded. "Could he have?"

"He didn't," Pat said with certainty. "I know Jose, and he didn't leave town. He would have said something to me if he'd been planning on leaving. Even if it was something unplanned, he would still have called."

"Where do you know him from?"

Pat looked at Mr. Peterson, and then back at Zachary. "We know him from the community. He's gay. Someone we get together with now and then to do something with."

They didn't often talk about their social life, so Zachary didn't know how large their group of gay friends was, or how long they had known this Jose. Zachary had never heard either of them mention him before.

"How long has he been missing?"

Pat swallowed and rubbed his forehead. Mr. Peterson patted his back and filled in the details. "As far as we can tell, it's been a week since anyone has seen him."

"A week." Zachary didn't like that. He could understand the police not being too concerned if it had only been a day or two, but a week should have been raising some red flags. "Have you talked to his work? His family?"

"He doesn't have any family here. He has a wife and kids back in El Salvador, he sends money home to them. Here, he doesn't have anyone... steady. Just friends, casual encounters."

"He's gay but he has a wife and kids in El Salvador?"

Pat shrugged and nodded. "Sometimes it happens that way."

Mr. Peterson had previously been married to a woman and had foster kids, so Zachary supposed he shouldn't have been surprised. People chose to do the socially acceptable thing, and then later decided that they couldn't maintain appearances.

"And work? Does he have a job?"

Pat nodded and took over again. "He did day labor, cash pay, but it was with the same company every day, not going from one job to another. I talked with the foreman and he said that Jose just stopped showing up."

"Was he surprised about that?"

"No... but that doesn't mean that he was right. If you had a worker coming in every day and then they just stopped coming without a word, wouldn't you be concerned?"

"I would," Zachary admitted. "But I don't deal with day laborers. I guess they probably have a pretty heavy turnover. Is he... legal?"

"No. Undocumented."

"So if there was trouble, he might have just disappeared."

"He could… but like I said, he would have at least given us a heads-up that something had happened."

"If he could. But sometimes there isn't any warning, they just get arrested and put into a facility awaiting deportation. You don't know that he would be able to call you. Or that he would. He might have been limited in the number of calls that he could make, or he might have figured there was no point. You couldn't do anything for him, so why bother?"

"I still think he would have told us if he could."

"Did the police check in with ICE? See whether he had been picked up in a sweep?"

"They haven't gotten back to us. I think if they had found his name on a list like that, they would have at least said that he was okay, even if they didn't give us any details."

Zachary nodded. In theory. But sometimes the police dropped the ball and didn't call back, especially if it were just a random friend and not the next of kin. Sometimes they got distracted by other cases or bogged down, and just clearing the case was all they could do, without making a bunch of reports to the friends or family.

"You don't think he went back to El Salvador? What if his wife said she needed him to come back? She or one of the kids was sick. Something that sounded like an emergency."

"He would have let someone know." Pat shook his head. "He didn't live by himself. Most of these illegals don't make enough money to get a place of their own. Especially when they're sending as much home as they can. So he had roommates. He didn't tell them where he was going. He just didn't come home one day."

Zachary found himself pulling out his notepad to start making notes. His brain was grinding through the possibilities. If Jose hadn't gone home, then ICE was still the most likely possibility. Someone had tipped them off and he had been nabbed on his way home from work, at a bar, or even at the grocery store.

But there were other possibilities. He was mugged or had an accident, and was in the hospital somewhere. Maybe under his own name and maybe as a John Doe. Similarly, he could be in the morgue. Going home to El Salvador was less likely. He would probably at least have told his roommates what was happening if he were going back home. There would be no reason not to tell them. He would have had to make arrangements; he wouldn't have just been able to hop on a plane and fly back in a couple of hours. Zachary scratched down a few thoughts. He looked up to see Mr. Peterson and Pat watching him intently.

"Do you have the name of the officer who investigated it? A case number?"

"Yeah. Just a minute." Pat got up and retreated to the bedroom to get the details.

Mr. Peterson gave Zachary a smile. "Thanks for this, Zachary. We've been very worried."

"You should have told me. I could have gotten started on it earlier."

"You have a lot on your plate. One undocumented worker disappears... it's not exactly at the top of the priority list."

"Not for the police. It would have been for me."

Mr. Peterson smiled. "Thank you."

They waited for Pat to return with the information about the policeman. "He and Pat were pretty close?"

"They clicked. Sometimes you just meet someone that everything falls into place with. You start a conversation with them, and it's like you've known them your whole life. You know?"

Mr. Peterson didn't sound jealous, but Zachary couldn't help wondering just how far the friendship went. He had never seen any cracks in the relationship between Mr. Peterson and Pat, but people hid that kind of thing. Zachary hadn't known that Mr. Peterson and his wife were getting divorced until he had shown up at the house one day to be told by Mrs. Peterson that her husband didn't live there anymore. He had seen, before that, that the two of them were not terribly compatible. They had very different personalities and viewpoints. If Mr. Peterson had had his way, Zachary probably would have lived with them longer than he had. Maybe not for years, but a few more weeks. They would have tried for longer to work things out. Mr. Peterson understood Zachary and his issues better. His wife had only been concerned about Zachary's behaviors and how they might affect the other foster children. As a mother, of course that was something that she had to consider.

Pat returned with a piece of paper. He handed it to Zachary. Detective Dougan, a phone number, and a case number.

"Thanks. Tell me the information you can about your friend. His full name, where he worked, where he lived, anyone else in your group I can talk to."

Pat sat back down. He pulled out his phone. "His name is Jose Flores. He worked for A.L. Landscaping." He read off a phone number and address for Zachary. "The roommate that I talked to..." He tapped around on his phone for a minute. "His name was Nando Gonzalez."

"Do you know him?"

"No. I hadn't ever met him before. I hadn't ever been in Jose's apartment. But I knew where it was. We had picked him up before and I knew what the apartment number was. So I just went and knocked on the door..."

Zachary processed this. He tried to envision what had happened, and how Nando might have felt about the broad-chested white man showing up without warning at his door. He would have been nervous. Anxious about being turned over to Immigration. Suspicious of whether Pat were actually a friend of Jose's, or someone playing a part. Nando probably wouldn't have told Pat everything he knew. Even if he knew from Jose that he and Pat were friends, he probably would still have hung back. Illegals had to be wary even of friends. There was no telling what Pat's true motivation might have been.

"Do you mind me looking into it? Going back and talking to him?"

"No, of course. Go ahead. I'd really like to know what happened to him. I'm worried. He wasn't that kind of guy, you know, the kind who would just disappear. I know some people do that. But Jose… he was dedicated to his job. He wanted to make things work in America. He wanted to help his wife and kids come here."

"This roommate that you talked to, he wasn't someone from your community, then?"

"No. We didn't know him."

"The two of them were not a couple?"

"No." Pat gave a smile and shook his head. "I doubt that he knew Jose was gay."

"Why not? Had he not… come out?"

It seemed like an antiquated term in a society where sexual orientation was no longer supposed to be taboo and gay marriage was legal. Was there still a reason for men and women to be in the closet and hide their orientation from their families and friends?

"It's different for men of color," Pat said slowly. "There is a belief that the word 'gay' only applies to white men. That it's not just sexual orientation, but race and class as well. The type of gay men that you see on prime-time TV. White, limp-wristed, lisping, middle-to-upper-class, sweater-wearing men. And people like Jose… aren't that. So they tend not to even identify as gay."

"Really?" It had never occurred to Zachary that the term meant anything other than a same-sex attraction. "I… I had no idea."

"How would you?" Mr. Peterson gave a smile. "Unless you spend a lot of time in those circles, you don't really hear what people think or what their prejudices are."

"So how would he identify himself?" Zachary asked curiously. "If he wouldn't say that he is gay, because only white guys are gay, then he would say that he is…?"

"MSM is a term they have borrowed from medical literature. During the initial years of the AIDS epidemic, medical practitioners found that a lot of non-whites said that they were not gay, even though they were having same-sex relations. So they had to change their language in order to properly identify the risk factors. Not 'are you gay,' but 'have you had sex with men?' MSM was the medical shorthand. Or WSW for the women."

Zachary wrote MSM down so he wouldn't forget it when he started to talk to people that Jose knew who might be part of the gay—MSM—community. Language was a powerful thing, and he didn't want to risk offending someone who might have information to share. Say the wrong thing, and he might never hear anything more from a witness.

Pat handed Zachary a photo. A group of men around a table. Pat and Lorne and others Zachary didn't recognize. Pat pointed to the Hispanic man beside him.

"That's Jose."

He was well-dressed, not what Zachary would have expected for an illegal worker. He had on evening wear, like the other men, a suit or dinner jacket and blue tie. He had a wide, pleasant smile, and looked comfortable, part of the group. Zachary raised an eyebrow at Pat, and when he nodded, kept the photo.

"Have you talked to his wife?"

"I don't know how to reach her. We never talked about it. I don't know her name or where in El Salvador she lives."

"Did *she* know that he was... MSM?"

"I doubt it. A lot of men like him keep it pretty quiet. Other than the people that they hook up with, they don't tell anyone. They live two lives, and keep them very separate."

"How did you meet?"

Pat and Mr. Peterson looked at each other. Not in a way that suggested they had something to hide, but just that they had to think about it and might need a memory jogger.

It was Mr. Peterson who answered first. "I think... the first time we met up was at a club downtown. There was a very popular lounge singer who was doing a night there... it was very busy, a lot of people wanted to see him. We went well ahead of time to get a table. The place was so packed, they were asking patrons to share tables. Jose ended up at our table, and we struck up a conversation."

"That's right," Pat's face cleared. "I'd forgotten all about that. We've done so many other things together. It was just one of those cases where everything fits together, and it was such a comfortable conversation... by the end of the night, it was like we had always been friends."

"And you've spent a lot of time together since then? How long has that been?"

"About... four months... five?"

"And the three of you together, or just Jose and you?"

Pat raised his eyebrows. "I'm devoted to Lorne, Zachary. This was not a hook-up."

"So the three of you?"

"Yes, the three of us. Usually other people as well. A group of guys getting together at a bar or club, or even a museum or gallery. Christmas shopping together. Just... things that friends do together."

Zachary nodded, getting a more clear picture of the relationship. "Can I talk to one or two of your friends? Or would that be intrusive?"

There were several seconds of hesitation, the silence drawing out.

"I'll have to talk to them first," Pat said eventually. "I'll get you names and numbers once I've had a chance to."

"Okay. Did the police talk to anyone else?"

"I don't know who they talked to. They didn't ask for the names of any other friends. Just for his boss at A.L. I think that's where the investigation stopped."

CHAPTER THREE

ORNE AND PAT'S HOUSE was a couple of hours north of Zachary's, and he was later getting back to his apartment than he had expected, but he was calm and hyperfocused on the investigation during his drive back. He could barely even remember his time on the road.

He was glad he had gone back in to find out what was wrong. If he hadn't, his own anxiety would have been through the roof by the time he got home, and he probably would not have slept that night. Going back had been the right choice. Zachary hadn't wanted to kick Tyrrell out to talk to Lorne and Pat privately, but he had needed to find out what was bothering them. It had been too obvious that something was wrong.

It was too late to start making phone calls on the case, especially not to the police officer. Zachary wouldn't even be able to get patched through. They would just tell him to call back in the morning.

But he could start by running Jose's name through the databases he had access to. He didn't expect to find much. Jose would not show up as a property owner or having a driver's license. He wouldn't have any arrest records. No credit history. But something still might pop up somewhere, on a news page, social network, or some other site. He should have asked Pat about an email address as well, which might have given Zachary access to Jose's email or social accounts if some of his data had been breached in the past.

There were a couple of social media accounts that might have been Jose's, but the avatars were cartoons rather than his face, so Zachary couldn't match them to the photo that Pat had given him, and their activity was private rather than public, so if he was to get into them, he'd have to have a password, or the police would have to deal with the providers to get access to them.

Eventually, his eyes were getting too gritty to look at the computer screen any longer, and he knew he needed to get to bed. He still felt wired, so he just took one sleeping pill and nothing else with a couple swallows of flat Coke from the fridge, and headed to bed. He would really get into gear in the morning.

He slept restlessly, but that was normal. If he got a few hours of sleep, he was doing well, especially with a new investigation buzzing in his brain. So when light started to make its way through his window signaling the impending dawn, he got up. He shuffled into the kitchen to put on some coffee, took his morning meds, and woke up his computer again. At least the computer didn't require a certain number of hours of rest. It was too early to call Detective Dougan, so Zachary checked his email. He hadn't checked it the night before.

There was a short email from Tyrrell saying that he had enjoyed having supper with Zachary and his extended family, and one from Mr. Peterson thanking Zachary for looking into Jose's case for them. Just casual, polite emails, but Zachary savored them, appreciating the touchstones. After all of the horrible email he'd gotten from Devon Masters before Christmas, it was a huge relief to be able to open his email inbox without feeling like he was facing the firing squad. Those casual little polite emails were the best remedy in the world. So he fired one back to each of the men and sipped his coffee. He took a glance at the morning news. Nothing much happening that would impact him.

He went back to his email and sent one to Kenzie as well. Nothing big or important, just touching base with her too. She had been a rock during his pre-Christmas depression, and now that things were back to normal, he wanted to pay her back in some way. There wasn't any big, life-changing thing he could do for her or give her, so for the time being, he would have to do the little things, and hope that they added up to something meaningful to her.

When she had first started seeing him, she'd had no idea what kind of a mess she was getting herself into. She'd been looking for a casual date, a fun time, and instead had ended up with him. She deserved a prize for not dumping him after the first confrontation with Bridget. Maybe part of that had just been the entertainment value Bridget provided, since Kenzie had never really considered her a rival, but had been amused that Bridget claimed to hate Zachary when, as far as Kenzie was concerned, Bridget was still attracted to him.

Zachary could have told Kenzie that wasn't the case—and had, in fact told her so several times—but Kenzie stubbornly refused to believe it. She said it was up to Zachary to boot Bridget out of his life, which wasn't something that he could do. It wasn't exactly polite to admit to his date that he still had feelings for his ex, but Zachary couldn't help that. He and Bridget had been apart as long as they had been together, but he still couldn't let go of the life that he had thought they would have together.

His current therapist had traced his inability to let go of the relationship back to Zachary's love for his mother and the fact she had abandoned him as a child, which was a pretty obvious parallel for anyone to draw, but being able to see the similarities between the two relationships and being able to get over his pining for Bridget were two different things. Until he could, Zachary was determined to 'fake it until he could make it,' to show Kenzie the attention she deserved and pretend that Bridget was out of his life and didn't mean anything to him.

Kenzie wouldn't be checking her email for a couple more hours, so he started to work his way through the stack of paperwork on his desk. If anyone had told him how much paperwork there would be as a private detective, he might not have set his sights on becoming one. He had never done well in school, his ADHD causing too many problems in any classroom setting. At least at home, he didn't have to deal with the distractions of thirty other people coughing and sniffling and shifting around in their seats. He worked through some routine skip traces, added paragraphs to reporting letters, and drew up invoices for cases that he had closed and needed to collect on. As much as he hated accounting, he wasn't going to get paid without them.

The hour hand finally crept around to eight—or since he didn't actually have an analog clock, the display on his phone and computer screen read eight—and he figured it was worth seeing if he could get Officer Thurlow Dougan. He dialed the number that Pat had given him and listened to the ringing, fully expecting that he would end up in Dougan's voicemail and have to explain what he wanted to the machine. He was scripting it in his head when the line was picked up, not by voicemail, but by a real person.

"Dougan."

"Oh, Detective Dougan. You don't know me," Zachary fumbled a little. He hated dealing with people by phone, where he couldn't read their facial expressions and body language. "I've been talking to Pat Parker about Jose Flores, the man that he reported missing...?"

"Right," Dougan said, his voice taking on an edge. Too early in the morning and he apparently didn't have his morning coffee on board yet. "And who are you?"

"Pat is my step-father," Zachary said, fudging the relationship a bit, but he knew Pat wouldn't mind. In fact, he would have been delighted. "And I'm a private investigator."

"I see."

"I know you're busy and you have plenty of other cases that demand your time and attention. I wondered if I could get a report from you on anything you were able to find, and then I'll do a little follow-up investigation, see if I can put Pat's worries to rest."

"I don't suppose Mr. Parker explained to you that Jose Flores is an illegal immigrant."

"Yes, he did. And I know that makes him a lot harder to trace through the usual channels."

"It makes him damn near impossible to trace. These guys don't leave a trail. Like I told your father when he made the report, this guy probably just got worried about an Immigration investigation and decided to move on to another location. Or he decided to go back home. It happens all the time. With undocumenteds, there's really nothing we can do."

"Yeah," Zachary agreed, trying to sound as sympathetic as possible, "and you've got plenty else on your desk to worry about."

"Darn right I do." Dougan sounded a little mollified. A few more minutes, and Zachary would have him volunteering everything he knew. The man didn't want to have to investigate it any further and he didn't want to waste his time in reporting to Pat that he hadn't been able to find anything. He just wanted it off his desk.

"I'm wondering what you were able to cover. Did you talk to his boss?"

"Sure. First place I went. As usual, the guy wouldn't admit that Jose even worked there. Of course he doesn't hire illegals. Everything he does is above board. But a little pressure and he did admit that he knew Jose, but hadn't seen him since your friend had. He just stopped showing up one day. Nothing unusual for these guys. They come and they go, and they don't say what they're doing. They just disappear. They're ghosts."

"Yeah. Pat said that he was sure that if Jose went back to El Salvador or to a different job, he would have said something about it, and he never did…"

"Pat doesn't deal with these guys on a daily basis. That's just not the way it works. It's pounded into these guys. *Don't tell anyone where you are or where you're going. It's too dangerous. ICE will get you. Don't leave a trail.* So even though Pat may think that it's a suspicious disappearance, that is not my opinion."

"Got it. And how about the roommate?"

"Roommates," Dougan corrected. "You never get just two of these guys in one place. You get whole families living in one room. With single guys, you get half a dozen or more in one apartment. They sleep in bunk beds, on couches, on the floor. Anywhere there's room."

"Uh-huh. Did you find anyone over there who was willing to talk to you?"

"Just got the same line everywhere. *Jose doesn't live here anymore. Maybe Jose went home. Maybe Jose found a better job.* Nobody knows anything. But they're not worried about it, either."

Zachary nodded to himself. It was going to take more digging to get anything more out of the roommates or friends. More time and effort than a police officer had to pursue such things.

"Did you find anything at all that indicated that he had planned to leave? Or anything that didn't jive with what the roommates were saying?"

"No. It was all pretty much what I expected. Nothing suspicious."

"Any enemies? Jealous—uh—lovers? Any risky behaviors?"

"No. No hint of any foul play. I gather from your, uh, step-father, that they were under the impression he was gay, but I didn't find any hint of that."

It didn't surprise Zachary that Jose had kept that part of his life a secret. It sounded like it was less acceptable in his circles than it was for Lorne and Pat. And they hadn't been comfortable with being openly gay for a lot of years.

24

"I'll take a closer look at that," he told Dougan. "Is there anything else that you would look at more carefully if you had the time to spend on the case?"

Dougan didn't answer immediately. Zachary wondered if he had pushed too fast. He didn't think he'd have Dougan's attention for long, so he didn't want to waste any time. He hadn't implied that the police weren't putting enough effort into the case, just that they didn't have unlimited time.

"I'd take a harder look at the roommates," Dougan said finally. "They're all undocumented, of course, so there's no way to check criminal records or follow their histories without getting federal agencies involved… but when you are trying to encourage them to talk, getting the feds involved is counterproductive."

"Yeah. That makes sense. Was there any roommate in particular that gave you a bad vibe? The one that Pat mentioned was Nando González."

"He seemed okay. But some of the others… I honestly couldn't even tell who was living there and who was just visiting. It seems like a free-for-all. If it was me, I wouldn't want to be living there with people coming and going in my room all the time. I wouldn't feel like I had any security."

"Yeah." Zachary thought about some of the foster homes he had been in, where there had been no sense of personal space or ownership, and if there was anything he didn't want anyone else to get their hands on, he had to keep it on his person. Like his camera. Places like that, the neck strap didn't leave his neck, not even while he was sleeping. "I wouldn't like that either." He let silence draw out for a few seconds. "Was there anything else that bothered you about the case? Anything that felt discordant?"

"We don't usually get missing persons reports for illegals. So that was a bit different. Not bad or wrong, just unusual. When we've got a case involving illegals, it's usually a body in the morgue, smuggling, human trafficking… we're not looking for immigrants that have gone missing."

Zachary jotted a few quick notes. "Great. Thanks for your time, Detective Dougan. I'll let you know if I run into anything you would want to act on. Feel free to call me if anything comes to mind later that didn't seem right or that you couldn't pursue at the time. Did I give you my number?"

He hadn't, but it was a way for Dougan to feel like he was still in control of the flow of communications. As if Zachary were acting for him, taking just one thing off of his desk that he didn't have to worry about anymore.

Dougan grunted that he hadn't, so Zachary gave it to him, and repeated his name, first and last. "And can I call you if I have any other questions? I promise I won't become a pest. But just in case something comes up that I need to get your read on."

"Yes, fine. I suppose. But if you do start harassing me, I'm going to block your number."

"Fair enough," Zachary agreed. Probably he wouldn't need Dougan for anything else, but he wanted to leave the lines of communication open and to

25

leave a good impression with Dougan in case Zachary ever had to deal with his department again. He knew how much cops hated investigators who interfered with their cases. He had both friends and enemies in his own local precinct. He couldn't always avoid stepping on toes, but he did the best he could to keep relations friendly.

"Thanks for all of your help, Detective Dougan. I appreciate you taking the time."

CHAPTER FOUR

MR. PETERSON AND PAT had never talked very much about their social life or the gay community in Vermont. Zachary had always assumed that they lived a fairly reclusive life, mostly doing things with each other. He didn't get invited to large dinner parties, and things like Christmas were always quiet, private affairs. Not that Zachary had ever been there for Christmas, other than the most recent one. He'd always turned down the invitations before. It wasn't because he didn't appreciate them, but Christmas was just such a difficult time of year for him, he could never bring himself to make plans ahead of time, and once Christmas Day arrived, he just wanted to recover his equilibrium.

But Pat and Loren obviously had a social life. They didn't just stay at home reading, cooking, and gardening. They went places, saw shows, and went out shopping with friends.

Zachary didn't imagine there was a big gay community in Vermont, though there were an increasing number of couples moving into the state following marriage equalization. Zachary fired up his browser and after anonymizing his IP address, started to do some research.

It occurred to him that if there were any foul play involved, even though the cops didn't think there was, there might be some hint of it in the community. Other people might have been targeted but never reported. There might be more information available if a more well-known gay white man had been targeted than there would be with an unknown, dark-skinned illegal. Zachary started with some general searches to see where the various gay bars, lounges, and other gathering places were in the nearby towns. There was a good amount that he turned up with just regular web searches. He could have someone else do some deep web exploration for him later on to see what was hidden in webpages that weren't cataloged by Google.

After making note of some locations, events, and festivals that were going on or had taken place recently, he started to dig deeper. Looking for signs of gay men or women who had disappeared, been assaulted, or murdered. If someone had targeted Jose, he was probably not the first person. More than likely, if there were a kidnapper or murderer out there, he had worked his way up gradually from threats and assaults, through other attempts and violent acts, until he had success on a higher level.

There were bulletin boards, many of them requiring a new account to get access. Zachary created a new email address and used it to apply for memberships. Most of them were automated and he was allowed immediate access. Not really secure if the participants really wanted any kind of shield between themselves and the general public. A couple of the boards indicated that his membership was pending, and he wondered whether there would actually be someone checking the profile out to see if he were a real person, or whether all the moderator would do was look at his name and email address and click 'approve.'

He started digging into the forums, looking for any sign of trouble. And it didn't take long.

Within half an hour, he'd amassed enough information to occupy a special task force. He wasn't sure how he was going to sift through all of it to find anything useful. There were specifics given about people who had caused disturbances at events, people who ordered gay prostitutes just to beat them up, neo-Nazis who had threatened violence and, in some cases, had followed through. It wasn't going to be a matter of trying to find someone who had committed crimes against the gay community, but sifting through all of the potential suspects to find someone who might be connected with Jose. He wasn't sure how he was going to do that.

It was late enough that Zachary knew Kenzie would be at the morgue, sorting through the email that had collected over the weekend, having downed at least one cup of coffee. She might be too bogged down to talk on the phone, especially if they'd had a number of bodies come in over the weekend, but he could leave a message and she could get back to him when she felt like it.

He dialed her number on the phone without looking it up or relying on a saved speed dial number. It rang a few times, but then was picked up.

"Zachary. Hey."

"Hi. How crazy is it over there today?"

"The bodies are practically walking themselves in today. I thought we were past the busy season once Christmas was over and done, but apparently some people managed to stick it out through Christmas, but couldn't stand the cold, dark months after that."

Zachary sighed. He could sympathize with her new clients. Christmas and the long, cold nights of January and February were daunting. Even those who were mentally healthy complained about how cold it was and how they were depressed by the snow and the cold.

"But, you don't want to hear about that," Kenzie said cheerfully, realizing that it wasn't the best approach to take with someone who regularly had problems making it through the cold, dark months. "I'm at your service. What's up?"

"Maybe I just called to talk."

"You wouldn't just call me just to talk on a Monday morning. You know it's a busy time, and I'm sure you have weekend emails and other jobs to catch up on as well. If you were going to call me just to visit, you'd wait until the end of the day."

"I suppose."

"So, what is it? You got a new case? Zachary Goldman is out to get justice?"

"Yes to a new case… though I don't know whether it will go anywhere or if there was any injustice done. For now, just a missing person."

"Okay. And what do you need me for?"

"You've taken some psychology courses, right?"

"Sure. I'm not as up with it as my forensics, but I can help with some basic questions."

"Okay, well, this one is about how to tell the difference between someone who's just blowing hot air and someone who really intends violence. Or has committed violence. How can I sort through possible threats to find the people who are really dangerous?"

"Yikes. You don't think that's a little deep for a Monday morning? I'm sure there are a lot of people who would like to know the same thing. But the fact is, you can't really tell. If you know enough about the person you might be able to construct a profile and have an idea of who is dangerous and who is not, but you couldn't tell for sure. Those TV shows you see where they build detailed profiles and predict who is committing a string of serial murders, that's fiction. There's no way to construct something so specific. People are going to do what they're going to do, and some of them are very good at masking what they feel. Or the fact that they don't feel."

Zachary thought back to the bullies and psychopaths that he had encountered in foster care or in school. Or even in the police force. Some of them were very good at looking innocent, even vulnerable. Some of the worst bullies hid behind their masks of age, femininity, or friendliness. They made you think that there was nothing to worry about, and then they brought down the hammer.

Someone like Mrs. Phipps at one of the group home he had been in would have the social worker eating out of her hand, thinking she was the sweetest little old lady anywhere, but as soon as the social worker was out of the house, would turn around and whale on Zachary with her cane for some infraction. Danger could lurk behind just about anyone's innocent-looking eyes.

"Can you think of some warning signs you might see? In, say, a serial killer or someone who had committed violence repeatedly, but managed to keep it under the radar?"

Kenzie made a clicking noise with her tongue. "I'm going to have to think about that one. Psychological profiling can give you some ideas. A serial killer is most likely to be a man, probably comes across as charming and self-effacing, maybe still lives with his mother or helps to take care of someone else. Sometimes it's someone who has a connection with crime, like a dispatcher or firefighter. Probably not a cop, but someone who would like to be, that sees things in black and white and sees themselves as the only one who can fix society's ills. As far as age goes, I can't help you there. Some of them start out very young. They've probably committed some kind of violence by their teenage years, if not actually killed someone, and either served time or got away with it."

"So, someone wouldn't just start at thirty or forty."

"Not as likely. They might not get caught until then, but chances are they started much earlier."

"And they tend to like a certain type, right? Like all of the victims are girls with long blond hair…"

"Maybe. But not necessarily. You'll usually see them sticking to one particular gender, maybe age range, but physical type is not as important as they make it out to be on television."

"Okay. I'm not sure how I'm going to get through all of this information, then. If you had to sort through a bunch of unrelated data to figure out who was a serial killer, how would you do it?"

Kenzie considered. He could hear her tapping away while she filled out forms. "Well… to tell the truth, I probably wouldn't use psychology at all. Because you're not going to be getting interviews and psychologist's report for each of the suspects, are you? Even if you were, I'm not sure it would help. What I would do is… I would try to match up their schedules with the victims'. Who doesn't have a good alibi? Whose long-haul trucking route or time off of work matches up with the distribution of the victims? You'll probably have a lot easier time narrowing it down that way than by a psychological profile. You're not going to be able to tell who is hiding behind a mask. You need to look for the physical evidence."

CHAPTER FIVE

I T WOULD TAKE A couple of hours to drive to Jose's residence. Zachary eventually bit the bullet and just headed out. He hadn't gotten far with the list of suspects from the discussion boards, but he had everything saved to the cloud so he could look it up on his computer, tablet, or phone when he needed to. If he happened to run across any of the accused bullies in Jose's apartment or at his work, he would at least have somewhere to start.

As it was, he didn't know where any of those names were going to lead or if any of them were going to be helpful. Other than to establish that there was still a lot of bullying and violence against the gay community, in spite of how it was supposed to be better for them now. He felt bad that there was still so much prejudice against gays. He remembered how careful he had been when he'd first met Pat, afraid of hurting his feelings—or worse, Mr. Peterson's—with the wrong reaction or by saying something insensitive. They were two of the nicest, most stable people that he knew, and he could never understand how people could be so prejudiced. Maybe it was because Zachary had grown up in so many different homes, meeting people of many different races and persuasions. He'd learned that everybody was just an individual, and to judge them by the way that they behaved and treated others rather than by any preconceived notion.

The address that Pat had given him was not in a nice area, which wasn't a surprise. Where else could the illegals afford the rent? It wasn't going to be a fancy neighborhood. Zachary drove around the block a couple of times getting the lay of the land before choosing where to park, a little distance away from the apartment, where it wasn't quite so sketchy looking. Then he walked back to the apartment, eyes peeled for any gang activity or other hazards. Eventually, he stepped into the building.

It was dim inside and he stood there blinking for a few minutes before his eyes adjusted to the lighting enough to go on. He didn't want to be walking in blind. The apartment was on the third floor, and there was no evidence of an elevator, so he climbed the two flights of stairs and looked at the numbers on the doors. Most of the apartments didn't have any numbers at all, so he counted them off and hoped he picked the right one. If he didn't, he supposed the resident would point him in the right direction. What were they going to do, beat him up because he knocked on the wrong door?

He knocked a couple of times before the door was answered. It was a short man with black hair and dark skin, Zachary guessed he could be Mexican or El Salvadoran or any one of a number of different nationalities. Zachary smiled and didn't make any movements that might be taken as aggressive.

"Hey," he said. "Is this Jose's place?"

The man looked at him suspiciously, then shook his head. "Jose doesn't live here anymore."

"So this is the right place. I wonder if I could come in and talk to you and any of the others who are around for just a few minutes. I'm trying to find out where he went."

The man shook his head and started to close the door. Zachary quickly stuck his foot in the crack to keep it from closing all the way. "I'm just trying to find out what happened to him. Once I know he's okay, that's it. I just want to make sure nothing happened to him."

"Nothing happen. He just go"

"I don't think that's true."

The man looked at him, brows drawing down. "Why?"

"Because he didn't tell anyone where he was going. If he was going to go back to El Salvador or off to another job, he would have told his friends."

"No. He not tell anyone. He just go."

"I'll just be a minute. Let me come in and have a look around, then I'll go and I won't bother you again. Are you Nando?"

"No."

"Is Nando here?"

The man looked over his shoulder. "Nando is out."

"When is he getting back?"

"Don't know."

"You must know something. Is he at work? Or did he go out shopping or to eat?"

"He just out. You go. You call him later."

"I need to talk to him. I'll just wait here." Zachary stubbornly didn't pull his foot out of the doorway. What were they going to do? Call the police on him? They wouldn't want anything to do with the cops. They wouldn't want to draw attention to themselves.

The man stood there, dithering about what to do, his eyes going up and down the hallway as if worried that someone was going to happen by. Finally, shaking his head in frustration, he opened the door and allowed Zachary to step in.

"Thank you," Zachary said politely. He looked around the apartment.

Detective Dougan had warned him that it would be crowded. He hadn't been kidding. There was no living room furniture in the room Zachary walked into, just cots and mattresses with barely enough room to walk between them. Zachary tried not to give away his shock at the conditions. The place smelled like onions cooked on a hot plate, mixed with stale instant coffee and body odor. Even though it looked like they were careful not to leave garbage around the apartment, Zachary could see cockroaches creeping along the floorboards under the cots. Anyone who had a mattress right on the floor was taking the risk of having them crawl right across him. Zachary gave a little shudder. But he pasted a smile on his face and forged ahead.

"Thanks for letting me in," he said, as if it had been the man's choice and he hadn't just been forced into it. "So, where was Jose's bed?"

There were other men there, all more or less the same racial profile and body shape. All men who spent the day working hard, who slept and ate little. They watched him with suspicion that Zachary pretended not to notice.

The man looked at him, rolling his eyes and shaking his head. "Jose not here anymore."

"I know that. Which bed was his? Was he in here or one of the bedrooms?"

"Who are you?" demanded one of the other men, older than the first, his face rounder as if he hadn't missed quite as many meals.

"My name is Zachary Goldman," Zachary said, offering his hand. "Are you Nando?"

The man nodded. He didn't take Zachary's hand. "And who is Zachary Goldman?"

"I'm a friend of Pat Parker's. Pat and Jose were friends, and Pat's been worried about what happened to him, so I came by to see if I could find anything out."

"Pat," Nando repeated.

"Yes, did you ever meet Pat?"

"No, I know Jose talked about a Pat." Nando showed rotten teeth with a grimace that might have been an attempt at a smile. "Pat and Lauren, a couple of girls that he went out with sometimes." He gave Zachary a wink. "I always thought he was doing pretty well to have two girls who would go out with him at the same time."

Zachary didn't correct his misapprehension. Jose may have told him that he was going out with girls because he hadn't been comfortable coming out about his status. If that was the case, it wouldn't do Zachary any good to tell Nando that he'd been lied to. That would just make him resentful and he wouldn't want to talk to Zachary or disclose anything else that he'd been told that might be a lie.

"Pat is worried about Jose," Zachary repeated. "Jose didn't say where he was going, he just disappeared without telling anyone. Pat wants to make sure that he's not hurt."

Nando shrugged his shoulders. "Jose goes where he goes. I don't know where he went. Maybe he went home."

"He wouldn't do that, would he? He needed to earn money here to send home to them. He wanted to take care of his family and maybe find a way for them to join him here someday, right?"

Nando pursed his lips. He folded his arms in front of his chest. "You don't know Jose."

"No, I don't. Tell me about him. Were you surprised when he left? Were you surprised that he didn't tell you where he was going?"

"No. People come, people go. Especially around here. Nobody stays forever."

"So you just came home from work one day, and all of his stuff was gone...?"

Something changed in Nando's eyes. He looked around the room as if he might have said something wrong, even though he hadn't yet answered.

"He did take his stuff with him, didn't he?" Zachary prompted.

"Who are you? Are you the one who sent that policeman around? We told the policeman; he took all of his stuff with him. Cleared everything out. There wasn't anything of his left behind here."

"Oh." Zachary considered that. He supposed that a place like that was probably similar to a foster home. Whatever you didn't take with you when you left, everybody else took at the first opportunity. Zachary had been taken out of the Peterson's home while he was at school. His social worker had packed his bag for him, but she hadn't known to pack his camera. She hadn't packed his meds either, but Zachary hadn't been concerned about those. He had only been worried about his precious camera. Mr. Peterson had kept it safe for him until he was able to go back and get it. At any other foster home, that wouldn't have happened. Whoever wanted the camera would have just taken it. "So what did he leave behind? Any personal papers?"

Nando looked around the room, meeting the eyes of others of the roommates, all of them trying to communicate by facial expression and body language as to what he should say or do.

"I don't care if you're using his things," Zachary reassured them. "I'm not going to take away blankets or clothes or anything. I'm just wondering whether there was anything personal. Anything that you were surprised he'd left behind?"

Nando scratched stubble on his jaw. "He didn't leave anything."

"What? Money? A journal?"

"He wouldn't leave money!" One of the other men barked with laughter. "Nobody leaves money here. If you have money, you keep it with you. You wouldn't leave it somewhere anybody else could find it."

"You don't have lockers or drawers or anywhere secure where you can store your own things?"

"Some people have a box," Nando said. "But you don't leave anything valuable here. If Immigration come one day… if you can't come back because something happened. Anything important, you take it with you."

"So, what did Jose leave?"

"He leave nothing," Nando insisted again. But every time he insisted, Zachary was more convinced that he was lying. Jose had left something behind.

Zachary took a slow look around the room. Then he headed toward the back hallway where the bedrooms were. Alarm showed in Nando's face and several of the others'. Zachary kept going. As long as they weren't physically stopping him, he was going to have a look around and find out what he could.

There were two bedrooms, and they looked pretty much the same as the front room, with cots and mattresses taking up the majority of the space. There were a few boxes, as Nando had said. Little cardboard boxes and a few metal boxes like a business would use for petty cash. There were no dressers and no clothes hanging in the closets. Extra clothes were neatly folded on each of the beds. Maybe to be used as pillows during the night.

There were no mattresses that were obviously unoccupied. Zachary looked at each bed carefully, analyzing whether there was anything out of place.

"You can't be in here," Nando said more urgently from Zachary's elbow.

Zachary keyed in on his tone. "I won't be long. Which bed was Jose's when he was here?"

"You can't be in here."

"Is this where Jose was?"

"He is gone."

Zachary took a slow walk around the room, watching Nando's face for some change in expression. Like a game of hot and cold. Nando was trying not to tell him anything about where Jose's bed had been, but he got more agitated as Zachary got close to it. Zachary bent down over one of the cots.

"This one?"

"No, you can't touch other people's things. It's time for you to leave."

Zachary picked up the clothes and shook each piece of clothing out, one at a time. Nothing hiding there. No cash in the spare socks. Nothing left in the pockets of the owner's pants. Zachary folded them again and put them down. He pulled back the blanket over the cot. Again, there didn't seem to be anything hidden there. There was a thin mattress over the top surface of the cot, and Zachary peeled it back to have a look underneath. There wasn't anything hidden under the mattress, but he could see a metal box underneath the cot. He got down on his knees to retrieve it and tried not to handle it any more than he had to, touching his fingertips to the corners in case there were other fingerprints that should be collected, such as Jose's or those of someone else who lived in the little apartment. Maybe someone who had something to do with Jose's disappearance.

It didn't have a lock, but it had a latch. Zachary flipped it up and opened the hinged lid. There were a few pictures, a little notepad, a piece of fabric that might have been a handkerchief. Zachary picked up the photos by the edges and studied them. A couple of young children, a woman in a flowered dress, smiling tiredly at the camera.

"Is this Jose's family?" Zachary asked.

Nando stared at him sullenly.

"That's his family," said another voice. Zachary turned to see a younger man in the doorway. He was maybe eighteen, no older than that. He had an easy smile and a friendly manner. "How did you know Jose?"

CHAPTER SIX

HOW DID I KNOW him?"
A look of realization crossed over the young man's face, but then was quickly gone. "My English is bad," he said humbly. "How *do* you know him?"

"I'm a private investigator," Zachary said, "looking into his disappearance."

The younger man looked at Nando and glanced around the room. "A private investigator?" the boy repeated with interest. "Like on TV?"

"Yes, like on TV," Zachary agreed. "And I'm going to find out what happened to him. What can you tell me about the day he disappeared?"

Nando shook his head at the boy, warning him.

"Why don't we go out somewhere?" Zachary suggested. "We can go talk somewhere more private. I'll take this," he indicated the box to Nando, "and keep it safe. Then you won't have to worry about it anymore."

The boy looked at Zachary and Nando uncertainly. He shrugged. "You want to buy me pizza?"

Zachary couldn't help laughing. "Of course, I'd be happy to buy you pizza."

He handled the box carefully, trying not to destroy any evidence. It had a handle on the top that he unfolded and hung on to with two fingers in an effort not to get more fingerprints on it. He and the boy walked back through the apartment and out the door. Nando didn't follow or make any threats. Zachary breathed a sigh of relief when he was out of the oppressive atmosphere of the apartment. While no threats had been made, they had not wanted him there. If they had decided to gang up on him, he wouldn't have been able to protect himself from all of them. As the apartment door shut behind them, he turned to the younger man.

"I'm Zachary."

"Philippe. Nice to meet you."

"Thank you for letting me know about Jose's box. I'm sure he would have wanted it to be taken care of."

Philippe looked sideways at him and didn't comment.

"How long has it been since you have seen Jose?"

"A week. Maybe a little more. Hard to remember, I don't keep track of him."

"No, of course not. You have a job and he has his and the two of you don't have a lot of time to hang out together."

Philippe nodded his agreement. "The days run together... I can't keep track."

"And Nando? He didn't want you to talk about it?"

Philippe laughed. "Nando doesn't want me to talk about anything. He is always saying to keep my mouth shut. *Don't talk to anyone about anything. Don't give them something to remember. Just keep your head down and don't make waves.*"

"I guess he has lots of experience. But still... you can't always live your life that way, hiding from everybody else."

"It's not normal for me," Philippe agreed. "I am a very friendly person; I like to talk to people. I like to have fun and have parties. Nando says *none of that. Don't let anyone see you.*"

"That would be very hard," Zachary said encouragingly. Though personally, he would much rather be holed up in his apartment alone most of the time, not out partying or visiting. But Philippe was naturally gregarious and it would be difficult for him to live that way. "So were you and Jose good friends?"

"We talked sometimes. He didn't spend much time at the apartment. But when he was around, we would talk. He liked to talk to people too."

"He was good friends with a couple of friends of mine."

Philippe cast a sideways glance at Zachary. He was following Zachary's lead back to where his car was parked, but didn't ask where they were going.

"What friends?" Philippe asked eventually.

"Pat Parker and Lorne Peterson."

Philippe nodded slowly. He didn't say anything to indicate whether he knew who they were or whether, like Nando, he thought they were girlfriends. Zachary decided to approach it from another direction.

"Jose had family back home?"

"Yes," Philippe nodded eagerly. "You saw his picture. A very nice family."

"It must have been hard for him to be away from them."

"Of course. He loved his wife and children very much. But he couldn't make the money they needed to survive in El Salvador. He came here to make a better life. They were supposed to follow him sometime."

"So when you didn't see Jose, did you think he'd gone back to El Salvador?"

"Back there? No, why would he go back? He needed to work here to support them."

"There wasn't an emergency back home? They didn't call him to say that he had to go back to see his family? Maybe one of his children was hurt or they were in some kind of danger?"

"No. Nothing like that." Jose shook his head, eyebrows drawing down. "Who told you that?"

"The first thing everybody says is, 'Maybe he went home.'"

Philippe shook his head with certainty. "He would never go back."

"Not even to visit? Not even if something had happened to his children?"

"If he went back, they would all be killed. He could never go back."

Zachary raised his brows. "He would be killed? By who?"

"He had trouble with one of the cartels. His family was safe as long as he left, but if he went back…"

Zachary thought that through. They walked in silence for a while. Zachary indicated his car as they walked up to it. "This is mine. I want to put this box away. Where do you want to go for pizza? Do you have a favorite place, or just anywhere?"

"Wherever you want," Philippe said agreeably.

Zachary stowed the box away and they both got into the car. He looked on his phone for a pizza place in a slightly nicer area of town and started the engine. He didn't want to ask Philippe too much until he was a captive audience. Once he was eating, Philippe wouldn't want to interrupt his meal just because the questions were getting uncomfortable. He'd want to eat all he could while he had the chance. Zachary suspected he was probably not getting enough to eat on a daily basis.

Once they were settled and the pizza was being baked, Zachary continued the discussion. "What do you think happened to Jose?"

Philippe pursed his lips, thinking about it.

"Nando says that people leave all the time. They can go on to another job or they might be running away. If ICE showed up at his work, he wouldn't stay around. He wouldn't go back to the apartment; he would just leave."

"The police officer who was investigating his disappearance said that Immigration was not involved. They don't have Jose and, as far as we can tell, they weren't investigating his work or anywhere that he was involved with. So why would he just disappear like that?"

"Nando says…"

"I want to know what you have to say. You seem like a bright young man. You seem like you were friends with Jose and care about what happened to him. I don't think Nando does."

Philippe didn't say anything for a while. "Nando does care," he said eventually. "But he is always worried about how things are going to affect him. He doesn't want to have to run away. He wants to make money. He makes good money because he works hard and he is the one who rents the apartment, so everybody's money goes to him."

"And he makes more than it takes to pay the landlord?" Zachary asked. There were a lot of beds in that apartment. If fifteen or twenty men were paying a hundred dollars apiece for rent, Nando could be socking away a good amount of money just from the rent.

"He is the one who runs the risk," Philippe said with a shrug. "So he gets paid something for it."

"Do you think that Nando had something to do with Jose's disappearance?"

Philippe looked shocked by this suggestion. His eyes widened comically, and he shook his head vigorously. "No, no, Nando wouldn't do anything to hurt Jose. He is a good man. He takes care of us. If someone is sick or hurt, he is the one who helps. He will get medicine or a doctor, or he can help someone escape, if there is word on the streets that someone is looking for him. Nando is a good man. Just very careful."

Zachary nodded slowly. The waitress brought out their pizza, and both men helped themselves. Zachary didn't see how he was going to be able to eat more than one slice of the huge pizza. Philippe could have his fill and take the leftovers home to the other men at his apartment.

"But Nando doesn't know what happened to Jose?"

Philippe shook his head. "He kept Jose's things. Didn't get someone else in there to replace Jose right away, in case he came back. But... he is not coming back."

Zachary chewed a mouthful of pizza, unable to answer right away. He swallowed. "How do you know he's not coming back?"

"If he was coming back, he would have by now. There wasn't anything to keep him away from the apartment. Not for this long. Maybe a couple of times he stayed away with a friend overnight. But not a whole week. And he didn't go to work. So... I don't know what happened, but I don't think he is coming back."

"Do you have an idea of why not? What might have happened to him?"

"This land... sometimes it just eats men up."

Zachary considered all that Philippe was saying or not saying. "Do you know Pat and Lorne Peterson?"

Philippe took another piece of pizza. Zachary wasn't even halfway through his.

"I met them," Philippe said finally, cautious.

"Nando thought that they were Jose's girlfriends."

Philippe laughed. "Jose did not have any girlfriends."

"He didn't date anyone here? Because he had a wife back in El Salvador?"

Philippe looked at Zachary over his piece of pizza, studying him closely. "You know Pat and Lorne?" he asked.

"Lorne was my foster father."

40

Philippe took another bite of his pizza, thinking about that. "You know that Jose dated men," he said finally.

Zachary nodded. "Yes. I know that. A lot of people might find that shocking, but I don't. Did other people in the apartment know that about him?"

Philippe shook his head. "I do not think so. The only people who know are people he goes with. Socially."

And that included Philippe himself, Zachary realized. He raised his eyes to meet Philippe's. "I'm sorry. I didn't realize you were that close."

Philippe nodded. "He thought I was too young," he confided. "He said I wasn't old enough to know what I wanted. But I have always known."

Zachary wasn't sure what to say. He let Philippe's words roll around his mind for a few minutes. He took out his notepad and pencil. "I need to write a few things down before I forget. I'm not going to write down your name. You can look, if you want to."

Philippe shook his head. "It doesn't matter. You can write my name."

"Do you have an idea what happened to Jose? Do you think he just left on his own?"

"No... he would not have left unless he was in trouble. And if he was in trouble, the rest of us would be as well. Me and Nando and everyone else who worked or lived with him. Or socialized with him."

Zachary nodded.

There was silence as Zachary wrote his notes.

"There have been other men," Philippe said.

CHAPTER SEVEN

Z ACHARY DIDN'T WANT TO misinterpret Philippe or put words in his mouth. He answered cautiously. "Other men?" he repeated. "You mean, you have seen other men?"

Philippe shook his head. "I have. But I meant... other men who have disappeared."

Zachary couldn't help readjusting his chair and leaning forward, wanting to connect with Philippe and not take any chance of misunderstanding him. "Tell me about these disappearances. Who has disappeared? Other undocumenteds, like Jose?"

"Some of them undocumented. Some with documents. But other men... who are not white... who are part of this community."

"Gay men?" Zachary pressed, then corrected himself. "MSM, I mean? Like you and Jose?"

Philippe nodded. He put down his pizza for a moment, which told Zachary that he was very serious about what else he had to share. He also leaned toward Zachary. "Jose was not the first one. There have been men disappearing... for some time."

"Did you tell the police this?"

Philippe's eyes flashed. "Why would I tell them anything? They haven't done anything. They think they solve the problem by arresting people. Having raids of bars and lounges and other places we gather. They don't want to stop the disappearances. Just the complaints."

"Do you think they know who is behind it? Or do you think the police themselves are behind it?"

"No. I just think... they don't want to hear it. They don't care if a few men go missing. It isn't worth it to investigate."

"Have you talked to others about this?" Zachary assumed that he must have. If men had been disappearing for years, then Philippe certainly wasn't old enough to remember them. He couldn't have been part of the community for more than a year or two, if that. Someone else in the community must have talked to him about it, and shared the information about the police cracking down on gays instead of trying to help them out.

"Yes. Of course."

"I'd like to talk to somebody who remembers about other men who have disappeared. I want to know what's going on."

"Nobody knows, though," Philippe said. "If they knew who it was, they wouldn't have to be afraid. They could turn them over to the police. Or they could do something about it themselves."

Zachary nodded. "I understand that. But if I can get information about the victims, these other men who have disappeared, I might be able to figure something out. A pattern. Somebody who knew all of them or was involved closely with them."

"How would you find anything out? If the police can't find anything, how would you? They are not going to give you their files."

"Did the police find out that Jose had left his box of personal items behind?" Zachary challenged.

Philippe shook his head. "No."

"And did the police find out that you and Jose were... close friends?"

"No."

"I found those things out. Today is my first day on the case, and I know more now than the police. I can investigate. I can't promise that I'll figure out who it is, but I can't figure it out if people refuse to talk to me. I need you and the other men in the community to talk about what's going on. I already have a list of men who could be involved. People who have made threats or who have been violent. I may not have the databases that the police have, but I have a start. And I can find out more."

Philippe raised his brows. "You have suspects?"

"Yes. Potential suspects. I need more details before I can point the finger at anyone seriously, but I have a start."

Philippe picked up his pizza again. He ate it more slowly, chewing thoughtfully. "I will ask around," he agreed.

"I need more than that. I don't live here and I want to be able to get started on the investigation today. I don't want to have to go home without anything, and then to come back in a few days when you turn somebody up who is willing to talk when the trail is colder. If somebody took Jose a week ago, and either harmed him or locked him up somewhere, then that person is here now. Close by. He's looking over his shoulder and thinking that nobody can punish him for what he's done. He's laughing at you."

"Not laughing at me," Philippe insisted, sounding offended.

"Yes, he's laughing at you and everybody else in the community who knows that something is going on but doesn't know who the monster is behind it. He's laughing at you and everybody else who is afraid to go out at night. He gets a kick out of it, out of knowing that he's smarter than you or anyone else."

"He isn't that smart."

"He is if he has been getting away with kidnapping or murdering men in Vermont for years. Enough men for the people in the community sit up and take notice. There are bound to be men that no one has tied to this guy too. People who were expected to go somewhere else, so they were never missed at the time. However many men you know of who have disappeared, you can bet there are more. Maybe twice as many. Serial offenders operate for years before anyone catches them. We never know how many victims there really were."

Philippe took another piece of pizza. "Why do you believe me?"

Zachary was taken aback by the question. He considered it from Philippe's point of view. He was young, barely old enough to be called a man. He offered a wild story about men disappearing with no corroborating evidence. As a young man and an immigrant, he was used to being ignored and pushed aside.

"I believe you because I believe Pat," he said slowly. "I've known him for a lot of years and I know he's not the type to get hysterical or imagine things or make them up. If he's concerned, then I know there's reason to be. He didn't tell me that there were other men who have disappeared, but that might just be because he didn't want to taint the investigation or sound like he was telling wild, unverified stories."

Zachary took a sip of his soft drink.

"And I believe you... because you took the time to answer my questions and you care enough about Jose to find out what happened to him. I'm not going to brush you off because of your race or your age. I've had that happen to me too many times. I believe you and Pat that Jose has disappeared. And I did my own preliminary investigating this morning; I know there are a lot of people who are making trouble with the community and could be dangerous. Just because it's not out in the open, that doesn't mean it's not there. There are still plenty of people who feel threatened by the growing acceptance of the gay community. A lot of people who would not balk at violence to stop it."

Philippe was nodding along with him. He took several big bites of pizza, so it was a minute before he could talk. "I will see if I can get someone to talk to you... if you really think you can find something out. I don't know what you can do when they just disappear. How would you find anything out? There are no clues."

"The more similar cases we can find, the more clues we'll have. We'll find a pattern. Somebody had contact with all of them."

Philippe stopped mid-bite, sudden realization crossing his face. "If it is someone who knew Jose... then it is somebody I know."

"Well... more than likely. We don't know for sure where they met or how well this guy knew his victims, but chances are... it's somebody who has crossed your path as well."

Philippe gave a shudder. "That is creepy."

It wasn't funny, but Zachary had to laugh at Philippe's accent and expression. "Sorry. Yes. It is. I wouldn't want to think this guy was looking at me."

"Looking at me..." Philippe repeated, shaking his head. "I do not like this."

"You need to know. You need to be careful... I don't want *you* disappearing."

"But how can I know who is safe and who is not?"

"We'll try to narrow down where they were when they disappeared. That will give us some clue. Just... try not to go places by yourself. Especially not when you're leaving somewhere that is known to... cater to men like you."

"It's more safe to be with someone? To look like a couple? That attracts more attention. People don't have to guess whether you are there for... purposes."

Zachary thought about that. "I don't know. I still think it is safer to be with someone than to be alone. The men who have disappeared, they haven't disappeared as couples...?"

"No," Philippe agreed after a moment, "only one at a time."

"Then I'd expect you to be safer walking with someone else."

Philippe nodded thoughtfully, but didn't immediately buy in. "It's a bad world," he said finally. "If you walk as a couple, you attract skinheads and other gangs who want to stomp out the... men like me. But if you walk alone, you might just disappear."

Zachary didn't like to think of what it would be like to live in that world. He'd been in dangerous situations before, but to be in danger just because of who he was dating or where he chose to drink or take in entertainment seemed totally unfair. Philippe and Jose and Lorne and Pat should all be able to walk where they liked and with whom they liked without being targeted.

"Be careful. We know there are predators out there, whether these disappearances are related or not, so please just be careful."

The boy nodded.

"Do you think you could get your friend on the phone?" Zachary suggested. "I'd really like to talk to him before going home again. If you'd like some privacy, I could go outside for some fresh air while you chat..." He motioned to the sidewalk in front of the pizza shop.

Philippe shook his head. "He won't be able to talk right now. He is working. You don't have anything else to do while you are in town?"

Zachary considered his options. "I need to talk to Jose's boss. And if there are places that you know Jose hung out, I'd like to visit them, ask some questions."

"You don't want to go these places," Philippe said, shaking his head.

"I need to. I need to talk to people who knew him, see what people saw, what they know. If he was being targeted because of his preferences, then there may be people around those places who might have seen whoever is… making these men disappear."

Philippe's eyes were big. "Why don't you say killing them?" he asked. "That's what you think, isn't it?"

Zachary looked for some other explanation, but couldn't find one. "With one person… he could have just gone somewhere. Or had an accident. Gotten hit in the head or mugged or even run away with someone. But if there is a pattern here, and other men like him are disappearing… then I have to think that yes, it is the work of a serial killer."

"But there are no bodies."

"Just because they haven't been found… that doesn't mean there aren't any. They just haven't been left somewhere that someone could discover them. He may have a field he buries them in, or a basement or storage warehouse. Who knows? Sometimes these guys kill for years and years before they ever get caught. They don't leave the bodies where they can be found."

"So you think Jose is dead."

Zachary met Philippe's eyes, dark and shiny with emotion. "After he has been gone for a week or more… yes. Now and then you hear about a kidnapper who has kept his victims alive for years… but that's pretty rare. And usually the victims are women. I can't think of any where men have been kept alive for years. If this is the work of a serial killer—and we really don't have any evidence of that yet—then I doubt he would have been kept alive for more than a day or two."

Philippe nodded his agreement. "I think this too."

"I'm sorry. That's not what you wanted to hear."

"I wanted to hear the truth. If I want to hear stories, I can go home and talk to Nando."

"What does he think happened?"

"That Jose just went away. He doesn't know about *us*. He doesn't know Jose at all."

"If he had found out, how do you think he would have reacted?"

Philippe smiled a little. "You want to know if he would have killed Jose?"

"I want to know what you think."

"No. Not Nando. He is my mother's brother. If he found out about Jose and me, he would probably kick Jose out and call my mother. He is supposed to be looking after me. Making sure I don't get myself in trouble."

"You don't think he would have blown up and attacked Jose? It's possible, you know, if he thought that Jose was taking advantage of you and that he had let your mother down. He could have blown his top."

"No. Nando, he talks tough, but he is not physical. He does not get violent. He uses words and his brain, not his hands."

Zachary nodded, but jotted the thought down anyway. If it turned out that Jose's disappearance wasn't related to other men in the community disappearing, it was possible that it was a one-off. Manslaughter when Nando discovered that one of the men he trusted had interfered with the nephew he was supposed to be protecting.

"I have the information about where he worked," Zachary said, "but I need you to tell me about the other places he went, whether he went with you or on his own or with others. I can ask Pat too, but I think you probably were closer to Jose and will be able to give me more information."

Philippe nodded. He was obviously reluctant to pass the information on, but he seemed resigned to it.

"I won't mention you when I talk to them," Zachary promised.

Philippe listed a few of the places that he and Jose had gone and Zachary wrote them down. He closed his notepad, and when he slid it back into his pocket, he pulled out a business card.

"Please call me once you have contacted your friend about the disappearances. I'd like to talk to him tonight if I can. It may already be too late… but I don't want to be accused of taking my time when someone might have been in danger. I think the chances that he is still alive are pretty slim, but I have to act like he is and time is of the essence."

Philippe agreed. He took the business card from Zachary and studied it. Zachary stood up, leaving plenty of money on the table. More than was needed for the pizza and the tip. He felt bad for Jose's young friend.

Zachary stopped, his hand on the back of his chair after he pushed it in. "Uh… one more question. Were you aware whether Jose was seeing anyone else?"

"Yes," Philippe admitted. "We were not exclusive. We both saw other people."

"Anyone who might have been jealous about Jose seeing someone else?"

"I don't know. I didn't hang around with any of his other… friends."

"Did he ever complain about domestic violence? Anyone who had hit him or choked him? Anyone he didn't want to have anything to do with anymore?"

Philippe shook his head. Then Zachary could see that he was reconsidering. Philippe looked at him, frowning.

"Choked him…" he repeated.

Zachary waited for him to process the memory. Philippe thumped his fingers on the table. "One day… he had bruises on his neck and he was hurt… his ribs…"

"Did he say where he got the bruises?"

"No. I asked, but he said it was nothing, not to worry about it. I kept asking him… and he said it was just rough play." Philippe shrugged, not meeting Zachary's eyes. "So I let it go."

"How long ago was this?"

"A couple of weeks ago, maybe a month."

"Not too long ago. It's worth looking into. Do you know anyone else he was seeing? Or anything about them?"

"We didn't really share that… we didn't want to hurt each other…"

"If you think of anyone, let me know. Even if it's just someone you got a vibe from… you know, you had the feeling that maybe they had met before or gone out sometime."

Philippe nodded. "Okay. I don't think so… but I'll think about it."

"Thanks. Put me in contact with your friend as soon as you can. I'll check out his work next, but that probably won't take long. We need to keep this moving as fast as we can."

CHAPTER EIGHT

ZACHARY REACHED A.L. LANDSCAPING and looked around. It was mostly just a front office with a receptionist on hand to deal with the public. There was storage space in back for materials and equipment, but it wasn't the type of place that had a storefront. The receptionist was white, apparently not an illegal immigrant. When Zachary came into the office, she raised her brows like she thought he had walked into the wrong place.

"Can I help you?"

"I'm looking for Art McDonald."

She looked surprised. "Do you have an appointment?"

"No, I'm afraid not. I'll wait if he's got someone else with him."

"Mr. McDonald doesn't see anyone without an appointment."

"Does he have any time this afternoon?"

She looked sour at this. She looked at her computer screen and considered her answer. "What is this concerning?"

"I'm looking into the disappearance of one of his workers."

Her eyes flicked over to him. "I beg your pardon?"

"One of his workers has gone missing. I'm a private investigator looking into it. We may have a situation on our hands."

Her hands left the keyboard and she stared at him. "A situation? What are you talking about?"

"I'm sure you want to keep everything quiet, but we may be dealing with… a serial killer."

Her eyes widened in alarm. "Are you pulling my leg?"

"Sorry, ma'am, I don't mean to scare you, but we really do need to address this immediately. I realize that he was an illegal immigrant, but I'm not here about immigration or your business practices. I'm here about a man's disappearance, maybe a whole series of deaths."

She looked unsure of what to do. Zachary tried to look impressive. She glanced toward another office, trying to decide whether to interrupt her boss, which was obviously something she wouldn't have normally done. After a few more minutes of hesitation, she stood up. "Please wait here," she instructed. She smoothed out her skirt, gave it a little tug down, and went into one of the other offices. Zachary listened, but couldn't hear her voice as she went to McDonald to explain the problem to him. In a few minutes, they were both back.

McDonald was a large man. Tall, florid red cheeks, too heavy around the middle. He looked strong, but also like he spent most of his day sitting around.

"What is this nonsense?" he demanded.

The receptionist looked around her front office as if there might be someone to overhear him, and that he should not be talking so loudly, but of course there was no one else there and he was the boss, so she couldn't exactly kick him out or tell him to tone it down.

Zachary offered a businesslike hand to shake and produced his business card for McDonald. "Zachary Goldman. Thank you for seeing me."

McDonald stammered something out that wasn't quite "I didn't agree to see you," but tried to be something more gracious. Then he returned to his previous line. "That is this nonsense about a serial killer? Is this some kind of joke?"

"No, I'm afraid not. I know that this is inconvenient for you, but if we're going to be able to prevent others from being killed, we need to find this guy. We need to identify him and get him off the streets so that he can't keep killing."

McDonald gave a distracted nod. He looked at his receptionist and then back toward his office. "I suppose you'd better come with me."

Zachary followed him back to his office. A tiny space, plain beige with few pictures or decorations. Lots of filing cabinets and loose papers. It looked more like an accountant's office than what Zachary would expect a landscaper's office to look. But he was a business owner, not the guy who was actually mowing lawns and designing flower borders.

"I really don't know what this is about, Mr. Goldman." He needed to look at the business card to prompt himself with Zachary's name. "But I can assure you that there is no connection between my business and any serial killer." He shook his head. "I wouldn't allow anything like that to go on!"

As if he thought that he would have any control over it.

"No, of course not. I'm certainly not accusing you of anything. This is just the latest development in a long chain of murders that has been going on for years. I'm not accusing you or anybody that you have hired. I'm sure this all went on completely outside of company time. But since the latest victim was one of your employees, I really do need to follow up with you and see if there is anything that we can find that might be helpful in our investigation."

McDonald sat down heavily behind his desk and motioned for Zachary to have a seat. Except that the chairs on the other side of his desk were all covered with papers. Zachary looked at them, trying to decide whether to shift one of the piles of paper somewhere else, then elected to stay standing. It gave him a psychological position of power over McDonald.

"I really do appreciate you taking the time to help me," Zachary said. Even though McDonald had agreed to nothing of the kind. "I'm sure you must know how hard it is to track down any information about illegals. You deal with them every day, so you must understand what it's like."

McDonald didn't take the bait. He just shook his head. "Who is it you're talking about here?"

"This is about Jose Flores."

McDonald's eyes flickered in recognition. "I already told the police; I don't know what happened to him. He just disappeared, didn't come in one day."

"But you didn't find anything suspicious about that behavior?"

"No. Why would I? These people come and go, they don't give any notice. They just leave you in the lurch. I have no idea where he was going or why."

"That puts you in a position, doesn't it? You rely on them to come in every day, you have everyone's schedules arranged, and then he just doesn't come in. Pretty inconsiderate."

"Yeah, well, that's just the way it is in this business. You have to be flexible. But there are always new people who are willing to work. You can find them as fast as you lose them."

"But then you have to train them."

McDonald nodded. "Yeah. That's true. It feels like a never-ending battle sometimes. But I'm trying to help these people out. It's not just something I do for myself."

Zachary balked at the idea that McDonald was just hiring illegals out of the goodness of his heart, that it was some kind of cause for him. Of course that was a big, fat lie. He just stared at McDonald for a minute, letting him feel foolish for having made such a statement, then went on.

"I realize that you already told the police everything you know; I just have a few follow-up questions for you. As you can understand, every little piece of information could be important. We don't have any way of knowing what may lead us to our killer."

"That Dougan was a pain in the neck. Treated me like I was breaking the law by hiring illegals. How am I supposed to run a business without workers? And how are they supposed to live if they don't get jobs? I'm keeping them off the streets. The government doesn't have to support them. People don't have to see them sleeping on the sidewalks and begging for money. It benefits everyone."

"I'm sure Jose was very grateful for his job. He had a wife and kids back in El Salvador that he was trying to support?"

"Yeah, something like that. One of those countries."

"He was happy working here, as far as you know?"

"I never had any complaints."

"And he was a pretty regular worker? He showed up here every day? Didn't just pop in casually now and then? Didn't miss Monday mornings because of a hangover?"

"No, he was here every day," McDonald said grudgingly. "He was reliable."

"That's what I'm hearing. How did he get along with the other workers? Were there ever any signs of trouble? People he argued with or wouldn't work with?"

"No, nothing like that."

"You never had any fights between him and someone else?"

McDonald considered for a moment, his eyes narrowing. Then he shook his head. Zachary wasn't sure whether he believed the answer. McDonald still seemed to be hiding something. "No, no fights."

"Nothing that concerned you?"

"I wasn't with them every day. I have foremen, designers, people who work with them every day. I'm just the guy that makes sure they have jobs to go to and that they get paid. I'm not the one working side-by-side with them."

"Who was? I should probably be talking to them too. And maybe to some of your other workers. They would know things about Jose that you would never have the opportunity to hear about, stuck here in your office."

"You're not talking to anyone else on my staff. I'm giving you my time and that's more than I think you deserve. I think this line about a serial killer is just that, a line. You don't know what happened to Jose. You don't know he's dead. You think I wouldn't have heard about it if the police found a body? Even if it didn't make it into the papers, the cops would still be back here waving their hands around and saying that I should have known."

"You couldn't have known that he was going to be targeted, and I doubt it had anything at all to do with his job. But we have to check everything out. It is possible that the killer first met Jose on the job. He could be another worker or he could even be a client. And at some point he made a connection with Jose, one thing led to another, and…"

"You're serious about it being a serial killer. Why haven't I heard about this before now? It seems to me if there was a serial killer, we would have heard about it. You can't keep something like that quiet."

"You can if everyone who is killed is undocumented and just looks like they have disappeared."

McDonald thought about that for a minute. "So you don't know it's a serial killer," he said finally.

"We've got a pretty good idea what it is that we're looking at," Zachary said seriously. "Just because we can't produce the bodies yet, that doesn't mean they're not there." He looked at McDonald significantly. "I'm sure you heard about that killer up in Canada who hid the bodies in landscaping planters."

The red color drained out of McDonald's cheeks. His eyes widened and he shook his head. "That couldn't happen here. We would know if anyone was tampering with planters. There's no way that could happen here."

"In that case, it was the owner of the landscaping business that was the killer. He had full access whenever he wanted."

"Are you accusing me? That's ridiculous!"

"I'm not accusing you. I'm just pointing out that... this is one of the first places we have to look at. Is there any possibility that the bodies might have ended up in garden plots? Concrete pads or borders? Planters? There are a lot of places that you could hide a body, if you were so inclined."

"But I'm not out there. Like you said, I'm here in the office all day long. I couldn't do anything like that."

"Maybe. You still have access to equipment and the work orders at night or on days off. But I'm not accusing you. There could be someone else on your staff... or it could be nothing to do with your business at all."

"There isn't anything. You know there isn't any connection with the business."

"I don't think there is," Zachary agreed slowly. "But I would like to have some questions answered."

CHAPTER NINE

S O A S K Y O U R Q U E S T I O N S , " McDonald barked. "This has nothing to do with my business."

"When did Jose come into work last?"

McDonald pulled out a handwritten ledger and looked at it, making sure that Zachary understood he was taking the question seriously and not just answering off the cuff.

"The twenty-third. That's a week ago last Friday."

"And he didn't tell you that he was going to be missing time or was taking vacation or going away somewhere."

"He didn't tell me anything. And as far as I know he didn't tell any of the supervisors either. But these people don't. They don't take vacations, and if they're leaving, they just go. They don't tell anyone."

"So you weren't surprised when he didn't show up for work the following Monday."

McDonald pursed his lips indecisively. "He had been a reliable worker until then, showing up for work every day. I was surprised to hear he hadn't shown up. But I wasn't concerned."

"Did you call him?"

"Call him? Why would I do that?"

"To see if he was sick or was coming back."

"No, I didn't call him."

"Did you have a number for him?"

McDonald glowered at him. But he got up and went to one of the filing cabinets and thumbed through the files there. He pulled one out and returned to his desk. He opened the slim file and looked over the information.

"Yes, we had a number for him. No way of knowing whether it was a legitimate number or not."

"You could call it and see if he answers."

McDonald said nothing.

"Did you give the police that number?"

"No."

"And you've never called him?"

"No."

"Could I get it from you?"

"I don't know about giving private employee information to anyone who asks. You are not the police."

"I can give you Detective Dougan's number and you could give it to him. Then either he could call it, or he could give it to me. Or you could call the number and see if he answers. It seems a little silly to sit on the number without *somebody* calling it."

McDonald could no doubt see that calling Dougan to tell him that he'd had Jose's phone number all along and had not provided it during their investigation would put him in a bad light. He'd already said that he didn't want to give it to a private party. That left only one option. He picked up the receiver on his desk phone and held it between his shoulder and his chin. He jabbed at in the numbers in his file, his irritation clear. He waited for a few seconds, then hung up again.

"Out of service," he said. "Probably it was a fake number from the start. They've usually got a burner phone, but they don't give the real number to anyone."

"Detective Dougan would be able to check it out and see if it's a real number and what the last few calls made on it were. You could say that it just came to your attention, or one of the other workers gave it to you because they were starting to get concerned about not having heard from Jose."

"I could," McDonald said morosely, not giving Zachary the impression that he would. But Zachary didn't want to push it yet, or he'd get kicked out before he got a chance to ask the rest of his questions.

"Did Jose have any friends in particular? Was he always on with someone else?"

McDonald shrugged. "No one that I'm aware of."

"What did he do? Did he have any particular specialty?"

McDonald looked at the file folder again, his eyes skimming over the information there. "He was a hard worker, did pretty much anything. Mowing, carrying, loading and unloading, handyman work. But he wasn't a skilled laborer. He didn't have any particular training or certifications."

"You don't know what education he might have had back in El Salvador? Did he ever say that he was an accountant or engineer or anything like that?"

"What would he be doing working at a landscaping company?"

"People do, you know. They get here and they can't use the education they had in their home country. Doctors and lawyers too."

"Well, he wasn't any damn lawyer, that's for sure."

Zachary gazed toward the open file on McDonald's desk. "I don't suppose I could get a copy of that, could I? Any information you could give me on Jose would be very helpful."

"You don't have a warrant. There's nothing in here you could use, anyway. There's hardly anything here."

"Do you have his next of kin? Contact information for his wife?"

McDonald looked at the file, then shook his head. "No. We have an emergency contact—I believe his roommate. But nothing back in El Salvador."

"Is the emergency contact Nando González?"

"Yes."

"Okay. I've already talked to him. Is there anything else? Anything that concerned you or that came up with the police?"

McDonald looked at his watch. "I think we're ready to wrap up here. I wish you all the best on your investigation, but I don't think there's anything else I can help you with."

Zachary waited for a few seconds, letting the silence draw out, seeing if there was anything else that McDonald had to contribute.

"How about that phone number? Do you want to give it to Dougan or me?"

"Why would I give it to you?"

"You might find it easier than talking to Dougan. Some people don't like talking to cops."

"What are you going to do with it if I give it to you? The number is no good. It isn't going to lead you anywhere."

"I may take it to Dougan myself and see if he can find anything out about the last people that Jose talked to, or if there was someone particular who had that number. It may not be a fake number. It may just have run out of minutes or battery by now. He's been gone for over a week. If it wasn't plugged in, the battery would be dead."

"If you tell Dougan it came from me, he's just going to be back here getting on my case and asking why I didn't give it to him in the first place."

Though that would be a good question for Dougan to ask, Zachary didn't want to antagonize McDonald. "I can say I got it from a friend of Jose's. Then it's off of your conscience, because you passed it on, but you won't have Dougan here asking questions. If you want to know the truth, I don't think Dougan is interested in putting any more time into the case. Not unless I can turn something up for him to look at."

McDonald pondered this for a few minutes, then shrugged. He turned the open file folder around so that it was right side up for Zachary. "There it is. You can copy it down."

Zachary skimmed the rest of the page as he slowly got his notepad out and flipped through it, looking for the next blank page to write the number down on. He wasn't a fast reader and he didn't have a photographic memory, so there wasn't a lot that he could get from the form in the time it took for him to write down the number. But he did his best, quickly skimming past Jose's name and address. No SSN, of course, and the birthdate was also blank.

The phone number that didn't work. Nando's name and phone number. A short list of the safety and hazardous materials training Jose had received from the company. There was nothing filled in under medical conditions and allergies. A few codes at the bottom of the page that Zachary didn't understand. Probably his pay level and other terms of employment. Zachary painstakingly scrawled out the phone number, reviewing the page for any other clues. When he was done, McDonald took the file back again.

"I appreciate you taking the time with me," Zachary told him.

McDonald stretched, then took a drink of his coffee, as if he'd just been released from a tedious meeting. "Tell me the truth… you don't think that Jose was actually killed by a serial killer, do you? That's just something you said to get in the door?"

"I'm afraid it is something I'm looking at. I'm meeting with someone shortly who can hopefully give me a head start on that. You'll let me know if you think of anything else? Or if anyone else seems to be showing interest in Jose and what happened to him?" Zachary slid another business card across the desk for him. "Just give me a call if you think of anything. It doesn't have to be proven. Random facts are fine. You never know what might trigger a connection."

McDonald nodded, but didn't pick up the card.

Zachary called Philippe to see where he was on getting ahold of his friend who had inside knowledge of the men who had disappeared. Philippe said that he had talked to him, but that he needed some time to prepare before meeting with Zachary. Zachary hoped that didn't mean that he was spooked and on the run.

"You're sure he's going to get back to us?"

"He will, he will," Philippe assured him. "He wants someone to listen. For years, he keeps telling everyone about these men disappearing, and no one will listen. He wants to talk to you."

"Okay. Well, I need to keep moving forward with the investigation, so have you had a chance to think about places that Jose might have spent time?"

"I don't think it's safe for you to go to these places. You were just telling me not to go anywhere alone."

Zachary had a hard time coming up with an argument to that. "I'll just be asking questions as a private investigator. Nobody is going to think that I'm gay."

"Who are you kidding? People see you coming out of a gay scene, they're going to think that you're gay."

"I'll be careful," Zachary promised. "Now, give me a few places to check out."

Philippe sighed and complied, giving Zachary the names of a few establishments and where they could be found. Zachary could practically hear him shaking his head. "But you be careful, bro…"

"I will." Zachary put his phone away. For a moment, he entertained the idea of calling a friend to go with him to the bars. But he was away from home and couldn't think of any friends that he would have invited to go to a gay bar with him anyway. All of the cops he knew well were out of the jurisdiction and weren't going to drive a couple of hours out of their way to humor Zachary's whims.

Tyrrell wasn't that far away, but Zachary couldn't imagine taking his baby brother into such a place. Mr. Peterson and Pat were, of course, the logical choices, but they were getting on in years and neither would want to be seen as being on the prowl. Being seen crawling gay bars with a much younger man like Zachary might irreparably damage their reputations.

So he went alone, like he had planned to do from the start.

CHAPTER TEN

WHEN HE GOT TO The Night Scene, it was just opening and there were only a couple of patrons there ahead of him. Zachary looked around, feeling a little awkward, knowing that he must stand out, both because he didn't belong there and because it was the first time he'd ever been there. The bouncer eyed him, but let him in without any questions. The long-haired bartender watched his approach with heavy-lidded eyes.

"Uh, hi," Zachary greeted. "Get a Coke?"

The bartender nodded and got out a glass. He filled it from the fountain, added a lime wedge to the rim, and placed it on a square napkin in front of Zachary. Zachary slid a bill across to him.

"Don't think I've seen you here before," the bartender commented.

"No. This is my first time."

"You meeting someone here?"

He had a feeling that the bartender was trying to figure out if he belonged there or had just wandered in from the street, thinking it was a regular bar.

"Actually, I'm looking for people who might know a missing man. Name of Jose Flores."

"Missing?"

"He seems to have dropped off the face of the earth more than a week ago. I'm trying to figure out what happened to him."

"That happens sometimes," the bartender said cautiously.

"Maybe so. If he's just gone on to something else, that's fine... but he has friends who are worried that something might have happened to him."

The man scratched the back of his neck. "That so?"

"Yeah." Zachary passed his card across the bar. "I'm Zachary."

"Paul." He didn't give his last name, but there was no reason he should. It wasn't like Zachary was the police or it was an official interrogation. He didn't need to provide any information he didn't want to.

"Nice to meet you, Paul. Did you know Jose Flores?"

"Might have. How do you know him?"

Zachary considered how best to answer it. He didn't know whether Mr. Peterson and Pat had ever been to the bar, or whether it was just somewhere for unattached young men to meet each other. Their names might mean nothing to Paul. But on the other hand, if he fudged on how he got the case, Paul might not see any reason to help him out. A private investigator looking into a disappearance for no obvious reason was very different from a private investigator looking into it for a friend who was concerned.

"A friend of mine asked me to look into it," he said slowly. "But I don't know if he has ever been here. I got the name of this bar from someone else."

"Who is your friend?"

"Patrick Parker. He is sort of a step-father to me."

Paul considered that, saying nothing. He polished a smudge on the bar counter that was invisible to Zachary. "He doesn't come around here," he said, "but I know him."

Zachary nodded, relaxing a little. "If you want to ask him about me, he'll confirm it."

"I believe you."

"So did you know Jose?"

"Not very well, but he did hang out here. Him and a couple of other immigrants."

"Was there ever any trouble that you saw? Anyone give him any hassle? Or did he ever get in a fight or cause trouble for you?"

"He wasn't that kind of guy. He was pretty quiet. Just wanted to meet people, have a drink and maybe a dance. Go somewhere else to take it any further."

Zachary breathed slowly. He took a sip of his Coke. "The guys he came with, they ever cause any trouble? Give you a bad vibe?"

"No. Nothing I can remember. They were regulars. Nothing suspicious."

"And was he always with them? Did he ever come by himself?"

"Might have. I didn't keep close track of him. As long as he was ordering drinks and not causing any trouble, why would I care who he was with or what he was doing? This is a place where you come to be yourself. We don't interfere with patrons unless they're being disruptive."

Zachary nodded. "When was the last time you saw him?"

"I couldn't say. A week. Two. Couldn't be sure."

"He's been missing from work for about ten days."

Paul nodded. "Somewhere in there."

"You ever talk to him? Discuss any interests? Home? Hopes and dreams?"

Paul chuckled. "Like I say, he wasn't here to talk to me. We never exchanged more than a few words."

"He was from El Salvador."

"Uh-huh."

"He never talked about it?"

"No, can't say he did."

"Never talked about going home?"

"Going home? No. Never. Nothing like that."

"You got the feeling that he intended to be here permanently."

"I don't know what his plans were, but I don't think going back to El Salvador ever entered into it."

"He had a wife and kids there."

Paul gave a grin. "All the more reason never to go back."

"I guess so. Do you get a lot of men in here who have families? Who hang around here but aren't... out?"

"Probably half the people who come in here, my friend. If they can't be themselves at home, they need somewhere they can be. This is that place for a lot of people. Leave the mask at the door and show who you really are and what you really want."

Zachary shifted uncomfortably. He looked around briefly. There were a few more customers trickling in, but things were not picking up yet. The music sounded too loud. Later, it would be drowned out by conversations. One patron, a big bear of a man with grizzled black and gray whiskers stared at Zachary, his face curious and challenging. He seemed to be a customer rather than a bouncer, but he looked like he would be perfectly happy running Zachary out of there if he felt like it was necessary. Zachary took a few more swallows of his Coke, trying not to let the man's stare unnerve him.

"Did he have any particular friends, other than the other immigrants that he sometimes came with?"

"No one particular. He hadn't settled down."

"So he didn't have a steady date."

"No."

"I was talking to Philippe earlier."

"I figured."

"How?" Zachary was taken aback that Paul would know who he had been talking to.

"Most people know to keep their mouths shut. That young pup Philippe... he hasn't learned yet."

"He's concerned about Jose. I'm someone who could help. It's not like he talked to someone untrustworthy."

Paul looked at him thoughtfully, then nodded. "Still... the boy needs more experience. I'm afraid he's going to say something to the wrong person. Something that will have consequences."

"Do you know who the wrong person would be? Is there someone around here you would not trust?"

"There's always people around here you can't trust," the bartender said slowly. "And once you say something, you can't take it back. Things could happen." He traced a white scar that ran down his neck.

"Is that what happened to you?"

"I was a young pup once too. The lessons can be harsh. Luckily, I survived. Not everyone does."

"Who cut you? Did you get in a fight? Were you attacked?"

"It was a long time ago. He's not around anymore."

"But there could be other people around here who would hurt someone like Philippe if he said the wrong thing."

Paul agreed. He left Zachary to attend to other customers, moving down the bar and then back again eventually. Zachary watched the patrons around him. He knew he couldn't tell who was safe and who was dangerous just by looking at them, but there wasn't anyone in the bar yet that he had a particularly bad feeling about. He would have felt comfortable talking to any of them. At least, under the right circumstances. Maybe not in a gay bar, but if they were sitting next to him on the bus or at a conference, he wouldn't have felt like they were dangerous.

"Philippe said that there have been other people who have disappeared. Other men like Jose," he said when Paul was back down at his end of the bar.

Paul busied himself with the till and the bar, serving drinks and making change as more people started to flow in through the doors. It was picking up faster than Zachary would have expected. Paul returned to where Zachary sat and leaned closer to him, bringing him a second Coke. "I wouldn't discuss that here."

Zachary looked around. The man who had been staring at him was sitting down, nursing a drink of his own, and no longer staring at Zachary, though he still glanced over while Zachary was examining him. Zachary looked around for anyone else who might be listening in or showing an interest in their conversation. No one looked particularly concerned with his being there.

"I don't suppose you'd want to discuss it another time and place," he suggested.

"No," Paul agreed. "So maybe you'd best just drop it. You don't need to be panicking people, making them think this is not a safe place."

"No, I didn't mean that. I didn't mean that anyone had disappeared from the bar. Just from town."

"People come and go all the time. Someone hangs out here for a few weeks or a few months, and then one day you think, 'I haven't seen that guy lately. I wonder whatever happened to him.' And probably, you never find out."

"Sure," Zachary agreed. "They find somewhere else they like to hang out, or they start a serious relationship and aren't here looking anymore. People aren't static."

"No. And it's best not to start talking about people disappearing, like something bad happened to them. There's a difference between disappearing and just not going back to the same bar."

Zachary drained his first Coke and pulled the second toward him. He needed to pace himself, or he was going to end up having to use the public restroom, and he really didn't think he wanted to risk that. He took a very small sip to show that he was still drinking and passed another bill to Paul to pay for the second drink.

"But Jose *did* disappear. He didn't just stop coming here. He hasn't been at work or at home. No one has seen him. The police have been brought it on it."

Paul cocked an eyebrow. He pushed the long hair on the right side of his face back over his ear, showing off several earrings. "The police haven't been around here."

"No, I didn't think so. I don't think they're actually very interested in finding out what happened to Jose. He's… a nonperson to them."

"We're all nonpersons to the police."

Zachary dragged his finger through the condensation on the side of the glass. "Is it that bad? The police don't get along with anyone who is gay?"

"I imagine some of them get along just fine with people who haven't come out yet. But the police departments and the gay community around here do not have a good track record."

"I'm sorry to hear that. The officer I talked to seemed pretty decent. He didn't put much time into it, but he didn't tell me to get lost. He didn't tell me that it didn't matter, even if he didn't believe that there was anything wrong. He still filed the report, did the initial legwork."

"Then they are doing more than they have done in the past. In past years… you try to get them involved in something, and you're more likely to get the wrong end of the baton, so to speak. It's best not to ask for help."

"There must be gay police officers. They don't treat you any better?"

"How do you think *they* would be treated if they did?"

Zachary nodded slowly. "I suppose if there's that much animosity, there would be resentments."

"As a cop, you don't want to be assigned all the dirty or dangerous calls. You don't want to be stuck at the bottom of the ladder and never able to advance. So you toe the line and you don't make allowances for people like us."

"I thought things would have gotten better since the Marriage Equality Act was passed. There has been an influx of gay couples…"

"Enacting a law doesn't change people's opinions. Not that quickly, anyway. There's a lot of resentment about that influx, if you're on the side of the Christians or the Nazis."

There were a number of curious glances in their direction at his words. Zachary felt his cheeks heating at the attention. "I'm sorry to hear that. I thought it would make things better."

"It has in some respects; not in others."

CHAPTER ELEVEN

THE LARGE MAN WHO had been watching Zachary picked up his drink and approached Zachary at the bar.

"Don't think I've seen you here before," he observed.

"Uh, no. I'm Zachary." On instinct, he didn't give his last name or the fact that he was a private investigator.

"You can call me Teddy."

It seemed a rather cuddly nickname for such a formidable man, but Zachary nodded and didn't ask why. He turned to look at Paul, but he had withdrawn to the other end of the bar and was serving customers there, not looking at Zachary.

"So are you new in town?" Teddy inquired. "Or just to The Night Scene?"

"I'm from out of town. I come down this way now and then to visit my father. A friend mentioned the bar to me today and I thought I would check it out."

Teddy's eyes raked him from head to toe, and Zachary had the uncomfortable feeling that the man saw him for what he was. Zachary knew that there wasn't any physical trait that could give him away as straight or gay, but he must look as uncomfortable as he felt hanging out in a gay bar and being approached by a stranger.

But Teddy didn't confront him and say he knew who he was and what he was after. He didn't even challenge Zachary on whether he was actually gay, or maybe had just ended up in the wrong bar.

Glancing around, Zachary noted that there were some women around. Or people he assumed were women. Everybody wasn't paired off. He could conceivably have walked into the bar without realizing that it was a gay bar. His so-called friend might have set him up there as a joke.

"So what do you think so far?" Teddy asked. "It will be a little while before everybody gets warmed up and the place will be hopping. Pretty quiet right now."

"I don't mind quiet. I wanted to get a feel for it before it was too busy."

"What were you talking about with Paul? You seemed to be having a pretty involved conversation."

Zachary shrugged. "Nothing, just small talk."

Teddy wasn't buying it. He motioned for another drink. Paul gave him a wave but continued to take care of drinks down at the other end of the bar.

"Are you a Vermonter?" Teddy asked.

"Yes. Just up north."

"And… unattached?"

Zachary considered the question. Teddy was moving a lot faster than Zachary would have expected. But if The Night Scene was a hookup joint, maybe that was expected. He found himself thinking about Kenzie rather than about the appropriate answer to give Teddy. They were closer than they had ever been, but Zachary had noticed a change since Christmas. Was it because she had been ready to take their relationship further when he had not been, too mired in his case and pre-Christmas depression? Or having had a taste for just how low he could go, had she finally decided that a relationship with him wasn't in the cards?

"Earth to Zachary…"

"Oh." Zachary brought his attention back to Teddy. "Uh, sorry, I was just thinking…"

"About who? That was a pretty deep dive."

"Yeah. Well… things didn't really work out between us the way I'd expected. Probably my fault."

"Maybe you just weren't compatible."

Zachary took a sip of his Coke. "Yeah. Maybe not. It's just that it looked promising for a while there… but maybe I'm not very good at long-term relationships." There was Bridget. He'd been with her for a couple of years. But that had ended up so disastrously that he couldn't consider it a successful long-term relationship.

"So maybe what you're looking for isn't long-term," Teddy suggested. "Maybe right now, what you really want is something quick and intense." He leaned closer to Zachary. Zachary couldn't help readjusting to increase the space between them. No matter what role he was playing, his reaction to Teddy being in his personal space was visceral.

Teddy grinned and drained the rest of his glass. He put it down on the bar with a hard thunk, attracting Paul's attention. Paul made his way back over to them and gave Teddy a refill. He glanced at Zachary. "And you're okay, Zachary?"

Zachary sensed the double meaning. Paul wasn't just checking on refills, but whether he was okay with the big man talking to him. He nodded. "Yeah, I'm good. Thanks."

"Let me know if you need something." He drifted back away, getting busier as the bar got more crowded. A couple of other bartenders arrived, tying up their aprons and positioning themselves along the bar so that Paul didn't have to handle everything himself.

"I was wondering if my friend was going to be here tonight," Zachary said, "But I don't see him."

"The night is young. The place barely opened. Who is your friend?"

"Jose Flores."

Zachary was watching carefully for Teddy's reaction to the name, but Teddy didn't betray any surprise or concern. "Oh, yes. Well, he's not here every night. Did he tell you he would be here tonight?"

"No. I was just thinking it would be nice if it worked out that way. Have you seen him lately? I hope he hasn't gone off again."

"No, I can't say I've seen him recently… maybe a few weeks. He's 'gone off' before?"

"Yeah, he kind of disappears from the scene every now and then. Maybe he's shacked up with someone."

"I wouldn't hang your hopes on seeing him tonight, then. Leave yourself open to… other possibilities."

He hadn't moved perceptibly closer, but Zachary again felt like Teddy was too close. The man was just being friendly. If Zachary had been attracted to him, he was sure he would have felt completely different about his proximity and the signals he was sending out. As it was, Zachary didn't think he could push the masquerade much further with Teddy. He should circulate and talk to a few other people. Get a feeling for who else might have known Jose or had concerns about what had happened to him.

Teddy saw Zachary's glance around the bar, and looked around himself. He jerked his head toward the door. "There's my date. I'll see you around. Happy hunting."

Zachary watched him make his way across the room to a younger man with a Hispanic cast to his features. They greeted each other warmly and found a table to sit down at. Zachary stared at them, a little shocked that Teddy had moved so quickly from flirting with him to cozying up with the man he was apparently there to see. The people Zachary normally spent time with were not the type to jump from one love interest to another in mere seconds, and it threw him off balance. He shook his head and had another sip of his Coke, looking around.

Zachary had asked a few other people about Jose. Everyone seemed to be friendly, but shrugged and shook their heads at his questions. It would seem that no one had seen Jose or knew where he might have gone. No one knew of any plans he'd had and, despite what Zachary had told Teddy, Jose had never dropped out of sight before. He didn't run into anyone who had been mentioned in the forums as possibly being dangerous.

It was getting late and the crowd was getting louder. Zachary had had enough of people standing too close or touching him while they talked. He just wanted his own space, peace and quiet.

He headed for the door, and was startled to have his way barred by a large man stepping into his path. He focused on the intruder and realized it was Teddy. He'd obviously had a few more drinks. His eyes were rimmed with red and his movements were sloppy.

"Come with me."

Zachary balked. "What?"

"Come. Come here."

Zachary looked around. Teddy grabbed his arm, pulling him back, away from the door. "Come on. Stay with me."

Zachary followed, resisting all the way, not wanting to walk right into some encounter with Teddy. Teddy pulled him over to the table that his date was sitting at and motioned to him and an empty chair.

"Here, sit down. Talk with Dimitri."

Zachary hesitated, looking at the other man. "Uh… Dimitri?"

The younger man nodded, showing off a row of very white teeth. "Hi."

"What is it… what is this about?" He still couldn't shake the instinct that Teddy wanted to pull him into something. A threesome, maybe.

"Teddy says you were talking about Jose. I know Jose."

"Oh." Zachary nodded. He sat down carefully, worried that doing so might mean he was committing to something more. "How do you know Jose? Have you seen him lately?"

"He's been very naughty," Dimitri shook his head, smiling at Zachary, showing off how charming he was. "He was supposed to meet me, and he didn't. I think he's avoiding me."

"When were you supposed to meet?" Zachary resisted the urge to pull out his notepad. He was there incognito; he would have to remember the important points to note down later. A casual friend of Jose's would not haul out a notepad and start taking notes.

"A week ago. But he never showed up. Left me here all alone."

Teddy nodded along. "I remember. Because I saw you later that night."

"At least Teddy doesn't stand me up. What happened to Jose?" Dimitri asked Zachary. "Do you know? Did he run off with some floozy?"

Zachary gulped. "I don't know. I haven't seen him. I thought he might be here tonight." Playing the part of a friend who had been out of touch, he couldn't very well say that he knew no one else had seen Jose within that time period.

"He hasn't been here. He must have some new beau who is keeping him busy." Dimitri's voice was falsetto, setting Zachary's teeth on edge.

"I guess he might have. I haven't been able to get him on the phone for a few days… Did you try him?"

"Every time I call, it just goes to voicemail. Like he's rejecting my calls."

"To voicemail?" Zachary sat up straighter. "What number do you have?"

It took some cajoling, but Dimitri eventually agreed to text it to him, which Zachary suspected was a ploy for Dimitri to get Zachary's number. Dimitri sent it through, and it was the same number as Zachary had gotten from McDonald. Zachary frowned. "And you get his voicemail? That's not what I was getting."

He tapped the number, selected 'call,' and listened to see what would happen. As McDonald had said, it went to a system message saying that the customer was not available.

"I get a message saying the phone is offline," he told Dimitri. "Do you remember what day you called him and got his voicemail?" Getting Jose's voicemail suggested that the phone had still been charged and online. That might give them a better fix on when Jose had disappeared. And if Dougan could get any information from the phone company records…

Dimitri shook his head. "I don't know."

"Can you think about it? What day was it when you tried to call him last?" Teddy was giving him a strange look, but Zachary didn't want to back down on the request. "It could be important."

"Why is it important? Obviously Jose doesn't care for me or for you. He's found some sugar daddy."

"Was it on the weekend? Or the week before? What were you trying to call him about? What day was he supposed to meet you?"

"Talk about needy!" Dimitri gave him a superior look. "Honey, if you're going to hang all over him like that, he's just going to kick you to the curb. If he hasn't already."

"Maybe his phone is broken," Zachary suggested. "Maybe he's not ignoring either one of us. Maybe he changed his number because someone was harassing him." Zachary opened his mouth to tell them about Harding, his last big case, and how he had tried to shake loose from his stalker by getting a new phone and number. But Zachary wasn't there as a private eye, so anything he happened to say about a case was going to come off sounding strange. "If his phone was broken, wouldn't he have called to give you his new number? And wouldn't he still show up here when you were scheduled to meet?"

"I would expect him to."

"You really don't know what day you called him and got his voicemail? When was your date scheduled for?"

Dimitri considered this. He gave Teddy a flirty look and made eyes at him, apparently wanting to impart to Zachary that Jose was not his competition. Jose was long gone, after all.

"Wednesday," he said finally. "Wing night. But he didn't show up. I called him, but every time it just went to voicemail. He could have just answered and said he couldn't come or changed his mind. He didn't have to treat me like that."

"No," Zachary agreed, trying to soothe his feelings. "You're right. I would expect better from Jose. He doesn't usually play games."

Dimitri nodded, fake-sniffling. "That was very naughty of him."

Zachary decided it was time to move on. He nodded to Dimitri and stood up. Teddy was still standing there, and looked for a moment like he wasn't going to let Zachary past, but then he gave a quick nod and stepped aside.

CHAPTER TWELVE

ZACHARY WAS EXHAUSTED AS he left the bar. It wasn't because he had been up too long or been doing physical work, but just the emotional effort it took to deal with all of the people and the noise and to act like someone he was not. And it was more than just letting people believe that he was gay. He was really not a 'people person,' and large crowds were difficult. A few close friends at a quiet venue was something he could manage for a while, but strangers were difficult, and especially having to deal with them in one-on-one interactions. He had stretched his social muscles about as far as they could be stretched.

He stopped near the doors of the bar to jot down a few more notes before going out. He didn't want to forget anything important.

He slid the notepad back away and stepped out the doors. In spite of the time of night, the street was brightly lit with streetlights and the signs of other nearby bars and venues. There were a good number of cars and people on the street, reassuring him that it was safe. He wasn't walking down a dark alley where predators might be waiting for him.

He had parked his car a little way away, though. He hadn't wanted to leave his car in the parking lot of a gay bar and risk it getting vandalized. So he'd found a place he could park a couple of blocks away.

At first, that didn't seem to be a problem. There were plenty of people around in spite of the cold weather. On their way home or going out to party. As he turned down the last street, however, Zachary could hear boot heels behind him. Nothing to be concerned about, just some woman in heeled snow boots. Zachary glanced back a couple of times, and couldn't see her. There was a small group of twenty-something young men behind him, and he thought the boot-heels came from behind them.

But the men, who had been talking, quieted when he looked back toward them. It was suddenly a little too quiet and he could still hear the boot heels and not see who it was making the noise.

He kept going. He wasn't far from his car. The young men would go on to wherever their vehicle was parked or to their clubbing destination and Zachary would be fine.

He started to walk just a little bit faster. Once he was in his car he could regroup. The speed of the footsteps increased as well and the group of young men seemed to be getting closer. Zachary risked one more glance back at them, noticing this time that they wore long brown coats and the sound of the boots was not a woman walking behind them, but one of the men wearing jackboots. Zachary swallowed. It was cold out and they were wearing hats, so he couldn't see for sure whether they were skinheads, but his instincts told him they were.

Skinheads who had followed him from a gay bar.

Zachary's short walk to his car had taken him farther away from the crowds and the bright lights. There were a few people around, but not many, and they walked quickly, heads down, not looking at each other. Zachary looked quickly around. He needed somewhere with more people. He would be safer in a crowd. The skinheads would get bored and go away, looking for other quarry.

But his walk had taken him away from the bars and storefronts into an area that was single family homes and low-rise apartment buildings. Nothing where crowds of people gathered. All was quiet and still, except for the clomping of the jackboots behind him.

If he ran, they would give chase and would bring him down. He'd never been a good runner, and since the car accident, he hadn't regained the ability to go much faster than a trot. The more he thought about his gait, the more likely he was to trip and fall. If he stopped to engage with them, they might draw the confrontation out longer, but they weren't going to be dissuaded from their goal by any argument from him. They would just be amused by him trying to talk them out of a beating, and then they would hurt him.

He tried to increase his speed just a tiny bit, so that they wouldn't notice. Put just a few more feet in between them by the time he got to his car. They didn't know which car was his, so they wouldn't know when to start closing in on him. If he could keep going at a quicker pace until he got to his car, he might be able to jump in before they had a chance to catch up. If he were lucky.

But he knew that wasn't going to work.

They could probably tell by his quickened pace and his narrow focus that he was getting close to his car. There were a couple of laughs as they spoke among themselves, planning out the fun ahead. Zachary swallowed hard. He fingered his phone in his pocket. He wasn't going to be able to get it out and call emergency or someone to help him before the skinheads managed to get it away from him. He couldn't figure out any other plan. Throw his wallet on the ground and hope that it distracted them and that one of them would go after it, giving him another half-second to get into his car? Yell at them like he was crazy and see if they were freaked out by it or he could attract the attention of some passerby? His throat was so dry, he didn't know if he'd be able to raise a croak, or if it would be like those dreams where he screamed and screamed and no sound came out.

His car was just three spaces away. Zachary found his keys in his coat pocket and pressed the unlock button.

The taillights flashed and his car gave a friendly chirp.

If he survived, he was going to have to take it to Jergens to get that feature disabled.

The skinheads were on him in a second, before he could get past the first car. A couple of them slammed him into the side of a red Nissan crossover with a crunch that shook Zachary from head to toe. He expelled a puff of air and a groan that sounded like a dying warthog. Zachary tried to fight back, to protest, but they had his arms pressed back against the car so the was spread-eagled, unable to move. He could try to kick them, but they'd know what he was doing as soon as he shifted his weight.

"What's going on?" Zachary demanded. "Let me go!"

"Little fairy thought that he was home free," one of them mocked, getting right in Zachary's face, eyeball to eyeball so that Zachary could smell his foul breath and see the tattoos inked all over his face. Swastikas, teardrops, numbers that Zachary didn't know the meaning of. He struggled to free himself, but they weren't going to let him go that easily.

"Thought no one saw him coming out of the den of iniquity," the man in his face crooned. "Thought that he'd pulled one over and no one would know what filthiness he'd been up to. Well, we know, little fairy. We know what you've been up to. And we're not going to allow it. It's an offense against God."

"I didn't do anything," Zachary protested. "I was looking for someone. A missing person. I'm not gay, I wasn't doing anything."

"*I was looking for someone,*" the man echoed in a high voice. The others were egging him on, throwing in their own remarks and encouraging swift and severe violence. "You were looking for someone, alright. Someone to fill your unwholesome desires."

"I'm looking for a missing person. He used to go to that bar."

They laughed again. Zachary tried to pull out of their grips, but he knew it was useless. His body wouldn't hold still even though his brain knew he couldn't get away.

"You want to know why he's missing?" the chief skinhead asked. "Maybe he's one of the ones that we got."

"Let me go. I don't have any problem with you guys. Just leave me alone."

"We have a problem with you. And you need to be taught a lesson. You need to be taught not to sin. Man shall not lie with man. It's right there in the Bible. We can't allow this to go on. Just because the government says that two fairies can get married to each other, that doesn't make it right. We're here to defend God and the Constitution."

Zachary knew they were just mouthing the words. They didn't believe in anything. He tried to tell them that Lorne and Pat were better people than the skinhead neo-Nazis would ever be. Simultaneously, he fought to hold the words back and his impulsive brain tried to push them out, so that he just stammered, which was probably the best possible outcome.

"Just let me go," he begged. "I'm not from around here. I'm not going to be back here again. I am just looking into a missing persons case."

"You're not no cop."

"No, no, I'm not. I'm just trying to help out a friend."

"Yeah, a friend," one of the skinheads sneered, and he was the first one to hit Zachary.

CHAPTER THIRTEEN

HIS FIST HIT ZACHARY'S cheekbone with a crunch and Zachary's head hit the van behind him. He saw bright stars and dark splotches and fought to stay conscious. Though why would he want to be conscious for the beating? The skinhead stood there shaking out his hand, obviously having hurt his poor knuckles on Zachary's face.

One of them pushed the first aside and kicked a knee up into Zachary's solar plexus. He would have hit the ground if he hadn't been supported by the gentlemen who had his arms pinned to the side of the van. As it was, he drew his feet up off the ground, all of the wind driven out of him, reflexively trying to curl up into a ball. There was laughter from the little group. There was nothing Zachary could do to protest or to fight back. He couldn't draw in a breath to reinflate his lungs. His legs were so weak that even when his feet touched the ground again, he couldn't hold his own weight or kick one of the men in the knee.

His head was spinning. There was a flurry of other blows. Zachary couldn't keep his eyes open or break the beatdown into a blow-by-blow analysis. They came from all directions at once and he couldn't even cry out.

There was a shout from somewhere. Zachary's head was spinning so badly he didn't even know which way was up.

"Let's go!" one of them said.

Another shouted something in German.

They dropped him to the pavement, kicked him a few times for good measure, then were off and running.

The Good Samaritan, whoever he was, didn't chase after them, but stopped to examine Zachary.

The first word out of his mouth was a curse, and Zachary knew he probably didn't look too good. He still couldn't get his breath back, and it seemed like a long time since he had breathed. His body should be reinflating his lungs and taking in oxygen, but he seemed to have forgotten how. Maybe the skinheads had reinjured Zachary's spine. Maybe there had been some small flaw in it that the doctors weren't aware of, and he would be paralyzed for life.

Which wouldn't be long if he didn't start breathing again soon.

"Can you hear me?" the man shouted, kneeling over him. "They're gone now. You're safe. I'm going to get help."

He clutched at the man's coat, not wanting to be left behind. If the man went to find help and left Zachary there on the ground, the skinheads might come back again and continue their lesson on morality.

"It's okay," the man told him again. He patted Zachary's clutching hand. "I'm not going anywhere. Just let me get my phone out."

Zachary loosened his grip and the man went through his various inside and outside pockets before he found his phone and called for help. He described his location and Zachary's condition the best he could, and then knelt there over him, murmuring soothing words and trying to keep Zachary quiet until help could arrive.

Zachary wasn't sure when it was he started breathing again.

"It's going to be okay," the man said. "Did you know those guys? Were they trying to mug you?"

Zachary shook his head, which made him woozy. "Skinheads," he breathed. "Thought I was… gay."

His savior swore again. He tried to make Zachary more comfortable, straightening out his splayed limbs and wadding something up under his head. "They shouldn't be very long. They'll take good care of you."

As Zachary lay there, he thought that it probably wasn't the worst beating he'd ever suffered. It was superficial. He'd have bruises for a few weeks, but no permanent damage. No broken bones. No internal bleeding. He'd be perfectly alright once he could get on his feet again. But it was going to be a while before he felt steady enough to get to his feet. He raised his hand and touched his face, feeling the sticky, warm cut over his cheek. It was bleeding. But it had been a punch and not a cut with a blade. Probably wouldn't need stitches. Maybe just a strip of suture tape.

"It's going to be okay," he whispered, unconsciously echoing the man's own words, trying to reassure him that there was no permanent damage. He was breathing.

When the ambulance approached, Zachary thought his head was going to split right open, the discordant sound of the siren bouncing around between his ears, making them pulse and his head throb and swell. Then the siren turned off, and the paramedics got out of their ambulance.

Ever so slowly. He didn't know why it was that on TV paramedics were always running and moving quickly, when in real life, they always seemed to go super slow, as if they were on a reduced speed from the rest of the world, carefully considering every step, getting their medical kits out, surveying the scene and discussing risks before they even got close. There was another set of sirens and a couple of police cars arrived. The cops moved faster than the paramedics, asking the rescuer what he had seen and if either one of them had any weapons.

"Weapons?" the man demanded. "Do you think I did this to him? Do you think he'd let someone do this to him if he was armed?"

"We have to ask," the cop said irritably. "You don't know how many times police get to a scene and find that people are armed when they aren't supposed to be and all kinds of bad stuff can go down. What about him? Are you armed, sir?" he asked Zachary loudly, bending down over him and opening up his coat so that he could check for himself.

"No," Zachary assured him, breathing heavily. The attack had happened too fast for him to get really scared and to think about what could happen to him in realistic terms. But the cops kept asking for more details, and each question ramped up Zachary's anxiety more. How many of the skinheads had there been? Which direction had they gone? Were they carrying weapons? Had they said anything? Were they known to him?

Once they had determined there were no weapons on the scene and that Zachary and his rescuer were not going to leap up and attack anyone, they allowed the paramedics to get in close to assess Zachary's injuries. They shone lights in his eyes, looked at his face and his head, and kept asking where it hurt the most. Zachary's head throbbed from the sirens and their demanding voices as much as from his injuries. He tried to shake his head, but that hurt too much.

"I'm okay," he told them. "I'll just go home."

"You're not going home. Where did they hit you? Just in the face? In the body?"

They felt all over his arms and legs and body, looking for blood and feeling for any breaks or flinching that would direct them to more serious injuries.

"Please…" Zachary just wanted them to stop touching him. "Please stop."

Eventually, they got a gurney out. Zachary didn't know where the police had taken the man who had rescued him, but once the paramedics had Zachary on the stretcher, the Good Samaritan appeared over Zachary's face once more.

"You're going to be okay," the man said, smiling reassuringly. "I'm sorry this happened to you."

Zachary gave his best attempt at a smile and thank you before the man disappeared from his range of vision again.

"He said it was because he was gay," he told the police as they continued to ask him for more details. "He must have come from that bar a couple of blocks away and they followed him. We don't usually have gang activity in this area. It's supposed to be a safe place to live."

Zachary tried to protest that he wasn't actually gay, but no one was listening to him. They couldn't care less what his sexual orientation was. The paramedics rolled the stretcher into the ambulance, and one of them got in back with him while the other got in front to drive.

"Hang in there, bud," the one in the back said to him, patting him on the shoulder. "You're going to be okay. We'll get you to the hospital and get you all checked out. You're safe now."

He felt a lot better when they got him to the regional medical center and got some Demerol into him. The pain receded to a more bearable level and his heart rate started to slow. He tried to relax his muscles, aware that he had been gripping the bars of the gurney tightly as if he might fall off. The nurses twittered over him and washed the blood off his face and put an ice bag over his cheek. He was parked in a hallway where they were waiting for someone to take him to x-ray. One of the cops towered over him, trying to get a coherent story out of him.

"I was in the bar," Zachary repeated patiently. "But I'm not gay. They just thought I was. The skinheads. But I'm not." He wasn't sure why it was so important for him to establish this point. He didn't think there was anything wrong with being gay. He admired Mr. Peterson and Pat for their devoted relationship and all of the good things they did with their lives. But he didn't want to be misidentified. He wanted them to see the person he really was, and not a role he had just been playing.

"Then what were you doing at the bar?" the cop asked impatiently, rolling his eyes.

"I'm investigating a missing person. Jose Flores. He frequented that bar, so I was asking questions about whether anyone had seen him or where he might have gone, if he disappeared on his own."

"You were investigating this. You're not a cop."

"No, I'm a private investigator." Zachary tried to slide his fingers into his inside pocket, but they wouldn't seem to work the way they were supposed to.

"May I?" the cop asked, his hand hovering above Zachary's.

"Yeah. Just... my pocket there..."

The cop inserted a couple of fat fingers and pincered Zachary's notebook and small stack of business cards between them. He drew them all out and looked at them. Zachary couldn't see them very well as the cop spread them out over Zachary's chest. His business cards, a few other cards he had collected during the investigation. His notepad. The cop picked up the notepad and started to flip through the pages without asking. Zachary supposed that he had already given the man permission to look at what he wanted to, so he held his tongue. It wasn't like there was anything incriminating in the notepad, or even anything very interesting. Just the messy, somewhat cryptic notes that he had made as he found out little tidbits about Jose's life and thought of more questions and avenues to investigate. He supposed it probably didn't look much different from the cop's own duty notepad. As the cop gathered everything back together into a stack, Zachary's phone started to ring.

"Can I keep one of these?" the cop asked, holding up one of Zachary's business cards.

"Yeah." Zachary patted at his pants pocket, trying hard to corral his phone. The cop didn't offer to help this time. Zachary eventually managed to pull it out and answer it before it went to voicemail. He saw Philippe's number on the screen. "Hello."

There was a silence for a moment from Philippe. Maybe he had already hung up, thinking that Zachary wasn't going to answer.

"Philippe? Are you there?"

"Is this Zachary?" Philippe sounded confused.

"Yeah. What's up?"

"You sound weird. Where are you?"

There was a call over the PA system for a doctor, and Zachary didn't think there was any point in trying to keep his location a secret. "I'm at the medical center. Did you get ahold of your friend?"

"Yeah. He says he'll talk to you. I told him it's gotta be tonight. Is that still okay? Did something happen?"

"That's good. Thanks."

"Why are you at the hospital? Did you find Jose?"

"No... I, uh, ran into some trouble."

"Are you okay?" Philippe's voice cracked like he was still thirteen. "What kind of trouble? Is it the guy you think killed Jose?"

"No..." Zachary looked at the cop, who was listening with interest, and wondered how much of Philippe's side of the conversation he was able to hear. "At least... I don't think so. I think if it was these guys, they would have just left him there, like they did me. I don't think they would go to the effort of dragging him away somewhere."

"These guys? What happened? What guys?"

"Skinheads. Neo-Nazis. Followed me from the bar."

"I told you to be careful! Didn't I tell you not to walk alone?"

"I never saw them until it was too late. I was being careful."

"You never know who is going to be hanging around these places."

"Yeah. Thanks."

Philippe didn't say anything for a minute. "Are you okay?" he asked finally. "You're talking, so you must be okay. Did they do any permanent damage?"

"I don't think so. Waiting for x-rays."

"So you probably don't want to talk to my guy tonight. You're not going to be able to see him."

"I still want to. Can he come here? I'm probably just going to be laying around here for hours until they decide I'm okay to go home or I sign myself out."

"Really? You want to see him at the hospital?"

"At least we will be safe. There won't be anyone hanging around like at the bar."

"Huh. Unless one of those skinheads broke his knuckles on your face and decides to go in to get them treated."

Zachary remembered the skinhead shaking out his hand after hitting Zachary in the cheek and didn't think it was so funny. He took a quick look around, nervous, but he couldn't see the emergency room waiting area from where he was. He couldn't see very much of anything from where he was. Just the cop standing over him, waiting for him to finish the call so he could ask more questions.

When he hung up, the cop raised an eyebrow. "Not much slows you down, does it?"

Zachary thought about how much he sometimes had to fight against himself just to get from one day to the next. Working through physical injury was nothing compared with fighting his own brain and emotional state.

"I guess. I mean, it's not that bad with the Demerol. I don't think anything is broken. I'm a little loopy, that's all."

"Who is this guy that you want to come talk to you tonight? What's that all about?"

Zachary didn't see what that had to do with his assault case, or what business it was of the cop's, but he answered anyway. Maybe there was a way to persuade the police that there was something to Jose's disappearance.

"A witness that says that more men have disappeared than just the one I'm looking for. That there have been a long series of similar disappearances."

"What does that mean?"

Zachary figured the cop already knew exactly what it meant. "That we might have a serial killer on our hands."

"We?"

"If there's a serial killer operating in Vermont, then the police are going to have to be involved sooner or later."

"What makes you think there's a serial killer? That's quite a reach."

"I don't know yet, not until I talk to this guy and look into it further. He says there have been others. That's all the information I have so far. That and my missing person... doesn't feel right. I don't think he just took off without telling anyone."

"Has a report been filed on him?"

"Yes. The officer in charge is..." Zachary tried to bring the name up, but the Demerol was having a bigger effect on him than he had thought. "McDougall? No—Dougan. I already talked to him. He doesn't think there's anything to it."

The cop grunted. "So, these neo-Nazis that attacked you," he said, going back to the investigation at hand. "Do you think they had something to do with your missing guy? Were they trying to warn you off from the investigation?"

"No, I doubt it. They wouldn't know about the questions I was asking inside, they just thought I was gay. Unless they have someone planted inside, and I don't think these guys are that subtle. They're just out to do some damage. Pick off easy targets."

"You might want to reconsider going to night spots like that. Especially alone. Take a friend with you. A few friends. Don't walk to your car by yourself."

Zachary sighed. He didn't exactly have anyone he could take with him.

The cop shook his head. "Well then, you might want to get a permit and start carrying. At least you would have a way to defend yourself."

Zachary had promised himself that he would never own a gun. It would be far more hazardous to his safety than it would be a benefit.

"Thanks," he said. "I'll think about it."

"That doesn't mean I want you going around shooting up every skinhead you see… but you do have the right to protect yourself."

CHAPTER FOURTEEN

SOMETIME BETWEEN WHEN THE cop left and when Philippe's friend made it to the hospital, Zachary fell asleep. He wasn't normally quick to fall asleep in strange places; it was hard enough at home. But the Demerol and the aftermath of the adrenaline rush apparently combined to make him sleepy, and he fell asleep right in the hallway as people walked by talking and shouting instructions to each other. He woke up a few times, but then closed his eyes again and just drifted off, feeling warm and comfy and drowsy.

He was eventually taken in for his x-rays, and then moved to another curtained area while he was waiting for the results. He'd been there for some time, sliding in and out of sleep, when a man showed up at his bedside.

At first, Zachary took him for a janitor or an orderly. A tall man with black skin and sharp, angular features. He looked down at Zachary and said his name a few times before Zachary realized that this was someone he actually wanted to talk to. Zachary tried to sit up and the man helped to readjust the pillows and raise the head of the bed. Then he sat down in a chair he dragged into the curtained area from somewhere outside.

"You are Zachary Goldman," he said firmly.

"Yes," Zachary nodded. "Sorry. I didn't mean to fall asleep there. You're Philippe's friend?"

The man looked at him suspiciously. "His friend, yes. I am."

"Good. He said that you had told him about other men disappearing, and I wanted to hear about that. It's important."

"I have tried to tell people that it is important, but everybody just blows it off." The man made a sweeping gesture with his hands.

Zachary nodded. He was starting to see how that was the case. No one yet had shown any concern over what had happened to Jose, other than Pat and Philippe. "Yes. But I want to hear. I don't know if I'll be able to do anything to make anyone else pay attention, but if these disappearances are related, I want to know about it. There's no point in chasing down dead ends if there are a bunch of related disappearances that could lead us to the killer. Or whatever he is."

Philippe's friend nodded.

"What's your name?" Zachary asked him.

"Jama Mwangi, but you can call me John."

"Okay, John. What can you tell me about these missing men?"

John had a soft-sided briefcase with him. He opened it up and pulled out a writing tablet which had a long list of carefully hand printed names in a column from the top to the bottom. Zachary took it from him, looking over the list. There were so many names. He had expected two or three more, not a full page. He scanned through the names. They were not names that he recognized. Nothing that had been in the news. A lot of them were Hispanic names, maybe some African or Middle Eastern. Zachary worked his way through them, trying to break them down by ethnic groups, to start seeing patterns even before he had any more information than the names.

He rested the list on his lap. "Are they all illegals?"

"No, not all. Some have documents. Some were even citizens, born here. But none of them were white."

Zachary thought about that, letting his mind drift. If they were all immigrants, or looked like immigrants, then the perpetrator had picked them because of that. He wanted men who would disappear more easily. Men that the police would discount, just as they had Jose, as someone who was *other* than they were. Someone who could be written off as unimportant and insignificant. People like that just came and went. They could just disappear one day, but there was no reason to be concerned. They just did that kind of thing.

"Can you tell me anything else about them? Did you know all of them? Did any of them get reported to the police as missing or end up in the news?"

John looked at Zachary, his eyes piercing. Zachary tried to keep his eyes steady and not to blush under the close examination.

"You believe about this?" John demanded.

"Yes, I believe it. I want to know if they're related to each other and Jose. I need more details in order to investigate them." He let his eyes run down the list again. "This is a lot of people."

"It is not all this year," John explained. "Only a few every year. Between two and six. But it has been going on for years."

"How did you find out? How many of them did you know?"

"There had been talk in the community. Rumors, stories that men disappeared and no one ever knew what happened to them. I didn't know what to think. I thought it was just urban legend. *You need to be careful, or the man with the hook will get you.*" He gave a laugh and looked at Zachary to see if he understood.

Zachary nodded. "A cautionary tale. Trying to help people to stay safe."

"Then there was Amelio…" John pointed to one of the names on the page, two thirds of the way down the list. "He and I were seeing each other… not exclusively, but regularly, every week or two… and then he stopped showing up. No one had seen him. I asked everyone. But he was just gone. They said that he had just stopped coming around. Maybe ICE got him…"

Zachary nodded. Same old story. "But you were sure that he hadn't been caught, or gone off somewhere on his own?"

"I couldn't be sure one hundred percent, but…" John gave a little shrug. "I knew him. I didn't think he would just leave without telling me. Or somebody. And there wasn't any word that it was Immigration. Usually, there are at least rumors. Someone saw it go down. Someone knew that they came to the apartment or to his work. But no one had seen or heard anything."

"Did he have a family? Here or wherever he came from? Back home?"

"No, he was single. There have been others… some of the men on that list had wives, children. Usually not here. Usually, they were still sending them money, or trying to arrange to bring them here."

"How many did you know personally? Just Amelio?"

John shook his head. "No. A few others…" He went down the list, pointing to each of the names after Amelio's, indicating how he knew them or knew about their disappearances. Zachary looked at him, feeling the deepening frown lines across his own forehead.

"How do you know so many of these men?"

Sometimes serial killers liked people to know what they had done. They liked to rub it in the face of the officials. Could John be one of those men, proudly showing Zachary all of the men that he had killed in the past years to see his reaction?

"I didn't know all of them," John said quickly. "I did know a few of them. I am… attracted to that type. Dark, slim, kind men… I was drawn to them. But they kept… disappearing."

As if someone else were drawn to them too. Zachary nodded. He had talked to Kenzie about the traits that the missing men might share. The type that the killer might obsess on.

"Do you have more details than this?" he asked, thinking of John's briefcase, which looked like it had held a lot more than just a few sheets of paper. John didn't look like a lawyer or accountant. "If I'm going to investigate it, I need to know everything. Trying to track down everything you already have would take time, and it would take that much longer to find Jose and whoever took him."

John let out his breath. "It's too late for Jose. Isn't it? Don't you think?"

"It may be," Zachary admitted, "but if you've already gathered data, I don't want to waste time trying to find out the same information."

John searched his face once more, then nodded. He reached into his briefcase and pulled out a thick pile of papers, all sorted into files and rubber-banded together. There were sticky notes protruding out the sides and tops of the folders. Zachary reached for it eagerly. It wasn't very often he had so much to go on. If John knew what he was talking about and wasn't just a paranoid conspiracy freak, the files were a treasure trove.

John laid the stack of files in Zachary's lap. Zachary pulled the rubber bands off and opened the top folder. Background notes on one of the more recently missing men. Surveillance records. Notes about his acquaintances and finances. Zachary couldn't believe his luck.

"You have all of this information and the police still wouldn't listen to you?"

John shrugged. "I haven't… exactly… gone to the police."

"How could you not give them this information?"

"If I went to the police, they would deport me."

"If you were helping them to solve a crime, especially one of this proportion, they wouldn't turn you in. They could help you get a visa to let you stay here, for helping them."

"They don't do that."

"They can," Zachary insisted.

"But they don't."

Zachary couldn't argue with that. He knew very little about what it was like to live as an illegal immigrant. John would know far better than he did how the police or government would respond to an illegal offering information and asking for asylum. Zachary had no idea how they would be treated. From what John and Paul the bartender had said, they wouldn't be welcomed with open arms.

"Can I borrow these files? Make a copy?"

John shook his head. "I don't want them out of my sight. You can look at them, but I don't know what will happen to them if you take them away. This is the only copy."

"We could go somewhere to copy them. A library. Office store."

"Nobody will be open this late. And you don't look like you are going to be going anywhere soon."

Zachary looked down at himself, still bruised and muddy and tired after his long night. He could get himself released, but he should at least find out whether he had any broken bones. And he probably shouldn't drive while he was still foggy from Demerol. His heart was thumping quickly, excited by the prospect of looking through all of the information that John had compiled about the missing men. But there was no way he would retain everything he read, even if he could read through everything in one night. What he thought he would remember might disappear as soon as the Demerol wore off. Drugs could do funny things with memory.

"I don't know… we need to find a way to copy them. Do you think that one of the nurses would let us use a photocopier?"

John raised an eyebrow, looking at Zachary and shaking his head slightly as if Zachary were crazy. And he supposed it had been a stupid question. The hospital wasn't going to let them borrow a photocopier. If he could just capture what was on each of the pages... but even trying to write down the important points on each page would take hours, and there was no guarantee that he would get everything relevant. At some point, he'd find he needed to go back to the originals, and that would mean arranging to meet John somewhere and then paging through all of those papers again for what he had missed.

"A snapshot," he said suddenly.

"What?"

Zachary started patting his pockets. He looked around. At some point, they had changed him out of his street clothes into a hospital johnny. They must have done that before taking x-rays, though he couldn't remember it. During that period that he'd been in and out of sleep.

"Where are my clothes? Do you see them?"

John opened a skinny cupboard. "In here."

"In my coat, check the pockets. I have a digital camera."

"A camera?" John repeated doubtfully, patting the coat.

"It's small. Smaller than a cell phone."

John looked through the pockets more carefully, and eventually found Zachary's tiny digital camera, which he always thought of as his spy camera. It was like the novelties listed in the backs of comic books when he'd been young, only it was far more sophisticated than anything that had been invented back then. Higher resolution than a cell phone camera. Removable storage cards so that he could take as many pictures as he needed to without filling the camera memory up.

Zachary checked it over. It was a little banged up after his encounter with the skinheads, but the lens and the viewfinder were unmarked, so it should work. Hopefully. He held it over the page of names and clicked the shutter button. A moment later, the document appeared on the LCD screen, edges smoothed and square, nice high resolution.

"Perfect. I'll take the pictures; you turn the pages. It will take a few minutes, but it's easier than finding a copy shop in the middle of the night."

John hesitated, taking the list of names from him.

"It will be okay," Zachary told him, trying to soothe any worries that John had. "You've done a lot of work and you probably don't feel like letting it go... but you want to do something for these men, don't you? You want us to be able to put them to rest, and to know what happened to them. And to catch whoever is doing this. We can't just keep watching from the sidelines as more men disappear."

John nodded his agreement. "Yeah, you're right... But you're sure you can use them? You can get the police to do something about it this time?"

"I will. I know cops and I'll find someone who will take another look at it. I'm not going to give up until they've taken another look at these cases. It's one thing when there's one missing man. But this many... we need to catch who is doing this."

CHAPTER FIFTEEN

T HE DOCTOR RETURNED TO find Zachary covered with John's papers while he photographed them to make sure that he had every last piece of information on the missing men as he could get. The doctor shook his head slowly.

"What's all this? Shouldn't you be resting?"

"I have work to do," Zachary told him. "Can I go home now?"

"The x-rays are clear. You don't have any bones that need to be set. But I wouldn't recommend resuming your normal activities for a few days. You're going to be pretty stiff and sore. You need to give your body the chance to recover before you go off… doing whatever it is that you do."

"Great. Do I get a prescription painkiller?"

The doctor pursed his lips, looking as if he were trying to decide whether Zachary was a drug-seeking addict. He looked down at the clipboard in his hand containing Zachary's chart, and nodded. "Yes, it would probably be a good idea, at least for a few days. I'm only going to prescribe a small number of pills. You'll need to go to your GP if you need a longer prescription, and he can decide what you need. You're on… other meds…?" he trailed off, apparently seeing the list of prescriptions that Zachary had provided.

"I don't take them all every day. But I figured you'd need to know all of them because of interactions."

"Yes, you're right." He looked at Zachary again. "You have someone who is managing this protocol? You're not getting different meds from different doctors?"

"Yeah. Just one doctor. You can call him if you want."

He nodded, looking relieved. "As long as you've got someone who knows all of what you are taking and is making adjustments when needed. I'll leave that to him." He took out a prescription pad and scribbled down the details of the painkillers for Zachary. "You're going to need to be careful if you're taking that with any kind of tranquilizer or sleep aid. Talk to your doctor or pharmacist first. I'll get the staff started on checking you out."

"Okay, thanks."

He was glad that he wasn't going to need to stay overnight. He knew that the Demerol was still masking the amount of damage that had been done to his body, but he didn't want to have to put the investigation aside while he recovered. Those missing men needed him. And other men who might be in peril if Zachary didn't figure out who the predator was.

"No driving," the doctor advised as he scratched his initials onto the chart. "You'll need someone to pick you up."

Zachary had been afraid of that. He looked at John, who shook his head. Zachary didn't know if he even had a car. He might have gotten to the hospital on the bus, or a friend might have dropped him off as a favor. Zachary could call a cab, but then the next question was where to stay. He didn't particularly want to be by himself in a hotel room. Not after the encounter with the skinheads. He wanted to be with other people, not walking down a lonely street again, listening to footsteps behind him.

"I'll... uh... I'll sort something out."

"If the nurses see you are driving yourself, they will call the police."

"I don't even have my car here. It's back at the bar where I got beaten up."

"Get it tomorrow when it's light out and you have someone with you."

He ended up calling Mr. Peterson. He hated to do it. He knew he and Pat would be in bed, and a ringing phone in the middle of the night would worry them. But if he didn't want to spend the night alone, there was only one couple in town that he could call.

"Zachary?" Mr. Peterson's voice was concerned. "Are you okay?"

"Yes. Everything is okay. I'm fine. But... I need somewhere to stay tonight. And a ride."

"Certainly, of course. Are you still working? It's got to be..." there was a pause as Mr. Peterson checked the time. "Three o'clock in the morning."

"Yeah. I'm sorry to bother you so late. I wouldn't have if I could have called anyone else..."

"You know that we're happy to have you over any time. Where do you need to be picked up?"

Zachary cleared his throat, preparing for further concern from his former foster father. "Well... I'm at the Regional Medical Center."

"The hospital?" Lorne's voice peaked louder.

Zachary could hear Pat in the background, asking about what was going on. Mr. Peterson muffled the phone while he answered Pat. Then he spoke to Zachary again.

"Are you hurt? Did you have a panic attack? Tell me what happened."

"I got hurt. It's fine. There's nothing broken, they're releasing me. Just a few bruises. I'll tell you all about it."

"We'll be right there. The hospital is about fifteen minutes away."

"Don't rush. It always takes an hour to get checked out. I'll be out front once I've been released. You don't even have to come in."

But he knew that wouldn't stop Mr. Peterson from coming in. He'd want reassurance from the staff that Zachary wasn't checking himself out against medical advice and to know whether there were any special instructions to follow. If they knew about the other medications. Zachary was a grown man, but bring his foster father into the picture, and he might as well have been eleven years old again, when he'd had a bad reaction to his meds and Mr. Peterson had been the one to rush him to the emergency room in his pajamas and sneakers.

Zachary went through John's papers one last time to make sure that he'd seen everything and captured it all on his camera. He brought up the images on the camera to make sure they were saved. Then he thanked John for all of the work he had done and for bringing it to Zachary in the middle of the night. Once John was gone, he dressed slowly and gingerly, and headed to the desk to sign all of the release forms and waivers.

He managed to get to the front doors at the same time as Mr. Peterson was walking up. Zachary smiled and waved and Mr. Peterson stopped where he was and waited for Zachary to exit the hospital. Even under the too-dim exterior lights of the hospital, Mr. Peterson could obviously see the damage done to Zachary's face. His mouth fell open.

"Oh, Zachary! What have you done to yourself?"

He took Zachary by the arm to walk him to the car where Pat was waiting, as if Zachary were the sixty-year-old instead of in the prime of life. They walked slowly, Zachary reducing his speed to accommodate Mr. Peterson's pace, and Mr. Peterson slowing his even more to adjust for whatever injuries he couldn't see.

"I'll tell you about it when we're on our way," he said. "I'll just have to repeat it for Pat otherwise."

He hobbled to the car, where Mr. Peterson insisted that Zachary get into the front where there was more legroom and more comfortable seating, even though Zachary was a small man and would have been just fine in the back.

Pat turned his head to look at Zachary as he got in, and exchanged looks with Mr. Peterson. They helped Zachary get his seatbelt on. Pat shook his head.

"Did you have a tussle with a bear, or what? You look awful, Zachary, and those bruises haven't even set yet. You'd better sleep with ice on your eye tonight, or you're not even going to be able to open it in the morning."

"It looks worse than it is. They hit my cheek, actually, not the orbital…" Zachary trailed off.

"They?" Mr. Peterson asked. "Who exactly is *they*?" He climbed into the back seat and pulled his door closed.

"I kind of got mugged," Zachary hedged. "It's okay. I'm fine and they didn't steal anything. They got interrupted."

"You're not fine. Where were you? Why were you out somewhere so dangerous late at night?"

"Err…" Zachary had hoped not to have to give them any details, knowing it would just make them feel worse. "I was… investigating…"

"Investigating what?" Mr. Peterson shot back. And then Zachary heard the intake of breath behind him as Mr. Peterson suddenly realized why Zachary would be in town conducting an investigation late at night. He swore softly. "Not Jose's disappearance?"

"Yeah."

"You shouldn't have… did you have to go out so late? You could talk to his roommate and his boss during the day. You didn't need to go anywhere else. You didn't need to go somewhere dangerous."

"It wasn't really dangerous. I was fine while I was there. It was just when I left… it was dark, and I didn't see… I was parked a few blocks away and I didn't realize that I'd been followed."

"By who? Do you know who it was that did this to you? Was it a witness? Someone trying to shut you down?"

"Just… no, nothing to do with the investigation. Just some kids looking for trouble, that's all. It was nothing. Really."

"Kids? Like a street gang?"

"No… a group… of young men. Not an actual gang, I don't think. Just the kind who band together…"

Pat looked over at Zachary as he pulled out of the hospital parking lot. "Zachary," he said, in a low, even tone that meant that they knew Zachary was trying to obfuscate. It was time to fess up and tell the truth.

"It was… a group of skinheads."

"Skinheads," Mr. Peterson repeated. "Why would you have any trouble from skinheads? You're white. You're not Jewish or…" He trailed off, understanding.

"They followed you from The Night Scene," Pat said flatly.

"Yeah."

Pat thumped the steering wheel in frustration. As a man who normally had endless patience and sangfroid, it was an emotional outburst. "This would never have happened if you hadn't been trying to find out what happened to Jose!"

"It's not your fault," Zachary hurried to reassure him. "It was just one of those things. It could have happened to anybody at any time."

"But it didn't. It happened to you when you were investigating a case that I gave you. And I'm not even paying you! You need to drop it now. It's not worth something happening to you. It's bad enough that Jose has disappeared, but I would never forgive myself if something even worse than this happened to you because you were following up on a lead."

"It's late and I got you out of bed," Zachary said. "You're tired. It's really not that big a deal. You'll feel better about it in the morning."

"I won't feel better about it. We'll talk in the morning, but you'll drop it. Wherever Jose has gone, we're not going to get him back. He's made his own choice."

Zachary was silent. He wasn't going to tell them that it was a serial killer. Not yet. Not until he knew more details. He had a lot of research to go over before he could come to that conclusion. But if it was a serial killer, there was no way Zachary was going to just let it go.

CHAPTER SIXTEEN

H E DID HIS BEST not to let Lorne and Pat see the extent of his injuries, but by the time they got back to the house, the Demerol was wearing off. Zachary got ready for bed and took one of the painkillers they had filled at the pharmacy on the way home. It was obvious he wasn't going to get any sleep without them. As it was, he had a restless night, tossing and turning to find a comfortable position when everything hurt. He was up by the time the gray light of dawn started to fill the room, hurting too badly to go back to sleep. His mind was already whirling as he tried to sort out the details he knew of Jose's life and his disappearance. He wanted to get started on John's research as soon as possible, but first he would have to get everything off of the digital card and print it out.

Mr. Peterson looked in on him when he got up and found him poring over his notepad, reviewing everything he had written down and trying to pull all of the threads into something that made sense.

"Up already?"

"Yeah, couldn't stop thinking about it."

Mr. Peterson shook his head.

"I know it looks bad." Zachary put his hand over his cheek and black eye, as if hiding them from sight would erase them from Mr. Peterson's memory. "But it really isn't as bad as it looks. I'm fine."

"You always say that. You won't admit when you are really hurt."

"Well…" Zachary trailed off, not sure what to say about that. He'd dealt with debriding and skin grafts following the fire when he was ten. That was a kind of pain he couldn't even begin to describe. When he compared that to the damage inflicted by fists and feet, even by several men, there was just no comparison. Even broken bones were not that bad. "It hurts if I move the wrong way or if I touch it," he tapped light fingers over the lump that was normally his cheek, "but I've had worse. The doctors checked to make sure nothing is broken and there's no internal bleeding. It's just a matter of time for the cuts and bruises to heal."

"Have you taken a painkiller already this morning? What can I get you? Breakfast?"

"Yes. I'm not hungry. Coffee would be good."

"You need more than coffee in your stomach if you're taking painkillers. You need real food."

"Just… just a piece of toast."

"Okay. I'll put it in the toaster in a minute."

Mr. Peterson went on to the bathroom and then in a few minutes was in the kitchen, getting the coffee and toast started. Pat was the usual cook for dinner, and Mr. Peterson for breakfast. Lunch was usually every man for himself. Mr. Peterson obviously got the light end of the cooking chores. Zachary was surprised that Pat wasn't up yet, but he might not have had a good night's sleep after having to get up in the middle of the night to fetch Zachary from the hospital. He'd been pretty upset when he'd gone back to bed.

Zachary wandered out to the kitchen as the smell of coffee started to waft through the house. He sat down at the table, continuing to read through his notes and make additional ones as Mr. Peterson put a buttered slice of toast in front of him. He put out jam and honey, but Zachary nibbled the toast without.

"What are you working on?" Mr. Peterson asked.

"Just looking through my notes; the interviews yesterday. Figuring out where I need to go next."

"You're not going to drop the case, are you?"

Zachary looked up at him. "No. I couldn't." He glanced in the direction of Pat's closed bedroom door. "It may be more than just Jose."

"What do you mean, more? You mean there is some kind of conspiracy?"

"No… someone who is… making people disappear."

"People?"

"Gay men of color, especially illegals… it's been going on for a number of years."

Mr. Peterson sat down. He stared across the table at Zachary. "You don't mean it."

"You haven't ever heard any rumors? Any talk about men disappearing?"

"I know there are people who have talked about it… but I always figured it was just tall tales. People seeing patterns where there weren't any. As a general rule… we like to classify things, give them names, sort out patterns. We're a species that likes logic and predictability and tries to create it."

"And that may be all it is," Zachary agreed. "I have to work through the data and see what I can find. Do you know if Jose was seeing anybody regularly? I have one young man who says they were, but I'm wondering if there was anyone else. Or if it was just random hook-ups."

"I don't know if I would say regular… but there were a few men. Probably more that I didn't know about. He didn't seem like he was ready for any kind of commitment. Men who have been married often fear settling down with someone again. Taking the risk of calling a relationship permanent."

Zachary wondered if Mr. Peterson had experienced that. It had seemed to Zachary that he had transitioned immediately from Mrs. Peterson to Pat, but Zachary hadn't been aware of anything that was going on while the Petersons were still married. What kind of relationships Mr. Peterson had pursued before the marriage broke apart.

"The boy I talked to, Philippe, he said that Jose had bruises on his throat one day. Like he'd been choked."

Mr. Peterson's face turned even paler than usual. He took a fortifying sip of coffee. "Who would do that?"

"I don't know. I don't know whether it was a regular partner, or someone he had just encountered. I don't know whether Jose normally participated in that kind of thing, or whether someone talked him into it or did it without his permission. Or as a threat or part of a fight. I just don't know." Zachary shook his head. He had more questions than answers; it was too early in the investigation to know anything.

"If he was into asphyxiation... I wasn't aware of it. But that's not something people usually share casually. I never saw him with bruises." He turned his hands palms-up and shrugged. "We talked about *music*."

Zachary nodded. Pat had said that they were just a social group. Jose had done his dating outside of that group, and perhaps they had not known each other as well as Pat had thought.

"Is Pat okay?" Zachary nodded toward the bedroom.

"He'll be alright. He's worried about you, but he still wants to know what happened to Jose. He was up most of the night after we got back, fussing about it."

"I'm not going to drop it. Especially not if this is a serial killer."

"If you have evidence that it is, you get the police to take over. You don't need to be putting yourself in some psycho's crosshairs."

"Sure, of course. You know me. I'm not a cowboy going in, guns blazing. That's TV, not real life."

Mr. Peterson nodded, and took a sip of his coffee, looking more reassured. "This thing last night has got us both pretty worried about you. We thought it would be a few inquiries on the phone, nothing dangerous. You getting attacked like that... brought it too close to home. We don't want you getting hurt. I don't know if you've looked in the mirror this morning, but you look like you collided with a train. I don't want you doing anything risky."

"I won't. The first thing I need to know is whether I could use your computer for a bit. I have some digital photos to process and it would be easiest if I could just do it here."

"Of course. Process away."

"You've got a digital memory card reader?"

"Doesn't everyone?" Mr. Peterson smiled.

Zachary had been introduced to photography by Mr. Peterson when he had given Zachary a used camera for his birthday. They had processed a lot of film together in Mr. Peterson's darkroom, even when technology had shifted to digital. Now they both used digital cameras most of the time, though they both still had analog cameras for more creative work.

Zachary ate a couple more bites of his toast and left the rest on the plate.

Zachary retrieved his camera from his jacket pocket and pressed his thumbnail into the card slot to pop the card out. It didn't come out. He tried again, and it still didn't pop free like it was supposed to. Zachary took a closer look to see what was going on. The camera had been banged up and dented during his altercation with the skinheads, but everything had seemed to be in working order when he had taken the pictures of John's documents the night before. Looking at it more closely, however, Zachary saw that one of the dents pressed into the card slot, and was pinning the memory card in place. Zachary tried to pry it loose with his fingernail, but that didn't work. He went into the bathroom and found a pair of tweezers, and tried to use them to pull it out. It still wouldn't budge. Zachary tried to push it farther in, and then to pull it out, but nothing was budging it. Zachary went back out to the kitchen where Mr. Peterson was reading the newspaper. Lorne looked up at him.

"What's up?"

"Have you ever had this happen before? I can't get the memory card out."

Mr. Peterson took it from him and examined it closely.

"Hmm... it certainly is stuck in there, isn't it? I'm not sure what I would suggest. Maybe take it to a camera repair store and see if they can retrieve it. Can you still access what's on the card?"

Zachary tested it, worried that after pushing and pulling the memory card around it would no longer be connected to the innards of the camera, but he was still able to pull the images up on the LCD screen.

"Yeah, see? They're still there."

"Can you transfer them to camera memory and use a USB cable to connect with the computer?"

Zachary looked over the camera. The mini USB port was just below the card slot, and it too had been deformed by the violent attack the night before. "I don't think that's going to work either. Even if we can bend it back into shape..."

"You'd best not mess with it. Leave it to the repair shop to take a look at, they have a lot more experience with that kind of thing."

Zachary sighed. "I'd better see if I can get hold of my witness again. Maybe meet him at a photocopy shop to get a hard copy of the documents. I thought taking the pictures was a good idea last night, but it seems like it was just a waste of time. I wasn't thinking clearly. Didn't even notice the damage."

"I'm sure they can still be recovered, but you might want to follow up with him just in case."

"Okay. Do you have a shop nearby that you'd recommend for repairs? My little place back home is pretty basic."

"Yeah, I can take you over there this afternoon. Why don't you see if you can get a bit more sleep this morning? You look all in."

Zachary shook his head. "I've got too much to do. And if this is the work of a serial killer, every hour could make a difference."

"Serial killers don't kill every day. That's not the way it works. You have time."

Zachary considered this. Mr. Peterson was right, of course. The difference between a serial killer and a mass murderer was the cooling off period between kills. A mass murderer might kill more people all at once in one angry rampage, but a serial killer killed, had a cooling off period, and then eventually ramped up to kill again. If Jose had been taken just over a week before, and John had suggested that two to six men a year had disappeared, then he wasn't likely to kill again in the next month. Zachary wasn't racing against the clock to get the case solved in one or two days. It would take longer than that to sort out what was happening and get the police onside.

"Okay. But I still can't sleep during the day. I slept at the hospital last night, too. Not just here. So I've had enough to get me through the day."

Mr. Peterson shrugged and shook his head, giving up.

Zachary returned to the bedroom and picked up his phone. He didn't have John's direct number, which meant that he would have to go through Philippe again, and if John were at work during the day, then he was going to have to wait until the evening again before being given an opportunity to talk and discuss his needs. But Zachary might as well get started right away. Maybe he would be lucky and it would be John's day off. He'd been at the hospital quite late, so maybe he had known that he wouldn't be at work the next day and could stay up late.

Philippe answered the phone after quite a number of rings, and sounded out of breath. "Zachary?"

"Yes. Sorry, did I get you at work?"

"Yes. It's okay for a minute, but I can't let the boss see me talking on the phone. What's going on? Is everything okay?"

"I wanted to get John's number from you. Or if I can't get that, if you would get him to call or text me. He's got my card, but I didn't get his numbers."

"You met with him last night, right? Why do you need him again today? He'll need to keep his head down. Not let anyone figure out what is going on."

That was probably a bit paranoid. There was only one killer, not a big conspiracy. The chances that John would somehow tip off a serial killer as to where he had been the night before and the information he had shared with Zachary was highly unlikely.

"I need to get another copy of his documents. I ran into a problem with the pictures I took. Can you let him know? I really need to start going through all of that information. See if I can verify his findings."

"I'll call him, man," Philippe said, sounding frustrated, "but I don't know if he'll be able to do that. He works hard, and he was already out last night. If he does too much sneaking around, someone will catch on. They'll know that he's up to something."

CHAPTER SEVENTEEN

ZACHARY DIDN'T WANT TO put the case aside while he waited for a response back from John, so he considered the information he already had, and then called Detective Dougan. The policeman answered his phone with a testy 'Dougan.'

"Uh, yes, Detective Dougan. It's Zachary Goldman. I wanted to talk to you about Jose Flores for another minute, if you have the time."

"I told you that if you harass me, I'm just going to block you. What is this about now? We just talked yesterday."

"Yes, sir, and I don't intend to harass you at all. I have had a couple of developments and I just wanted to follow up with you and keep you informed."

"Have you been drinking?" Dougan asked suspiciously.

Zachary paused, frowning. "No. I haven't had anything to drink today."

"You sound like you're slurring. You haven't had anything at all?"

"Oh… no. I ran into some trouble last night, and I have a fat lip… that must be what you're hearing."

"You ran into some trouble?"

"It's unrelated," Zachary said, not wanting to have to explain again or to distract Dougan from the case at hand. "I don't want to take up any more of your time than I need to."

"Okay. Go ahead. What have you got?"

"During the course of your investigation, did you get Jose's cell phone number?"

"No, I was told he didn't have one. I figured it was bull crap. Everybody has to have a phone number these days to hold down a job. But he wasn't the registered owner of any phone number, and his landlord said he didn't have one."

"I got it from his boss and Dimitri, a friend. Same phone number from both, so it looks like it's legitimate. Dimitri says that it was working up until Wednesday. It was going to voicemail, but it was still in service. Sometime since then, it has started getting the 'not in the service area' message, so I'm assuming that's when it ran out of juice."

"I doubt it will help to shed any light on the case, but go ahead and give it to me and I'll take a look."

Zachary read the number off to him. "I thought maybe you could see who he's been talking to on the phone… maybe someone on his call logs will know what happened to him."

"Yeah. Possibly. But probably a wild goose chase. Give me this *friend's* number as well."

Zachary gave him Dimitri's number. "I'd offer to go through the logs myself, if I thought you'd give them to me."

"Unfortunately, not something I can do. We'll have to run them down ourselves. Is that it, then?"

"I wanted to ask you… and this is only very preliminary, not something I have any proof of… but has there been any investigation into rumors of gay immigrant men disappearing over the past few years? Like maybe there is someone targeting them…?"

"What?"

"I am hearing talk of quite a number of men who have disappeared in the last few years. They say that the police won't pay any attention, but I don't know if that means that the police have looked into it and discounted it as a possibility, or whether that means that they haven't looked into it."

"First I've heard of it," Dougan growled. "I can check to be sure, but I think I would have heard about it if there was an investigation underway. I don't like to get involved in finger pointing, but you should understand that every time there is a bust at one of these lounges, the gay community immediately starts whining about relations between the police and the gays and how we're always too quick to bust them and slow to listen to anything about how they are being victimized. So yeah, you do hear about violence against them whenever there is a bust. But that doesn't mean that there's anything to it."

"No, of course not. There are always going to be a lot of… different perspectives on community policing."

"Yeah. If you want to put it that way."

"I don't have anything on this yet, but… I am going to be looking over some documents on these disappearances. So this is just a heads-up that I might have something to discuss in a day or two, once I've had a chance to go through the data. I don't want to surprise you."

"You're going to find out that there's nothing to it, I can guarantee that."

"Good. I hope there isn't. I'd rather not think that someone could have been operating here for that long. I'd rather not think of the friends and family who have been left behind finding out now, years later, that it wasn't ever dealt with at the time."

"Is that a threat?"

"No." Zachary bit his lip. "I didn't mean that at all. I'd like to put this to bed just as much as you."

"I doubt that. Let me just warn you, if you get anything, you'd better be bringing it directly to me, and not discussing it with anyone else along the way. If something like this leaks out to the public, there will be widespread panic. I do not want to have to deal with the consequences of something like this getting out into the wild."

"I think you'll find that it already is in the gay community. But maybe not in the mainstream. I'm not going to give the information to anyone else. Just to you."

"See to it."

Despite his assertion to Mr. Peterson that he'd had enough sleep and wouldn't be able to sleep during the day, Zachary fell asleep while he was holding an ice pack across his eyes. He had apparently been conked out for a couple of hours when Lorne came into the room to see if he was ready to go to the camera repair shop.

"Do you want to sleep longer? We can put this off for another time."

"No." Zachary blinked his eyes, trying to clear his vision, knowing that if he rubbed them, the bruises would make him regret it. "I want to get those pictures processed as soon as I can. I haven't heard back from Philippe yet about what John said." He picked up his phone from the bed beside him and looked at it. There were several missed calls from Philippe. The ringer was turned off and with the phone on the bed, the vibration hadn't been enough to wake him up. "Oh, I guess he did. Hang on a sec, I need to see what he has to say."

Rather than checking the voicemail messages that Philippe had left, Zachary just called him. Philippe answered almost immediately this time. "Zachary? Where the hell have you been? I thought he got you too!"

"Thought who got me?" Zachary asked, a knot tightening in his stomach.

"I've been calling John and calling him. He doesn't answer. I checked with one of the guys who works at the same site as he does and John didn't show up today! He never misses work, but he didn't show up today. No one knows where he is. Every call just goes through to voicemail, and he's not returning any of them. It's just like with Jose, Zachary! What's going on?"

Zachary looked over at Mr. Peterson, who could probably hear Philippe's panicked voice, even though Zachary didn't have it on speakerphone.

"I don't know what's going on. Maybe he is sick today. Do you know where he lives? Or who he lives with?"

"They said he didn't go home last night. He went out to the hospital to see you, and then he never went home."

"He would have had to go home," Zachary said blankly.

"I know, but he didn't!"

"He had all of those papers. He would have gone home to put them away somewhere safe. He had put all that time and effort into all of that research. He wouldn't have let anyone else get their hands on it."

"He's missing!" Philippe insisted.

"I hear you... are you going to report it to the police?"

"He wouldn't want me to."

"Why not?"

"Because, we don't report each other to the police. If he was just somewhere else... I would get him in trouble. I don't want to get him in trouble."

"He could already be in trouble. Not with the police, but with someone who intends to do him harm. You need to report it."

"No, I can't. Nando told me to stay out of this. He'll kill me if he finds out that I talked to you and that I've been talking with John. I'm just supposed to be going to work, not getting myself in the middle of something like this!"

"Nando would want you to tell if you knew people were being victimized. He'd want to know about Jose and the others."

"No, he wouldn't! He would tell me to mind my own business unless I wanted to disappear too!"

Zachary didn't know what to say to that. He let the words just hang in the air. Did Nando know something about what had happened to Jose and the missing men? Or did Philippe?

"I'm going to have to get the police involved," he said finally. "They can do more if they start while the trail is fresh."

"You're just going to cause more trouble!"

"Then I'm going to cause more trouble," Zachary agreed. He hung up the phone. He looked at Mr. Peterson. "You heard?"

"Who is this John? He's the one who let you take pictures of his research?"

"Yes."

"Maybe he changed his mind. Maybe he decided that dealing with you was too dangerous and he needed to go underground."

"I hope so. I'd much rather think he was in hiding than that something had happened to him."

Dougan didn't answer the phone when Zachary called him again. Zachary wondered whether he had already blocked his number, or whether he would because Zachary had called twice in one day. But he tried to stay calm about it, left a message about John and his unexpected disappearance, and he got ready to go to the camera repair place.

Pat was up and gave Zachary a careful hug, trying to be mindful of all of his bumps and bruises. "You're a good man, Zach. Please be careful and don't do anything risky because of this case. I wouldn't want anything else to happen to you."

Neither of them had told Pat yet about the call from Philippe. Zachary was still hoping it was a mistake, and that they would soon hear that John was okay.

"I'm just fine," he assured Pat. "I know it looks bad, but… I've dealt with worse. We're just going over to the camera store. Nothing is going to happen there."

"I've been to the camera store with Lorne," Pat said, his eyebrows drawn down in a dramatic scowl, "and every time he goes, they empty out his wallet."

Zachary laughed. "Well, I can't promise they won't do that," he agreed. He might find one or two things he needed to add to his collection while he was there too. There was nothing that was quite so much fun as a camera store, especially if they had vintage cameras and parts as well as modern digital.

"I don't know if it's a good idea turning the two of you loose in a camera store," Pat said. "It's akin to taking a couple of alcoholics to a wine tasting."

In spite of Zachary's reassurances, Pat still patted his shoulder and clucked over him like a mother hen, always protective of his family.

"We won't be long," Zachary promised.

"Oh, I've heard that one before. You won't be back until you've cleaned the whole store out."

The owner and staff at the camera store gaped at Zachary's ugly bruises, and then tried to pretend they weren't staring every time they looked at him. Zachary tried to ignore the looks and just to talk to them as if everything were normal. Mr. Peterson greeted the owner as an old friend, then gestured to Zachary.

"Rocky, this is one of my of foster kids, Zachary. The only one who inherited my love of photography."

"Hi," Zachary shook hands with him. "Might have had something to do with the camera you gave me for my birthday."

Lorne waved his hand. "I knew you had the eye. That's why I gave it to you. You were a watcher, always observing everything."

"Well, it was the first birthday present I ever got, so even if I hadn't had an innate talent for it, I think I still would have pursued it as a hobby."

Mr. Peterson cocked his head. Zachary replayed what he had just said in his head. "What?"

"You mean it was the first birthday present I ever gave you?"

Zachary shook his head. "No, the first birthday present I ever got. First one I can remember, anyway. Maybe I got things as a baby, from welfare organizations, but our parents never had any money for gifts."

Mr. Peterson considered this seriously. "I never knew that."

"We didn't always have enough *food* to get by."

"Well… I guess I'm glad I got you that camera."

Rocky, the owner spread his hands in inquiry. "So, what can I do for you today?"

Lorne explained. "Zachary's got a camera that's had a little accident. We need to recover the pictures on the memory card."

"Let's have a look."

Zachary brought out the little camera and showed Rocky the card slot, with the digital memory card wedged firmly in place. Rocky examined it and also the damaged mini USB port, his mind following the same logic as Mr. Peterson's. He pulled out some tools.

"How important are the pictures and how important is the camera itself?"

"The pictures are more important. If the camera has to be replaced, I can deal with that. But the pictures are of some important documents, and I don't know if I'll ever be able to get my hands on the originals again."

Rocky nodded. "We'll see what we can do, then." He started unscrewing the tiny screws that held the camera together.

Zachary browsed through the store, not wanting to stand there staring at Rocky as he worked on the camera. He would do his work best without someone hovering over him. In a few minutes, Zachary was lost in the world of photography accessories just like a kid in a toy store.

His phone ringing pulled him out of his happy wandering. He pulled it out and looked at the display, which was a blocked number. He answered the call, his heart speeding.

"Zachary Goldman."

"It's Detective Dougan, returning your call."

"Thanks for calling back. Did you get my voicemail...?" He wasn't sure whether he needed to start at the beginning or if Dougan was already up to speed.

"Let's skip the preliminaries. I believe your John Jama Mwangi matches up with my John Doe."

"Your John Doe?" Zachary repeated, heart sinking.

"Deceased black male, six foot four, slight build, mid-forties to early fifties."

"Yes... that could be him. What happened?"

"Vehicle fire. He's in the morgue."

Zachary was shocked. He was horrified, but at the same time, relieved that John's disappearance did not follow the same pattern as the rest of the disappearances. It was just a coincidence. It was horrible, but a victim of the serial killer would have just disappeared.

"How did it happen? An accident?"

"I would say not. Looks like the car was torched with him in it. It will be some time before we hear from the medical examiner whether he was alive or dead when the fire started."

Zachary's legs went weak. "When did this happen? Where?"

"It happened in the hospital parking garage, early this morning."

He looked for somewhere to sit down, and hobbled over to a chair that had been set up by a camera on a tripod, struggling to catch his breath.

"But that's... he came to see me at the hospital last night. He must have... that would be right after he left..."

"Sounds like it," Dougan agreed.

"But... what could have happened? It wasn't an accident? It was torched?" Zachary echoed Dougan's words, trying to make sense of them and to form a picture of what had happened.

"I'd like to know how this connects up with your missing persons investigation."

"He is a witness... he believed that these other missing men were all related. He had done a bunch of research into all of the other disappearances, tried to tie them all together."

"And you believe him? That they were all related?"

"I don't know. I haven't had a chance to read through all of his research yet."

"You have his papers?"

"I took digital photos of them. He didn't want to part with the originals."

"And he had them in his briefcase?"

Zachary thought of the papers in the car. In his mind's eye, he saw the briefcase full of papers catch fire. The whoomp as the fire reached the bundle of papers and started to burn higher and brighter. How the flames would rise and jump and spread to the upholstery, consuming the whole car.

And then he was there. Not in the car, but in his childhood home as the Christmas tree went up in flames, the fire jumping to the curtains, furniture, and carpet, consuming everything in its path. The air was sucked from the room and Zachary was burning up in it, trying to crawl under the couch and to protect his face with his arms, while the fire roared around him like a living monster.

CHAPTER EIGHTEEN

ZACHARY, YOU'RE OKAY. COME on back. You're not there. You're in the camera store. Open your eyes. Look around."

Zachary became aware of Mr. Peterson's gentle touch and his calm, even voice. If Mr. Peterson was there, then the fire was long extinguished. He could breathe again. Zachary sucked in lungfuls of cool, sweet air. He pried his eyes open and took in the camera store around him, a couple of the employees gawking at him like he was some sideshow freak. Zachary held Mr. Peterson's arm, trying to ground himself back in the present.

"You're okay," Mr. Peterson repeated.

Zachary nodded, unable to speak yet. He focused on breathing slowly in and out, trying to slow the pounding of his heart. Mr. Peterson stood there waiting patiently.

"Sorry," Zachary apologized.

"You have nothing to be sorry for. You can't control the flashbacks."

"I should be able to. After this long, I should know better than to let myself think…" he trailed off, trying to force his mind away from thoughts that would take him back down that hole.

"See anything you're interested in buying today?" Mr. Peterson looked around at the shelves of camera accessories, trying to distract Zachary.

"Plenty," Zachary agreed, forcing a smile. "Just like Pat said, I could spend all of my money here."

"I'm thinking of a macro lens."

"Yeah. Those are cool."

"Were you… talking to someone?" Mr. Peterson nodded to the phone in Zachary's hand. He looked down at it and realized the call was still live. He put it back up to his ear.

"Uh—hello?"

"Mr. Goldman? What the hell is going on? Where are you?"

"I, uh… I get flashbacks sometimes. Sorry."

"Flashbacks to what? Were you a soldier?"

"No. A fire." Zachary tried to gloss over it, to focus on other aspects. "So everything was destroyed. All of John's original research."

"I would say so. Did he have a suspect? Who knew he was coming to see you?"

"I don't know who might have known about it. Just me, and him, and Philippe as far as I know. He didn't have a suspect... not that he mentioned. I'll have to see what's in his papers, but I would think that if he had a name, he would have told me, even if he couldn't prove it."

"And Philippe? Give me his info."

"He was a friend of Jose's. He's not the one."

"You can't rule out anyone Jose knew. It's a lot easier to get someone alone if they trust you."

"He's just a kid. Eighteen, maybe."

"I need to talk to him. Whether he is a suspect or not, I need to know who he talked to or who might have overheard him. If only three people knew where our vic was going to be, then one of you either torched the car or told the person who did."

Zachary sighed. He knew it was true, but he couldn't imagine Philippe having anything to do with Jose's death, not even because he had accidentally let slip to the wrong person where John was going to be. He reluctantly gave Philippe's information to Dougan.

"I want copies of all of the papers you took pictures of. They could be the key to this case. How soon can I get them?"

"As soon as I can. The camera got damaged and we're trying to recover them right now."

"The camera got damaged."

"Yes. The photos are on the memory card, they're still just fine. But we can't get the card out. I'm just at the repair place."

"You want to tell me what happened last night?"

"I told you, John came to see me at the hospital. I took pictures of his research. Then he left, and I guess that's when—"

"Back it up. I want to know the rest. Why you have a fat lip and were in the hospital last night and how your camera got damaged."

"Oh. That."

"Yes. That."

"I had... an encounter with the local skinheads."

"I see. Did you report it?"

"I talked to a cop... I don't remember his name. I might have been a little doped up on Demerol at the time."

"How badly were you hurt?"

"Cuts and bruises. Nothing broken."

"Except your camera."

"Yeah," Zachary agreed.

"As soon as you recover the photographs, I expect you to get them to me. Can you email them?"

"Sure, of course. The minute I get them."

When Zachary ended the call, he bowed his head, letting out a long breath. Mr. Peterson was still nearby, browsing the accessories and keeping an eye on Zachary. He glanced over and raised one eyebrow. "Okay?"

Zachary nodded.

"I've got it out," Rocky announced. Zachary looked over at the service counter and saw Rocky holding up the memory card with a pair of tweezers. Zachary got up, his legs still a little wobbly, and went over to him.

"And everything is accessible?"

"Let's have a look." Rocky inserted the card into a card reader and watched the computer monitor. "Looks like it's loading."

They watched the file list populate the screen. Zachary breathed out a sigh of relief. "Can you print them out so that we have a hard copy?"

"There's quite a bit here." Rocky changed the view to thumbnails. "Are they all documents? Cheaper to print them on copy paper rather than photographic paper."

"Yes. Copy paper is fine. I'm just anxious to have a hard copy right away. It's easier for me to read than a computer screen. And could I borrow your computer to email out a copy?"

Rocky hesitated. "I don't normally let customers use my computer. It's not a public terminal."

"It's important," Zachary insisted. He pulled the first page from the printer as it dropped into the tray. "Look," he showed Rocky the list of names. "These are all missing and probably murdered men. I need to get copies of all of this to the police for them to use in their investigation."

Rocky's eyes widened as he took in the length of the list. He looked at the printer as it whirred and continued to drop pages into the tray. "You can just take it home and email it from there."

"Just let me use your computer for thirty seconds," Zachary snapped.

Rocky looked taken aback. Mr. Peterson shot Zachary a surprised look from across the store.

Rocky stepped back from the computer, turning it a few degrees toward Zachary for him to use. Zachary opened the web browser and uploaded them to his cloud account then logged into his email and shared them with Dougan.

Rocky had moved away to talk with Mr. Peterson, and Zachary realized they were discussing Rocky's fee to retrieve the memory card and print the files.

"I'll pay for that," Zachary said quickly. "You don't need to do that."

"Zachary, we asked you to look into this case. If we were proper clients, you'd be billing us back for your expenses anyway, wouldn't you? There's no reason you should have to eat the costs just because we're family."

"But…"

"Zachary, let me cover it."

Zachary gave in. He was exhausted after the flashback and wanted to go somewhere he could be alone to recover. He had sent the files to Dougan. The police would be reviewing them and they would open an investigation into the missing men. Zachary would review the files too, in time, but in the meantime, the police could get started on the information John had compiled. They would probably tell Zachary to stay out of the case altogether, and his involvement would be at an end.

CHAPTER NINETEEN

H E LEAFED THROUGH THE papers as Mr. Peterson drove home, making sure that everything he could remember from the night before was there, captured from the camera. The digital memory card was safely in his wallet. He wanted to analyze everything and start figuring out the case, but his head throbbed and he was tired from the flashback. He just wanted to close his eyes and recover. Mr. Peterson had been talking, but Zachary hadn't been listening to him. He looked over when Lorne stopped talking, startled by the silence.

"Are you okay?" Lorne asked.

Zachary swallowed. He nodded. "Yeah. I'll be fine."

"I know you will be… I just want to make sure."

"Yeah. It always tires me out… but that's all. It will be okay."

He sat and listened to the radio and looked through the papers again, worrying that there would be one page missing, the key to solving the disappearances. John's copies were gone. If Zachary hadn't taken pictures the night before, then they would have been completely in the dark when the originals were destroyed. Even the list of who had disappeared. Men were forgotten after a while. They had no families and no one knew what had happened to them, and eventually everyone forgot they had even existed.

Back at Mr. Peterson's house, they reported to Pat on the recovery of the files. Zachary skipped supper and went to the guest room where he had spent the night before, shutting the door so he could let himself go without being observed. He knew his foster father was not far away if he needed his stabilizing influence, but his immediate need was for space to just be alone with his own thoughts and memories. The next day, he would start compiling the evidence and seeing what he could come up with.

Zachary awoke in the morning to his ringing phone. He had taken a sleeping pill the night before and had slept through the early dawn when he usually woke. But it wasn't late. Zachary rubbed his gritty eyes and looked at the screen. It was a blocked call. Dougan.

"Zachary Goldman."

"Goldman, I should throw your butt in jail. What do you think you're doing, spreading your theories to a reporter?"

Zachary blinked and tried to figure out what Dougan was talking about. "What?"

"You act like you're being helpful and cooperative, and then you throw the police department under the bus! How are we supposed to conduct a proper investigation when you tell everybody what's going on? If we ever had a chance to get close to John Mwangi's killer without alerting him to our suspicions, that's out the window now. I can't believe that you would be so irresponsible!"

"Detective Dougan… I don't know what you're talking about."

"You don't. No one else had this information. It could only have come from you. You couldn't even give us a few days to look at the evidence and pull things together. You just jump in with both feet and put everything in jeopardy."

"I don't know what you're talking about. I haven't talked to any reporter. I haven't talked to anyone."

"That's clearly not true. It wasn't Mwangi who went to the press. He didn't have time after talking to you. And he's been sitting on this information for months already. Why would he suddenly release it after talking to you? He wouldn't. Because *you're* the one who did."

"I haven't talked to anyone."

"You're the only one who had the documents."

"Yes. As far as I know."

"Then how did they get all over the morning paper? That list of names has gotten everyone in a panic. The phone has not stopped ringing. They want to know how the police could have sat on the news of a serial killer for so long without letting the public know the risk. We haven't even determined that there is a serial killer! That's your theory, and it hasn't been proven in any way."

"It's not even my theory. I haven't gone through everything yet either. I haven't even verified that all of the men on the list are missing."

"Well, you've thrown it all into the public eye now, and that doesn't make it easier for us to investigate, it makes it harder."

"I didn't give it to anyone." Zachary tried to sort out what Dougan was telling him. "They had the list? I don't understand… As soon as we got the documents off of the memory card, I printed them off and I emailed a copy to you. That's it. No one else has seen them."

"Who else has access to your computer?"

"It wasn't my computer."

Zachary's heart sank as he realized that it must have been Rocky or someone else on his staff. Zachary had lost his cool and told them about the missing and murdered men. Rocky had either copied what was on the card onto his hard drive, or Zachary had left his email box open in the browser, giving him access to what he had sent to Dougan.

He swore under his breath. "I didn't want to wait until I could get to another computer to send it to you. So I borrowed the camera shop's computer to email them to you right away. He must have kept a copy."

Dougan swore as well. "Brilliant, Goldman. Just brilliant."

CHAPTER TWENTY

ACHARY OPENED THE WEB browser on his phone to look up the local news site to see how bad the exposure had been. Maybe it would just blow over and after the initial panic, everyone would just go back to whatever they had been worrying about before the story broke. If people hadn't cared about the missing men before, then why would they worry now? After the initial shock wore off, people would decide that they were in no danger themselves and would go back to their own lives.

But the story had broken big. He immediately saw that it was not only on the local news, but had been reported in the national papers' websites as well. They were all just regurgitating what the local paper had said and adding that the police had no comment, but it was everywhere. It wasn't going to just blow over.

Some of them had done a little digging and had sidebars on Zachary's attack by the skinheads and on the fire that had killed John. Once the first one had reported that Zachary had been attacked after leaving The Night Scene, the rest of the articles had reported that he was gay himself, and that was what had sparked his interest in the case. Pat's and Lorne's names were also mentioned, reported as being 'prominent men in the gay community.'

Zachary felt sick.

He opened the bedroom door and walked to the kitchen, where Mr. Peterson and Pat sat with their coffee and a newspaper. Zachary could only hope that the story hadn't made it to the printed news before the deadline.

But Pat's ashen face told him that his hope was vain.

They both looked at him without a word. Without the usual cheery morning smiles.

"I'm sorry," Zachary said. "I didn't talk to anyone. I swear. It wasn't me."

"How did they get this, then?" Mr. Peterson asked.

Zachary licked his dry lips. He glanced over at the coffee machine. "It must have been Rocky or someone on his staff. They had the recovered files."

Mr. Peterson shook his head slowly. "Good grief. I never would have expected Rocky to do something like that. That's my fault, Zachary. I should never have taken you there."

"You had no way of knowing. We just went there to get the camera fixed. They shouldn't have used it for their own purposes."

"No."

Pat was still looking at Zachary with wide eyes. "Do you really think this is the work of a serial killer?"

"I don't know. I haven't spent enough time going through the documents. I don't even know yet if John was right and they are all missing. Some of these guys could be reading about their own deaths right now and be pretty surprised. I need to go through and verify everything."

"I would guess the police will be doing that now. They have more manpower than you do."

"They haven't even opened an investigation into this," Zachary said. "They just got the information yesterday, and like I said, it has to all be verified before we go jumping to any conclusions. I do think… that it is more than coincidence that ties all of these men together. It looks too much like a pattern. But it's way too early to tell."

"The paper says there is an investigation underway."

"I know… but they're wrong. There are two investigations right now. Jose's missing persons case and John's death. I don't know if any missing persons files were ever opened on any of the other men. But there is no serial murder investigation. There's no task force, at least not as of five minutes ago. And just in case you're wondering, I am not gay."

Pat cracked a smile at that. "I think I know that. I get your point. They haven't gotten all of the facts right. This is just so shocking." He shook his head in dismay. "I had no idea, when we talked to you about Jose, that it would lead to any of this."

"How could you? I'm just following the evidence, seeing where it leads. There wasn't any way to predict it." Zachary poured himself a cup of coffee. "I guess I'd better hit the books."

"Do you need any help?" Mr. Peterson asked. "Reading, collating information, anything?"

He knew that reading wasn't Zachary's strongest suit. But Zachary's skills had grown and developed as a private investigator, and he had gotten accustomed to reading and managing large amounts of paperwork when he had to.

"I'll take my ADHD meds so that I can focus on it, and I'll start a database or wiki on the computer to tame all the facts. It's a big job, but I can manage it."

"Well, if you need anything, just let me know. You can rest your eyes and I can read some of it to you. I'm not so much good on the computer, but you can bounce ideas off of us. Talk about theories, see what fits."

"Thanks. I'll let you know." He had worked out how to make his computer read digital documents aloud to him, so he didn't need Mr. Peterson for that. But he might take him up on brainstorming ideas together.

"And you need more for breakfast than just coffee."

"One piece of toast," Zachary conceded.

"You eat the whole thing."

"I'll try."

When Zachary walked through the living room to get back to the guest bedroom, he saw unusual activity out the front window and stopped for a closer look. There was an assortment of trucks that didn't belong there, with satellite dishes on top and people milling about with cameras and boom mikes. Zachary stared at them.

"I see you've noticed our visitors," Pat observed.

"How long have they been here?"

"Since before we got up. That security system of yours woke us up when they got too close to the house, so I chased them back over the property line. They've been pretty good since then, but we're leaving the system armed so we know if they start getting too close again."

"Why would they be here?"

"To interview you."

"Or the prominent citizens in the Vermont gay community," Mr. Peterson added, smiling.

Zachary rubbed his temples. "Oh, man... I'm so sorry about this."

"This isn't anything you did, Zachary. This is something that we all walked into. It's part of finding out what happened to Jose. If he was the victim of a predator who has been killing other gay men for the past few years... then this is what we need to do. We can't back down just because it's inconvenient."

"I should have been more careful, though. I should have made sure that Rocky hadn't copied anything to his hard drive. Made sure that I logged out and cleared the web browser. I shouldn't have emailed the files from there at all. I don't know what I was thinking. Just that the faster I got them to Dougan, the sooner we could start getting some answers."

"Zachary, we're all in this together. Pat and I fully support you on this. Pat asked you to look into it. I took you to the camera shop. None of us could have predicted this outcome, or we might have approached it differently. But you didn't do anything but follow the evidence. If you've found more than the police did, that just shows what a good investigator you are."

Zachary remained hyperfocused on John's papers for most of the morning, pulled out of it once or twice due to the whoops of the security system when the crowd outside got too close to the house. He had his phone turned to airplane mode so he wouldn't be interrupted by reporters or other curious inquiries. When he took a break, he turned his phone back on to collect his messages. He saw that one of them was from Kenzie and gave her a call back.

"Oh, so you are deigning to speak to the rest of us common folk?" Kenzie teased when she picked up.

"Sorry. Had to turn the phone off to get anything done this morning."

"I don't doubt it. I thought your questions about profiling the other days were theoretical. You actually took on a serial killer case?"

"Well… not intentionally. It was just the disappearance of a friend that Pat asked me to look into. But I guess you know now he wasn't the only one to disappear."

"Me, along with the rest of the country. You made the news in a big way. And the fact that you've solved a couple of murders in the last year gives you a bit of credibility."

"I'm not the one who leaked it. That was… unintentional. I wasn't looking for any publicity."

"You've certainly caused some waves. Phone lines are all lit up looking for comments from officers who have had contact with the great Zachary Goldman on other cases."

"No one is going to talk to them, though, right? Just a lot of 'no comments.'"

"That's the official line. I don't know whether they'll be able to wring a quote out of anybody anonymously, but there won't be anything official." She paused. "And then there are people who know that you and I have been seeing each other for the last year and are now confused by the report that you're gay."

Zachary felt himself flush. "You know that's not true."

"Well, it would explain a few things…"

"Kenzie, I just don't want to rush things—"

She was laughing. "After your experience with Bridget, I don't blame you for not wanting to rush things. But then, I wouldn't blame you for going off of women, either…"

"I was at the bar for the investigation. If I'm investigating the disappearance of a gay man, doesn't it make sense to investigate the places he frequented?"

She gave another laugh and let him off the hook. "Okay, okay. Really, I wasn't calling to bust your chops. I just thought I'd check in with you and see how you were doing. So how are you?"

"I'm okay." Zachary considered. "I'm not as anxious about the publicity as you would think."

"That's good, but I was more worried about your trip to the hospital. How badly are you hurt?"

"Bumps and bruises. Nothing broken or ruptured."

"Still, you must be pretty sore. How many were there?"

Zachary thought back. It had all happened so fast. He tried to slow it down in his brain. "Maybe... six. Two guys were holding me, and..."

Kenzie swore. "You're lucky you're still in one piece. How did you manage to get away?"

"A bystander interrupted them."

"Lucky for you."

"Yeah, it was. Could have been a lot worse."

"How are Pat and Lorne handling the publicity? I don't imagine they were expecting to have a spotlight shined on their lives."

"There are reporters camped out outside their house. They're handling it pretty well, but I hope it doesn't go on for too long. Another story will break, and the reporters will have to go somewhere else."

"Serial killers are good copy. They won't give up for a while."

"Thanks."

She chuckled. "Just had to bring a little ray of sunshine into your life. But seriously, you're okay?"

"Yeah. Thanks."

"And I know you probably aren't as far along in the investigation as you were hoping to be, but do you have everything you need on serial killers?"

"I'm going on your advice and trying to match up suspects with opportunity, rather than a psychological profile."

"That will give you the most solid information. You can get a behaviorist to try to create a profile for you, but they're not as accurate as you see on TV. It might help you to focus on a smaller group of suspects, but you wouldn't be able to rely on it like an alibi."

"Motive, means, and opportunity. That's what I'm going to focus on."

"Good. Are there many suspects?"

Zachary thought of the people he had already talked to. None of them had struck him as serial killers, but wasn't that what they always said? *He was the nicest guy. He was so quiet. Always helpful.* And then there were the names he had pulled from the online forums.

"I don't really have a handle on it yet. I'll be looking for connections between the victims. Did they frequent the same places, live in the same area, have mutual friends, that kind of thing?"

"If this guy has been hunting the same waters for a few years... he's going to be hard to spot. Or he would have already been discovered."

"Yeah."

"You should probably just let the police investigate it. They aren't going to want you getting in the way, and you can't exactly hide your investigation from the killer now. I wouldn't want you to be a target."

"I'm just reading files right now. And the police haven't yet opened an investigation, despite what the reporters are saying. They have an investigation open on Jose's disappearance, and on my informant's death, nothing on a serial killer. We're all a bit behind the eight ball. No one was expecting this to go public so soon."

"This informant… that's all a little spooky. He comes to you with this theory, and then he gets murdered within an hour? No one can tell me that's a coincidence."

"I know." Zachary had been trying not to focus on this issue as he worked his way through John's papers. He just kept telling himself how much he appreciated the work that John had done and how lucky he had been to find him.

"You need to be careful, okay? Neo-Nazis and burning cars… you're taking risks."

"I'm at home with Pat and Mr. Peterson. They have a state-of-the art security system. We're surrounded by reporters eager to get a picture of something they can publish. We couldn't be much safer."

"Okay. Well, you be careful. It's really the job of the police department, not you, so let them do their thing."

"I will," Zachary agreed.

CHAPTER TWENTY-ONE

ZACHARY DIALED PHILIPPE'S NUMBER with the list of possible victims in front of him. Philippe hadn't been around for long, but he might have known the last few people on John's list, since the two of them were acquainted. And he might have the names of some of the other men who would know the earlier victims.

The phone rang immediately through to voicemail. Zachary hung up and looked at his phone.

There was no reason to jump to the conclusion that something had happened to Philippe. If any of the news articles had linked him to Zachary or Jose, he was probably dealing with calls from reporters and, like Zachary, had either turned his phone to airplane mode or turned it off. Or he had seen Zachary's number and sent it to voicemail or had blocked it. There was no reason to think that something had happened to the boy.

He looked up Nando's number and it also went to voicemail. Chances were, the illegals were spooked. Now that Zachary's name had shown up in the news, they wanted nothing to do with him. They didn't want to be caught in any investigation, whether by the police, or Zachary, or news reporters. They knew how to go underground to avoid inquiries.

Zachary went to talk to Pat, and found him busy in the kitchen making sandwiches.

"Be ready in a few minutes," Pat promised.

Zachary wasn't hungry, but he knew Pat was right and he should probably eat soon, so he didn't argue. "I was wondering whether you had talked to your friends."

"What friends, Zach?"

"I asked if I could talk to some of your acquaintances who knew Jose. You said you needed to talk to them first. So I'm wondering whether there's any way I could talk to them now…?"

"All of the publicity complicates things. I don't know how far you'll be able to get with them. But I've got a couple who said yesterday that they would talk to you."

Zachary let out his breath, relieved. "Good. And I have some names I wanted you to look at, when you're not busy…"

Pat glanced at him. "The names of the missing men?"

"Uh, yeah. I wondered whether you knew any of the others."

"There are different social groups in the community, just like with any population. Jose moved between the music scene and some… riskier places. Most of the people Lorne and I do things with are stable older couples or bachelors. Not young pups who are polyamorous. The newspaper articles blurred the last names of the missing men, but I don't think I knew any of the others. Not well enough to know anything about their lives, anyway."

"I'll show you the unmasked list, just to be sure. It might trigger something."

Pat nodded. "Just don't get your hopes up. If this guy has avoided discovery, it's by targeting men who aren't in committed relationships. Otherwise, their partners would have talked to the police."

"Even if they're illegals?"

"Hard to say," Pat admitted, "but I would think some of them would have, considering the number of names on that list."

Eric Naylor had agreed to talk to Zachary, but it was obvious he was still leery of the idea. Zachary arrived at his used clothing store at closing time, as Naylor had suggested, and when Naylor got a look at him, Zachary thought he was going to lock him out. The swelling on Zachary's face was going down, but the bruises were setting in and the split cheek and lip were still livid. Despite the fact that he looked like a victim rather than a goon, Naylor still looked hesitant about letting him in. Eventually, he steeled himself and opened the door wide for Zachary, then closed it and locked it behind him, turning the sign over to 'closed.'

Naylor was an older man, probably in his sixties, slim and neat and expensively dressed. He had long, tapering fingers and a prissy manner.

"I appreciate you agreeing to see me," Zachary told him. "I know you probably aren't too eager to talk about what might have happened to Jose, especially in light of all of the stuff in the news today."

"I think, actually, that seeing it in the news made it seem more real. When Pat said that he was afraid something had happened to Jose, I didn't think it was anything. He could have just gone away without telling anybody. But seeing all of those names… if this really is a serial killer…"

"We don't know yet. But we'd like to catch the guy if it is. Before he hurts anyone else."

Naylor nodded. He busied himself with tidying up the store as he talked to Zachary, his fingers always moving.

"Do you recognize the names of anyone else on this list?" Zachary handed him the printed page.

Naylor's eyes went over it, working their way down the page. "I don't think so," he said. "Sometimes you know someone's first name and not their last, but I don't recognize anyone."

"Okay, thanks. So you were part of the group that hung out sometimes with Pat and Lorne? And Jose?"

"Yeah. We like our music," Naylor made an abbreviated motion in the air, as if he were leading a band. "When there was someone good playing or singing, we made sure we were there."

"In mixed groups, or just LGBT venues?"

"Mostly LGBT. That's where we can fit in and not have to worry about being harassed. But if there was something we just had to see at a bigger venue, we would."

"Were you and Jose close?"

Naylor flashed him a look. "Is that what Pat told you?"

"He didn't say anything. I'm wondering."

"We were friendly. We did things with the group."

"You never saw each other outside of the group?"

"We didn't date."

Zachary filed that away for future reference. "What did you talk about?"

"Music. Other things. Small-talk. Work."

"Did he talk to you about his job?"

"No. He asked about the shop sometimes, I'd tell him anything interesting that had happened. You know, interesting customers, estate sales, bell-bottoms."

"Sure." Zachary looked around the store. It was higher than thrift-store quality. Vintage or designer, mostly. An upper-class used closing store. "You look like you carry some good stuff."

Naylor smiled, looking around his shop. He nodded. "It's a good place. I enjoy the work."

"You must not be here by yourself."

"Right now, yes. But not during the day. I have several employees. I close up on my own, spend time on administrative tasks. Things like that."

"Did you ever consider hiring Jose or any of the other immigrants?"

"Uh… no… I liked Jose, but I wouldn't hire illegals. I don't want to get in trouble with the feds. That's a good way to ruin a business."

"They're cheap labor, if you don't get caught. Better margins."

"Not worth the risk."

"What did Jose talk about? His family back home? What his plans were for the future?"

"Not much. He would mention them in passing, but we were… in a different space than all of that. It was an escape. He could be himself instead of a family man, someone who was responsible for others… he could relax."

"Makes sense. Did he ever talk to you about his other friends? People he saw outside of your group?"

Another sideways look. Naylor made a show of trying to remember any such conversation, then shook his head. "No, I don't think he ever did."

Zachary let the silence draw out for a few seconds. He raised a brow at Naylor. "I don't get the feeling you're being completely honest with me."

"What do you mean? I'm answering your questions."

"Yeah. What I mean is, whenever I ask you something about your personal relationship with Jose, I get the feeling you're lying or avoiding the question."

"I don't know what you're talking about."

"You're lying to me about something."

"What did Pat tell you? I am not in a relationship with Jose."

"I don't think *anyone* is in a relationship with Jose anymore. This has nothing to do with Pat. I just asked him for names of other people in your circle of friends who would talk to me about Jose. He didn't say anything about your relationship. But your body language whenever you talk about him... is wrong."

Naylor just stared at him challengingly, not changing his tune.

Zachary leaned on one of the clothing racks, studying Naylor's expression. He watched for any change. "One of Jose's partners told me that he had bruises on his throat one day. Like someone had choked him."

Naylor's eyes got wide.

"Was that you?" Zachary asked.

"No, it certainly was not!" Naylor's tone was heated. His voice had a satisfying ring of truth. He did not like hearing about Jose getting hurt. Or he didn't like hearing about one of Jose's other partners.

"Did he tell you who it was? Or did you already know?"

"I didn't know anything about it."

"You must know some of the men that he's gone with. He talks with you. He must mention his social life sometimes."

"There are rules. You don't talk about people's other partners."

"Ah." Zachary nodded at the confirmation that they *had* been seeing each other. "That's one of the rules. And it never gets broken? It would be easy to slip up now and then, or maybe someone didn't like the rule and wanted to talk about others."

"No." Naylor shook his head. "No, we follow the rules."

"Who else was Jose with?"

"I don't know."

"Just because you didn't talk about it, that doesn't mean you don't know."

Naylor's eyes narrowed. He looked down at the floor, worried.

"Jose is gone. I don't know if he's alive anymore or not," Zachary said. "After more than a week... probably not. Don't you want to find out who did this to him? Don't you want to know who it is that's taking other men in the community? You can't just turn a blind eye to it and pretend it's not happening." Zachary paused, analyzing Naylor's expression. "Or maybe you don't care, as long as he doesn't come after you. You're not dark-skinned like the others. You're tall and fair. Not the same physical type at all. So maybe you don't care about any killer, as long as he doesn't come after you. You and the rest of the community will just stay quiet and let him prey on immigrants, because they don't count."

"Of course they count!" Naylor said hotly. "They are people just like anyone else. Being from another country or being dark-skinned or dark-haired doesn't make you less of a person. They matter just as much as anyone."

"Then help me. Lying to me isn't going to help Jose. It isn't going to help the other men. If you tell me the truth, you might be able to protect others in the future. Maybe other current partners. How many of the men that you are seeing now meet that type?"

"I'm not here to talk about my personal life," Naylor said stubbornly.

"So you don't really care about saving anyone else's life. You're just worried about your own reputation."

"I... I am a business owner. I can't have people looking at me as if I'm just a... I am a mature, responsible member of this community."

"I don't see what your personal practices have to do with any of that. And I'm not going to tell anyone what you tell me now. I'm just trying to find out what happened to Jose. I want to know who it is that's taking these men. It's been going on for years. Maybe you don't care if it keeps going on. What's another five or ten years? Twenty to sixty men. Your community will tolerate that kind of loss. There are always new immigrants, and new couples moving in because of the marriage laws. They refresh the pool."

"You can't talk about them like that, as if they're just playing pieces and don't matter!"

"That's how you're treating them. Like your reputation is worth more than they are."

Naylor slammed his hand down on an accessories table, sending a number of small pieces flying. "You don't have any right to talk to me like that!"

"Then tell the truth. How hard is it to admit that you and Jose were together?"

"Yes, okay. We were together. Sometimes. Privately. Not in public."

"That's fine. I don't care if you never went out with him in public. I want to know who was seeing him and what you know about it. You know that the person most likely to harm him is an intimate partner, don't you? Statistically speaking, the person most likely to kill him is a lover."

"I did not kill him."

"Maybe not, but who else might have known where he was or might have had reason to be jealous of him? Who were his enemies? Ex-lovers? Did his wife know he was seeing men while she was waiting for him to bring her here?"

"I don't know who else he was seeing."

"I thought you were going to start telling me the truth."

"I am."

"Who else?"

Naylor growled. "Philippe. You already knew that. John Mwangi. Honore Santiago. Others. I didn't always find out if it was just a one-time encounter. Even if you don't talk about it… you get a feel after a while. Suspicions. The way people react around each other."

"And do you know who choked him?"

"No."

Zachary believed it. "Did you ask him about it?"

"He said it was off-limits," Naylor's tone was sullen.

"Philippe still talked to him about it. Demanded to know who it was."

"Philippe is a boy. He doesn't always follow the rules." Naylor gave Zachary an appraising look. "What did Jose tell Philippe?"

"He suggested it was consensual."

Naylor frowned, shaking his head.

"You don't think so?" Zachary asked.

"I don't know. It was… out of character."

"Do you think he was lying?"

"I thought…" Naylor fiddled with the clothing in a rack closer to Zachary, adjusting the spacing between the garments. "I thought he was afraid."

"And what did you think of that? What did you do?"

"I wanted to know what had happened, how he had gotten hurt, but he wouldn't talk to me about it. He said it was off-limits, but I thought he was just saying that to make me stop asking."

"So what did you do?"

"I stopped asking." Naylor gave a shrug. "What was I supposed to do? I wanted to spend the time with him. I didn't want a fight. So I figured he could take care of himself. He was an adult. If there was trouble, he could handle it." Naylor shook his head, eyes glassy. "Would it have made any difference if I had done something? What? Tell him to go to the police? Force him to tell me who it was and confronted them? There wasn't anything I could do if he didn't want to talk about it."

Zachary nodded. "I don't know what you could have done. He wouldn't go to the police because he was illegal."

Naylor sighed. "It makes them so vulnerable. How would you like to be invisible? Disposable? He didn't have any rights."

Zachary did know what it was like to be invisible and disposable. "It must have been very difficult." Zachary waited a few seconds, watching Naylor's face, curious about whether he would let the tears fall or force them back.

Naylor looked away. "How long was this before he disappeared?"

"A week, maybe two. Long enough to put it out of my mind. I don't think it could have been related."

"What did you think happened when he disappeared?"

"I thought… he was gone. He must have taken off. Immigration caught wind of him or he decided to move on somewhere else."

"Did he ever talk about going somewhere else? Was there somewhere he would have liked to have gone?"

Naylor gave a little laugh. "Somewhere warmer. Hawaii. He never talked about it seriously. Just one of those things you fantasize about. What you would do if you had the money and the means. Retire somewhere warm and live the good life. It wasn't something that was ever going to happen to him."

"And there wasn't anywhere else, somewhere he might really go? Somewhere there was better work? A friend or relative who could help him?"

"No. Not that we ever talked about."

"It didn't occur to you to go to the police when he disappeared?"

"No. He wouldn't want that."

"But you didn't say anything to Pat when he went to the police?"

"He didn't ask *my* permission. I didn't know he was doing it. I would have told him not to bother, but that's all."

"He didn't know about the two of you?"

"Not that he ever said. But he and I didn't discuss personal relationships. I knew that he and Lorne were happy together and weren't looking for anyone else. When we got together as a group, it was just as friends, and Jose and I never showed any special affection in public."

"Do you think that there is someone out there who is killing these men? Or do you think that they just disappeared by their own choice?"

Naylor fiddled with the buttons on the front of a jacket on display. "I don't know. There are rumors. People say not to go out alone. To make sure you have someone to walk you to your car. I always thought it was a little bit 'Big Bad Wolf.' Something that people said to make sure you didn't go wandering in the woods alone. Not a real threat. Something to keep people alert and avoid encounters with skinheads and other gay-bashers."

Zachary ignored the subtle jab. His eyes were following Naylor's fingers, distracted by his fidgeting. He looked at the jacket, trying to capture the thought nagging in the back of his brain. He concentrated.

In the picture Pat had given him, Jose had been dressed up. When Zachary had seen Jose's possessions in the rented apartment with Nando, there had been no sign of formal clothing. Not on Jose's bed, and nothing hanging in the closets.

CHAPTER TWENTY-TWO

"I S THAT JOSE'S JACKET?"

Naylor stiffened. He turned his head and looked at Zachary.

"He might have worn it once or twice." He ran his hand down the jacket nostalgically, as if remembering it lying over Jose's chest. He looked back at Zachary again. "With a store like this, do you think I'd let him show up at La Rouge in a t-shirt? He always came here before we went out."

Zachary looked around the store with new eyes. Serial killers sometimes kept trophies. Was it possible that any of the clothes on display had belonged to or been worn by any of the other missing men? How would anyone ever know? Though, if Naylor were keeping trophies, surely he wouldn't have them out front where other people could buy them. Maybe on a special rack in the back of the store, carefully protected in garment bags. Or was it a game for him, watching to see who would buy them? Maybe getting to know the men who bought them.

It was a morbid thought, and Zachary knew he was letting his imagination run wild. He needed to focus on the evidence. What could be proven. Not flights of fancy.

"Did you date—or see—any of the other missing men?" He'd already asked Naylor if he knew any of the other men on the list, but wanted to touch on it again, now that Naylor had admitted his relationship with Jose.

Naylor shook his head. "No. I don't know many of the immigrants. Jose was... special."

"Have you dated any men who disappeared who are not on the list?"

"People come and go... go in and out of circulation... but I don't think so."

"If you did, you should tell me now. It wouldn't be good if it came up later," Zachary warned.

"You think I have something to do with these men disappearing? That's ridiculous. Whoever it is, if there is a serial killer, it's not me. He's not anything like me. There are plenty of people out there bashing gays. You should be looking at them, not at me."

Zachary tended to agree with him. Naylor's name had not popped up in any of John's papers or with any of the people Zachary had questioned at the club. There was no reason to suspect him of having anything to do with the disappearances.

"I just want to be sure. We don't want there to be any confusion over who you knew and who you didn't." He used 'we' as a reminder that he wouldn't be the only one asking questions about the missing men. The police too would want those answers, and if they got a different answer from him than from Zachary, it would bring up more questions and suspicions.

"I don't remember meeting any of them. Maybe we ran into each other at some social event. I can't say I was never in the same room as any of them or talked to them. But I didn't have a relationship with any of them. Only Jose."

Unlike Naylor, Honore Santiago, rival for Jose's affections, didn't want to meet Zachary at his place of business or at home. He wanted neutral ground. Neutral turned out to be La Rouge, the gay lounge that Naylor had mentioned, so it wasn't nearly as neutral as Zachary would have liked. So close on the heels of the attack by the skinheads, it was about the last place he wanted to be seen. Maybe that had been Santiago's hope when he suggested it.

Climbing right back into the saddle was probably the best thing for Zachary. It meant he didn't have the time to develop a phobia of gay venues. He would go, nothing bad would happen to him, and his brain would learn that it wasn't an innately dangerous place to be. If Mr. Peterson and Pat ever wanted to take him to some show they loved, he would want to be able to go and not to be held back by unwarranted fears.

He planned to do the opposite of what he had done at the bar, having his car valet-parked so that he would be able to step right out the front door and not walk along lonely streets to get to it.

He hadn't expected to run into any issues. He had gotten into the bar without any problems; it had looked just like any other bar and people had walked by it on the street without another look. La Rouge was a different story. There were all kinds of people up and down the sidewalks in front of and beside the lounge. Not patrons, but protesters and reporters.

There probably wouldn't have been reporters there if not for the news of the serial killer. They wouldn't be hanging around La Rouge waiting for something to happen or to get pictures of gay celebs. But the word was that there was a serial killer targeting gay men in the state, and where else would such a killer go? Obviously he would go somewhere gay men hung out. La Rouge might not be quite the kind of place that the MSM immigrant men hung out, but the reporters wanted photo ops, and La Rouge was big and flashy and recognizable.

Apparently, it was also where the gay bashers had gone to make their voices heard. As Zachary got closer, he could see some of their signs citing scripture and sin and burning in hell. There were women there with children. It was the last place that Zachary would have brought children, especially at night. He supposed the protesters thought that they would be less likely to be arrested if they had children with them, since the police wouldn't want to have to deal with screaming children and figuring out what to do with them while their parents were arrested. Or maybe the children were supposed to make the gay men feel guilty in some way. Embarrassed to be seen at such a wicked place by innocent children. Or sad that they could not have biological children as a gay couple. They must have had some logical reason to bring children there, other than their entertainment.

The traffic slowed to a crawl, which gave Zachary time to reconsider meeting there. He could call Santiago back and suggest that they meet somewhere else, since it was such a circus at La Rouge. He didn't even have to use the reporters or protesters as a reason not to go. He could just say that he had run into traffic, or that something had come up.

But he didn't want to give himself an excuse to avoid the lounge and to reinforce to his brain that it was a dangerous place to be. By confronting it head on, he would teach himself that it was nothing to be afraid of. So he stayed in the lane inching toward La Rouge, texting Santiago that he was going to be late but would be there as soon as traffic allowed.

Giving his car to the valet meant that he had to get out right in front of the reporters. There was no easy way to avoid them. He hadn't planned for a trip to La Rouge; he didn't have a tux or a black suit or any kind of fancy dress. He had a button-up shirt and a jacket, and had borrowed a tie from Pat, so he was dressed decently, but his face attracted immediate attention. Zachary heard a collective gasp when he got out of the car and handed the valet his keys, as people saw his bruised face and then started to talk to each other, pointing him out. It wasn't long before he was hearing his name in their comments. They had clearly made the connection between his beaten and bruised face and the man in the news.

A wave of reporters surged forward as he got close to the front doors, shouting their questions and holding up cameras. Security was already on hand and did their best to restrain and subdue the intruders, and one of them was quickly at Zachary's side, sweeping him inside.

"Sorry about that, sir. We don't usually have this much trouble. Everyone is going crazy over the articles in the news today, about the possibility of a serial killer, did you hear?"

He looked at Zachary and his eyes widened at the condition of Zachary's face.

"Uh... you look like you've already experienced worse than being harassed by reporters and Bible thumpers! Are you alright?"

"Yeah, thanks. Sorry for all of the disruption."

"It's not your fault." The security guard passed him off to the maître d', with a murmur of "Welcome to La Rouge, sir."

The maître d' was skinny like a greyhound, with the same alert, quivering-with-expectation look. The guy was going to have a stroke by the time he was forty if he didn't chill.

"Welcome, sir, welcome. Are you meeting another party here today, or are you alone?"

"I'm meeting someone. Santiago?"

"Monsieur Santiago..." The maître d' looked down at his appointment book and nodded vigorously. "Of course. You have a private dining room. I think you will find that quite acceptable. This way, sir."

Zachary followed the greyhound through the busy lounge until he came to a series of small, private dining areas. Each one had a room name beside the door, and the maître d' stopped beside one labeled 'Presidential.' He knocked lightly on the door, waited two seconds, and then opened it a crack. He peered in through the crack, then swung the door wide for Zachary, giving a grand gesture. "There you go, sir."

CHAPTER TWENTY-THREE

ZACHARY ENTERED THE SMALL, dark-paneled room. The lighting was dimmer than he had expected, but it wasn't dark. There was a dining table, a sideboard with drinks, and various paintings and plaques on the wall. The man standing at the sideboard pouring himself a drink was, he assumed, Honore Santiago. He was a tall man, darker than the Hispanics but not as black as John. He was luxuriously dressed in clothing that Zachary was sure had designer names he wouldn't even recognize. The thread count was probably higher than he could count, and it had all been hand-woven by children in some third-world country with twig-thin fingers. He was slender, but not whippet-thin like the maître d'.

"Mr. Goldman," Santiago said. "It is a pleasure."

He offered his hand to Zachary, but when Zachary held his hand out to shake, the tall black man instead grasped it with one hand and brought the other hand in to caress the back of Zachary's hand, holding his sandwiched between them. Zachary jerked reflexively to pull away, but the older man held on, giving him a wide, bright smile and pressing Zachary's hand between his own firmly. Zachary nodded, gave a little squeeze, and then managed to extricate himself from the man's grip.

"Nice to meet you too, Mr. Santiago. But you can just call me Zachary."

"Delighted. Won't you have a drink?"

"I can't mix it with my medications," Zachary said, indicating the bruises on his face. "Just something fizzy, no alcohol."

"Of course! Coke with a twist? Or do you prefer sparkling water?"

"Coke is great."

He stood near Santiago's elbow, not sure whether he was supposed to sit down, prepare his own drink, or stand there while Santiago prepared it. Apparently, the third was acceptable, and he took the cold glass from Santiago once it was prepared. Santiago then motioned to the table set with sparkling china and silverware.

"Won't you have a seat, my good man. I don't imagine it's good for you to be on your feet for too long after what you have been through."

"I'm fine, really. It's worse than it looks."

"Not according to my sources. You're lucky you didn't have internal bleeding or a ruptured spleen or kidney. You're supposed to be taking it easy."

Zachary sat down where Santiago had indicated and put the Coke by his plate. "I am taking it easy. I'm sitting down."

"You're running all over town pursuing a serial killer. That's not exactly taking it easy."

Zachary didn't point out that the reason he was running around town was because of where Santiago wanted to meet with him. "I'm sitting down to talk with you. That's all. Then I'll go home and hit the hay before midnight."

"Ah, we'll see about that. You really should stay and take in the floor show. At least part of it. I don't know how many chances you will get to see the divine group that is playing today. The next time you hear of them, they'll probably be on a world tour, sold out before it even starts."

Zachary shrugged. He didn't have that much interest in music, or theater, or cabaret or whatever La Rouge was showing that night.

"We really don't need to do dinner," Zachary said, gesturing to the plates. "I don't have much appetite. I just thought we would have a discussion and then I'll be on my way. You don't need to entertain me or to feed me. Really."

"Nonsense. How could I not?" Santiago sat down and put down his old-fashioned glass. He leaned forward in his seat, lacing his fingers together with his elbows on the table. "Now, where has that naughty Pat been hiding you? You are the most fascinating person! He should have told us about you *ages* ago."

Zachary tried to ignore Santiago's dramatic, flamboyant manner and just talk to him as if they were businessmen having a routine discussion. He didn't want to get wound up by all of Santiago's nervous energy and enthusiasm. If he did, he would either be exhausted once the night was over, or bouncing off the walls so hard that he wouldn't be able to sleep for a week. He took a couple of deep breaths, mentally coaching himself before speaking.

"I've known Pat for more than twenty years. He is my foster father's partner."

"Ah, so Lorne...? I didn't know that he fostered."

"It was a long time ago. While he was still married to... his wife. I was only with him for a little while, but we kept in touch, and I met Pat later on... when they moved in together. It was all a little shocking at the time."

"Back then? It would have been," Santiago agreed. "And foster parenting. I don't imagine his agency was too happy about that. Allowing homosexual men around children was a big no-no. Hard for them to be approved even now. People still have that prejudice that we're all attracted to little boys and just won't be able to help ourselves. Really." He rolled his eyes. "As if we have no self-control whatever."

Zachary nodded wordlessly, unable to think of any response to this.

"Tell me," Santiago said in a confidential tone. "In foster care, in your experience, did you never run into any predators? You were never abused?"

Zachary caught his breath. He stared at Santiago, waiting for him to realize what an inappropriate question it was. Santiago waited. Zachary tried not to think about any of the men, women, and older children that he'd had to deal with during his growing-up years, defending himself against their abuse when he was far too small and weak and outclassed to succeed. He didn't need to go back to any of those places in his memory and he certainly didn't need to detail them to Santiago.

"I would expect that anyone who spent any length of time in foster care has run into that kind of thing," he said flatly, as if it were not an emotional topic at all.

"Exactly," Santiago agreed. "And were they gay men? Any of them?"

Zachary shrugged. He had never put himself into the heads of those predators. He didn't know what turned them on, whether it had anything to do with his gender or just his helplessness. He didn't know whether it was a physical attraction or the desire to bully and control someone, to torture him and own him completely.

"No. I don't know."

"That's right. They think that by keeping gay men from becoming foster parents that they are protecting the children? When you look at their track record over the last hundred years or however long the foster care system has been around it should become blazingly obvious that it isn't gay men who are perpetrating the crime."

"No," Zachary agreed. "Now if we could get on to the topic at hand..."

"Oh, I didn't mean to take us so far off-track. It's just so interesting that you got to know Pat and Lorne as father figures. That's just so fascinating to me. I've never seen them that way. It's a whole different perspective that I had never considered."

Zachary nodded, hoping to move things alone. "They've both always been great examples. Even though they weren't the ones taking care of me, they were so kind and patient and caring... to each other and to me. I suppose it would have been different if I had been their foster child. I wasn't easy to get along with, and they probably would have had too much of me before very long. But as it was, just having them around when I needed some help or someone to talk to... They've been very good to me."

"What was your biological father like? How well did you know him?"

"I was with him until I was ten. Him and my mom."

Santiago nodded encouragingly.

"He was... physically abusive. Didn't have much use for kids. We pretty much just tried to stay out of the way when he was home."

"Nothing like Pat and Lorne."

"No. I don't know that I've ever heard either one of them raise his voice, much less his hand, in anger."

Santiago smiled and nodded, looking happy with that comment. "I've always thought they were a very nice couple. Never a cross word to each other. Almost too good to be true."

Zachary shrugged. He knew that Mr. Peterson and Pat still got on each other's nerves just like any heterosexual couple. They weren't perfect and were sometimes irritable and cross. One of them might be stubborn and the other hurt, but in the end, they always made up, and they never had to apologize for physical harm or to try to take back cruel, hurtful words.

"Why don't you tell me about Jose?" he pressed Santiago, trying to get back on topic. "Tell me what your relationship with him was like."

"Oh, you're rushing me. This should be an after-dinner discussion, not something that we're rushing through now."

Zachary knew that no one had promised Santiago that Zachary would have dinner with him, and he should just make that point and get on with it. He took a breath. "I'm not here to eat. Why don't we——"

"You must have something. What's the point of my booking a private dining room if I have to eat by myself? You have to at least allow me that."

"I'm not up for much. My stomach really isn't recovered yet from yesterday." Zachary touched his side with an exaggerated wince.

"We'll just get a couple of appetizers, then. That's not a problem."

Santiago pressed a button recessed in the table, and in a moment, a waiter opened the door and entered.

"Gentlemen, you are ready to order?"

"Just some light fare," Santiago said. "A variety of canapés and amuse-bouches. If you would."

"Certainly, sir. Anything specific for either of you?"

"No," Santiago shook his head and looked at Zachary. "Escargot? Caviar?"

"Nothing rich," Zachary protested. "Just… crackers, fruit…"

Santiago rolled his eyes. "A cheese platter too, then, and some berry parfaits, bowls of grapes…"

The waiter nodded. "It will be just a few minutes then," he agreed. He scribbled down his notes and withdrew from the room.

"You really should have thought of something more challenging," Santiago said. "I'm always trying to stump the chef." He laughed. "It's so much fun."

Zachary nodded. He was starting to understand that they were not going to get to the topic of Jose and Santiago's relationship until Santiago was good and ready. If he said they would have to eat first, then Zachary would have to wait until the various canapés and amuse-bouches arrived. Then they'd get down to brass tacks.

"So what is it you do?" he asked. "I didn't ask Pat about your background."

"I'm sure you would have been very amused if you had! Yes, I'm a bit of a black sheep around here." He indicated his cheek to point out his skin tone, in case Zachary didn't notice the pun. "There are really not enough non-whites in circulation. It can be a little frustrating if your tastes run to dark meat. But I digress. I am an entrepreneur. A business owner. I have my own little kingdom, with hundreds of men under me."

"Oh...? What is it you do?"

Santiago grinned, showing off his brilliantly white teeth again. "I own and run the Peaceful Retreat Funeral Home and Cemetery."

Zachary stared at him, slowly processing the words. It was so unexpected; his brain was puttering along behind him and hadn't caught up. He stared at Santiago. "A... cemetery? You run a..."

"I run a cemetery. A graveyard. A boneyard. Yes, sir. That's me. I have many men *under* me. You see?"

Zachary barely refrained from groaning. But even though his brain seemed to be running on super slow speed, it was still generating all kinds of possibilities.

A cemetery? A funeral home? What better way to dispose of men you never wanted found again? He could dispose of the remains so completely that no one would ever find them. If the funeral home also had a crematorium, he could burn up all of the evidence, and then bury the ashes in the graveyard. How could anyone ever find any sign of them again?

Even without a crematorium, how easy would it be to dump a body in a grave and bury it? Who would ever know the difference?

Santiago was chuckling to himself, pleased at having surprised Zachary.

CHAPTER TWENTY-FOUR

S ANTIAGO WAS STILL LAUGHING when the appetizers arrived. He helped himself, and Zachary put a few on his plate. They didn't actually look too bad. He wasn't hungry, but the little bites looked interesting and tasty and he wouldn't be required to get down a full meal. He popped one little canapé in his mouth and chewed, nodding at Santiago.

"It's good."

He didn't ask what it was. After Santiago's suggestion of escargot or caviar, he didn't want to know what he was eating. The fruit that accompanied the other platters was cool and fresh and he popped a couple of grapes into his mouth.

"So, tell me about Jose," he suggested.

Santiago sighed. He stretched and leaned on the table plucking up various different fruits and canapés throughout the conversation.

"Jose was a very pleasant companion to pass the time with," he said. "I'm sure you've heard from others that he was easy to get along with, friendly, a good conversationalist. He spoke English well and blended easily with most company. He was… open to new experiences, to trying new things. Enjoyed music, food, nice clothing, and jewelry. For a working-class illegal immigrant, he was surprisingly well-educated and up on the latest news and trends. He didn't come across like a farmer or a janitor."

Zachary nodded. "And how long had the two of you been seeing each other?"

"Some months. I really couldn't put a date on it… between six and ten, maybe?" He shook his head. "I'm not always good with timelines."

"You knew that he had other partners."

"Oh, of course." Santiago waved the question away as if it were of no concern. "No one expected him to be exclusive. Nor am I."

Santiago was not part of Pat and Lorne's circle of friends, though obviously Santiago was familiar enough to comment on their character. Pat had said that most of their group of friends were stable couples. Unsurprisingly, Santiago didn't fit in as part of that group. What was surprising was that Jose did, when it was apparent that he had multiple partners and no interest in settling down.

"Was there anyone that he was seeing that... concerned you? Maybe you thought they weren't right for each other, or that he might be in danger?"

"No. I wouldn't have interfered with his social life. He could see who he wanted. I wasn't jealous, if that's what you are getting at."

"Was anyone else? Maybe someone who *did* want to be exclusive?"

"I didn't get involved in his other relationships. We didn't discuss it."

Not quite Naylor's 'off-limits,' but close enough.

"And you don't think there was anyone who was interested in him who might have been resentful because they were rejected or had broken up?"

"I can't think of anyone. I don't know who his exes are. When we were together... it was just the two of us. Not all of those other relationships. We just focused on one another."

Zachary doubted that their relationship had been quite as ideal as Santiago made out, but he let it go.

"Do you know if any of Jose's other partners ever hurt him?"

"Hurt him?" Santiago shook his head. "No."

"You never saw him with bruises, like someone hit him or choked him?"

Santiago showed no reaction to this. "No."

"Others have said that they saw bruises on his throat. Like someone had choked him."

Santiago shrugged. "Different strokes. That's the whole point of having multiple partners. Different people go for different things."

"I have a list of names that I'd like you to look at."

Santiago shrugged and picked up another canapé. Zachary handed the list across the table and Santiago looked at it while he continued to pick at the food. "Yes, I know some of these names..." His eyebrows went up. "Oh, I had forgotten..." He shook his head. "It's funny just how quickly one can forget. These men were part of our lives, part of our community, and then... they were gone. Without a word. We moved on, but there they all are... there are so many when you see all of their names together."

"How many did you know?"

"Mmm..." Santiago's eyes went over the list. "I would say maybe half. That doesn't mean that I had anything with them, just that we knew each other. Could sit and talk at a bar or a show."

"How many *did* you have relationships with?"

Santiago looked up at Zachary for a moment, his eyes calculating, then back down at the list again. "Maybe... half a dozen." He flicked the paper back over to Zachary. "And don't bother asking me when I knew them and when the last time I saw them was. I told you I have difficulty with timelines. You know, I've never really felt like I move linearly through time..."

Zachary wasn't about to tackle that one. He picked up the paper and put it back into his folder. Santiago was definitely on the suspect list. He was the first one to admit to knowing so many of the missing men. Though why Santiago would want to hurt Jose or any of the others was beyond Zachary.

"Who else would have known a lot of the men on that list?" Zachary asked. "So far, everyone I talk to says they don't recognize them. But you knew half of them. Who else ran in the same circles and might have known more of them?"

Santiago had a swallow of his drink. "You don't want to go back to The Night Scene," he indicated the bruises on Zachary's face, "but I imagine if you were to try there or The Blue Goose, you would find that they were familiar to those crowds. Didn't anyone at The Night Scene say they knew them?"

"I didn't have the list when I was there. Just Jose's name. Didn't get the others until after."

"Ah, well there you go. You have to go the right places if you're going to find people who knew them."

"Yeah. So they all tended to circulate at The Night Scene or The Blue Goose?"

Santiago drained his glass and again pressed the button on the table. "Those that I *knew*," he said pedantically. "I don't remember everyone on the list."

"But those that you remember, you would have seen them there?"

"Yes. That's right."

"And is there anywhere you don't go where they might have circulated? Maybe The Night Scene one day, and The Blue Goose another day, and then... where...?"

The waiter appeared and Santiago handed him the glass, motioning to the sideboard. "Fill me up."

The waiter took the glass from him and nodded, going to the sideboard to prepare another drink. Santiago leaned on the table, helping himself to some cheese and some of the fruit. He wrinkled his nose at the grapes, like maybe one of them was sour. He waited until he had his drink to wash the taste away and the waiter was out of the room before answering.

"There are a few other places they might have hung out. I prefer to hit places with a little more class," he gestured to indicate their surroundings, "but some people's tastes run to... grittier establishments."

"Grittier?"

"My boy, The Night Scene is one thing. Despite your experience upon leaving there, it is a pretty safe environment. Mainstream. There are other places where people who are interested in other sorts of encounters might hang out."

"Meaning what?"

"You'll find that the people who come to places like La Rouge are more interested in the arts, in good food, in long-term relationships where you know each other and respect each other's boundaries. At a bar like The Night Scene, you're still going to see a lot of dating couples. People who are getting together and getting to know each other and see how they get along together. More casual. You could go there with someone, or to meet someone new, have a few drinks together, and see how you got on. But there are other places where you wouldn't be looking for a regular date. You might never even know the other person's name."

"Just a one-night hookup?"

Santiago nodded. "Yes... or something anonymous. Someone you saw occasionally, but didn't have a relationship with. There are all sorts. In the straight community as well as the gay."

"Sure, of course," Zachary agreed. As a private detective, he was often hired to follow cheating spouses, and some of the venues that he had walked into made him not only want to wash the residue of the place off of his skin, but to strip off the first layer of skin altogether. He gave an involuntary shudder. He'd seen places that catered to all sorts of unusual and taboo tastes. Zachary could envision a predator trolling places like that, looking for his next victim. "Did Jose go places like that?"

"I wouldn't know. We never discussed them. But Jose was exploring, seeking out new experiences. I wouldn't be surprised if he explored some of the seamier elements. He wanted to have a... full range of experiences."

"Where are these places? Are they public? Do they have names?"

Santiago's eyes glittered with interest. He obviously hadn't expected Zachary to be aware of how things operated on the underbelly. "I'm sure your police friends would know some of the places to look. If they're really interested in finding a serial killer, they should look under a few rocks. It's always of great interest to see what crawls out of dark places."

CHAPTER TWENTY-FIVE

ZACHARY FINALLY MANAGED TO extricate himself from the dinner with Santiago. It had been a very long day, and he had already decided there was no way he was going to one of the seedier bars to ask after the missing men. He'd had enough excitement at the 'classier' joints and would leave that job to the police, as Santiago had suggested. People might not be as quick to provide a policeman with the information as they would to a friend of a friend, but the cops would be safer there than Zachary.

He made his way back out to the main entrance, aware that people turned and watched him the whole way, curious about his battered appearance or recognizing him from the news articles. He'd been in the news with previous cases, but usually it wasn't until the end after everything was sorted out, when publicity wouldn't have an effect on the investigation.

He handed his valet ticket to the attendant who appeared beside him.

"We'll have you just wait here, sir, until your vehicle pulls up outside the door. We're having a little trouble tonight. Not usually like this."

"Thanks."

After a short wait, his car pulled under the canopy in front of the door. Zachary nodded to the attendant and went outside. As before, it was only seconds before people recognized him and surged forward, waving their signs or holding out their mikes and shouting at him. Zachary held up his hand to ward them off, indicating that he wasn't answering any questions.

"Are you assisting the police in their investigation?"

"Are you making any progress in finding the serial killer?"

"The holy scriptures say that God shall strike the sinners dead! It is the wrath of God!"

Zachary turned toward the religious nut. There were a lot of serial killers who had claimed to be doing the will of God by killing gays or prostitutes. He couldn't afford to ignore a credible threat.

A man in blue jeans and a t-shirt with more religious rantings stenciled on it waved his sign at Zachary, pressing against the guard who held him back. His already wide eyes popped when he saw Zachary was looking at him.

"They shall all be stricken with a plague!" the nut shouted, thrusting his sign forward. "They shall all die!"

"Do you know something about the men who disappeared?" Zachary demanded.

"Just keep moving, sir," the valet told Zachary, pressing his keys into his hand. "Don't give these guys any attention."

"I want the police called. They need to talk to him."

"Police can't do anything about protesters. They'll just tell them to stay behind the line, unless there's violence going on when they arrive."

"This guy is a suspect in the serial killer case. They need to talk to him."

The valet gave him a look. "A suspect? He's just a nut job."

"He thinks God should strike all gay men dead. You think he wouldn't take that into his own hands himself?"

"No. He's just a screamer. You ignore them, eventually they go away."

"You didn't hear about that policeman in Russia? How many was he convicted of killing? Seventy women? Because he decided they were loose women and God wanted them dead."

"I doubt he announced it in public." The valet hooked a thumb at the protester, who was released after he'd been pushed back behind the property line.

"He was quite willing to confess everything to the police when he was caught. Who knows whether he told anyone else before that? You really do need to get the police here."

"Not up to me. I'll pass it up the line, but don't hold your breath. You have a nice night, sir."

He was clearly waiting for Zachary to get into his car so he could go and get the next car in line. Zachary looked back at the protester. He was just one of many. How could they tell the ones who were dangerous from the ones who were just kooks? The valet was right that serial killers, while they might enjoy the spotlight, didn't generally announce their intentions to the public. They picked out a cop or news reporter and started feeding them little clues, getting a kick out of how much smarter they were.

The valet touched his cap, again saying goodbye to Zachary and trying to get him on his way. Zachary got into his car. The valet shut the door firmly, again wishing Zachary a nice evening. Zachary pulled out and headed back to Mr. Peterson's house, moving slowly past the protesters and reporters.

Zachary didn't even turn on the radio on the way home, needing the silent space of the car to unwind. The verbal repartee with Santiago, the shouting protesters and reporters, and the valet who refused to listen all sucked the energy out of him. He knew he was going to have to spend some time visiting with Mr. Peterson and Pat when he got back, letting them know how the investigation was going and that he was making progress. If he was. He did have a couple more places for the police to look, some suspects for them to check up on, and the protesters at La Rouge. He still couldn't point to one suspect and say that he was the killer, or even prove that the missing men had been murdered. But maybe what he had found out would help to lead the police to the solution.

At least the police were being forced to take Jose's disappearance seriously.

Zachary pulled into Mr. Peterson's street. Even before he turned the corner, he could see red and blue lights bouncing off the houses. He hit the brake, almost coming to a complete stop, as he looked at the squad cars stopped in front of Mr. Peterson's house. His mind flashed back to a similar scene at Bridget's house when she had been kidnapped. Marked cars and unmarked cars parked in front of the house and pulled up on the lawn, all of them with lights flashing.

He took his foot off the brake and hit the gas, shooting down the street and then hitting the brakes again hard with a screech of tires when he reached the house. He threw the car into park and bailed out, rushing the door.

He should have known that the police wouldn't let anyone go belting into the house like that without first verifying his identity, but he wasn't thinking logically. He was just reacting to the police presence and the memory of what had happened to Bridget.

He had almost been too late for Bridget.

"Whoa, stop right there!" Hands grabbed him and he was pushed to the side, the impetus of his run for the door redirected to slam him into the side of one of the police cars. They pinned him, feeling for weapons. Zachary struggled to break free of them.

"No, let me go! What's happened to them? Let me see! Let go!"

"Zachary. Zachary, it's okay." Mr. Peterson made an appearance on the front step, speaking urgently over the shouting. "We're okay, Zach. We're both fine."

Zachary stopped fighting and slumped against the car, hitting the bottom of his chin. The policemen finished frisking him, and by the time they were done, Dougan was on the step with Mr. Peterson, telling them to let him go.

Zachary hurried to the door, where Lorne pulled him in for a hug. "It's okay, Zachary. Everybody's fine."

Zachary gripped him tightly, trying to convince himself it was true, and looked past Mr. Peterson into the house.

"Where's Pat?"

"He's inside. Let's go in." Mr. Peterson released him and they entered the house together, both squeezing through the doorway at the same time. Pat stepped into Zachary's line of sight.

"You okay, Zach? We tried to call you. We didn't want you coming home to this unexpectedly."

Zachary gave him a quick hug as well, relieved that neither one of them had been kidnapped or killed. His heart was still thundering, but he knew they were both okay.

"What happened? Why are all the police here?"

"It's just the protesters. Things got out of hand. Damage to the property. A rock through the window." Pat gestured and Zachary saw the windowpane with a piece of cardboard taped over it. "We'll get it fixed in the morning. Nothing permanent, just a nuisance."

"Was there... a note with the rock?"

That was the way it was done on TV. A rock through the window with a threatening note attached to it. That was the way it always started, before escalating to gunshots or Molotov cocktails.

At the thought of flaming bottles being thrown into the house, Zachary swayed on his feet. He tried to focus on Pat, on the fact that neither of them had been hurt, instead of the idea of the house going up in flames.

"Come sit," Pat insisted, pulling him a couple more steps over to the couch. Zachary sat down and tried to control his breathing. Dougan had already been privy to one flashback, Zachary didn't want to break down when they were face-to-face.

"There was a note," Mr. Peterson admitted, drawing Zachary's attention back to the present rather than letting him focus on what could happen or what had happened in the past. "Nasty bit of hate mail."

"I need to see it."

"You don't want to, Zachary. No one wants to be reading that garbage. Leave it to the police."

"Let me see."

They exchanged looks with each other, weighing the possible consequences of allowing Zachary to see the note against refusing to. Eventually, Mr. Peterson nodded at Dougan, who said a few words to one of the other cops traveling in and out of the house, and the note was brought to Zachary, pressed flat in a plastic page protector.

Zachary swallowed and looked down at it. The messy writing spidered across the page in wandering lines. It was difficult to read, which made it an excellent distraction. Zachary worked through it a bit at a time, then nodded and pushed it away. It wasn't a mocking note from the serial killer. It wasn't a threat that he had to get off the case and keep quiet, or else. It was just a horrific bit of hate mail aimed against homosexual men.

"There were eggs earlier in the day," Pat sighed, and it took a moment for Zachary to realize he was talking about vandalism, not what he'd made for dinner. "Cleaned that up... the reporters were gone by dark... the alarm went off a couple of times, but we couldn't see anyone. Then the rock through the window."

"I'm sorry… I feel so bad that this investigation leaked out and ended up causing you trouble like this. It's been such a nice neighborhood, and now…"

"It will go back to normal as the story dies down," Mr. Peterson assured them. "It's just a temporary disruption. It isn't from our friends and neighbors, it's from strangers. They think they can vent all of their crap and stay anonymous. That's nothing new."

Zachary took a deep breath in and let it out. He rubbed his eyes, careful of his bruised, tender face, and looked around.

"You came because of the vandalism?" he asked Dougan. It seemed like it was a little out of his purview. Why would he be assigned to look into such a minor charge?

"The vandalism, making sure that everyone was safe, talking to each of you again about Jose, and whatever else you've been stirring up."

"I haven't been making any trouble," Zachary protested. He had been gathering information that might be useful to the police, not interfering with their inquiries. He hadn't cause them any extra trouble.

"Then why did I get a call from La Rouge about protesters over there?"

Zachary blinked. The valet had done as he said he would and passed the information along the line, and the management had actually decided to do as Zachary said and call the police department.

"I didn't think they would. There was one guy over there who was spouting all of this stuff about how they deserved to die… I just… wasn't comfortable with just ignoring it, pretending he couldn't possibly be serious."

"Well, I sent someone to pick him up, so if he is guilty of something, we'll find out. The good thing about these nut jobs is, they're perfectly happy to tell you everything they have done. They're not calling for lawyers and asserting their rights, they're begging to tell you everything they know."

"I don't know if he's dangerous, but he rubbed me the wrong way."

Dougan nodded, not looking upset about it. Pat and Mr. Peterson sat down and everybody got comfortable. Zachary shifted. "Could I take a break? I need to check my voicemails and… just catch my breath."

The police officer seemed unperturbed. "Go ahead. I have some questions for your two friends, and it's probably best if they feel like they can talk freely."

Zachary opened his mouth to point out that Mr. Peterson and Pat had talked to him voluntarily and wouldn't feel like they needed to hide anything from him, but Dougan beat him to the punch.

"I know, you're all open and talk about these things; it's just good practice. If I have to ask anything awkward, they can answer knowing that it won't get back to you. They can figure out whether to share it with you later."

Zachary shrugged and shook his head as he walked away. There was no point in arguing about it, since he'd been granted the time he needed to check his messages and get himself back together again emotionally.

He went to the bathroom first, looking at the horror show that was his face before taking a painkiller. He had a new bruise and cut on the bottom of his chin from being pushed up against the side of the police car. There was only a trickle of blood, so he pressed a wad of toilet paper to it and waited for it to stop.

CHAPTER TWENTY-SIX

WITH HIS BEDROOM DOOR shut, Zachary sat down on the bed and played his voicemails.

The news of his investigation had been nationwide, and it hadn't taken people long to connect his name up and start calling him. He'd had the call from Kenzie right at the beginning, and had pretty much ignored the voicemails he had been getting since then, other than taking a quick glance at the name or number attached to each one to make sure that there weren't any from Philippe or other witnesses who he needed to talk to. Others could wait.

Rhys Salter's grandmother, Vera, had left a halting message. Zachary had investigated the death of her daughter, Robyn, and had made friends with Rhys, an emotionally broken and usually nonspeaking teen during the case and kept in touch with him afterward. Zachary hadn't received any messages from Rhys recently, which he hoped meant that Rhys was just living his life and getting through one day at a time and didn't need to check in with Zachary.

Vera hadn't called to say that Rhys needed Zachary or that there was anything to be concerned about. Instead, she was worried about the publicity. "I don't think you'd better be seen anywhere with Rhys," she said in a near whisper. "I didn't know that you were gay, and it doesn't matter to me, but you can see how people are going to talk about a gay white man taking out a teenage black boy, especially with all of the teasing Rhys has to put up with for being mute and his momma being in prison. He doesn't need that. So I would appreciate it if you don't meet with Rhys without talking to me first. You can message with him, I know he enjoys that, but please don't offer to take him anywhere."

If she were there, Zachary would have explained to her that he wasn't gay, but that he understood how it could be harmful to Rhys's reputation, so he wouldn't do anything that could be misconstrued as an inappropriate relationship with the boy. But she wasn't there, and maybe by the time he saw her again, the whole thing would have blown over and there would be no need to even mention it. He deleted the message and went on to the next.

A short greeting from Kenzie, just checking in to make sure he was okay. "Give me a call sometime to let me know you're still alive," she joked. Zachary smiled and went on to the next.

There were several hang-ups. Probably reporters. Then a couple of reporters who had left long detailed messages urging him to call and get his story out there as soon as he could.

He was really hoping that one of the numbers he didn't recognize would be from Philippe, but so far none of them had been.

There was a call from Campbell, a more senior cop back home. Zachary hadn't expected to hear from him, but he supposed Campbell had seen the news coverage like everyone else and was curious about it or wanted to razz Zachary about the inaccuracies in the articles.

"Zachary," Joshua Campbell's voice boomed even on the small phone speaker. "Helluva life you're living these days. I gather you're down south rather than here, but give me a call when you've got a few minutes. I got a call from a Thurlow Dougan down there, and he's asking a lot of questions. I've told him you're okay, of course, but call me to talk things over. You know the number."

Zachary made a couple of notes to himself so he wouldn't forget who he needed to call. So Dougan had checked up on him. Called home to see how the locals felt about him. Zachary hoped that he had been satisfied with the answers.

There was a brief, teasing call from Tyrrell. An attempt to be lighthearted, but Zachary heard real concern behind his words. They had just been reunited, and Tyrrell wasn't sure how to take his big brother being splashed all over the national news. And he probably didn't know how to take the conflicting information he was reading about Zachary. It was a pretty confusing way to get to know a long-lost sibling.

More junk calls. Hang-ups and nut jobs. He shouldn't have made his phone number quite so easy to find.

Then there were the calls that Pat had said they made to warn him about the police circus at the house. Pat first: "Everything is fine, Zachary. Just a heads-up to make sure you're not worried if there are still police cars here when you get home. We've just had some damage to the property. We're both okay."

And then later, Mr. Peterson's carefully measured tone, "Just checking to see when you're planning to be home, Zach. Give me a call when you're on your way."

The call from Bridget had come early on, but he had left it until last, pretending to himself that it was because he didn't want to hear what she had to say, when the opposite was true. He wanted to listen to her last, just like he left the cherry on a sundae for last, as one final treat to savor.

"I guess you know why I'm calling, Zachary," she said in a disapproving tone. "I couldn't very well help seeing all of the coverage. I just wanted to say that I am not one who subscribes to the theory that all publicity is good publicity. This coverage, with all of its inaccuracies, could really be damaging to your reputation as a private investigator. I know it's none of my business and I don't have any right to advise you on these things… it's just a bug in your ear. Something to think about. I have a friend who is a publicist, if you want some help in dealing with this."

She hung up. Zachary sat there, listening to her voice in his head. Even when she called him to criticize, he still longed to be with her again. But she had made it clear. That wasn't going to happen. He needed to accept it.

He'd believe it if she ever stopped calling. Then he'd know it was really over.

He sat for a few more minutes, trying to get himself into the right frame of mind to talk to Dougan, then took out his notebook and went back out to the living room.

The living room discussion between the three men being conducted in low voices stopped when Zachary stepped into the room, and they all looked up at him. He sat down on the couch, and the discussion didn't resume.

"Okay, then, Zachary?" Mr. Peterson asked with a reassuring smile.

"Yeah, all good. Thanks for leaving those messages for me… sorry I didn't pick them up before coming back."

"I'm sorry you didn't. We didn't want you to come home to police cars and panic. But…" He gave a shrug. "All things considered, you didn't do too badly."

Meaning at least Zachary hadn't ended up a heap on the sidewalk in a full-blown meltdown. Lorne had seen worse reactions from Zachary before. Zachary's response to finding the house surrounded by police cars had been pretty normal, just like any man coming home and worrying what had happened to his family might have.

Zachary shrugged and didn't look at the pane of the window that had been covered with cardboard. He looked at Detective Dougan. For an instant, his own words came back to him, about the cop in Russia who had been convicted of dozens of murders. *He decided they were loose women and God wanted them dead.* Zachary had no doubt that the Russian officer's bosses and colleagues had had no idea what kind of a monster he really was inside. He'd had a wife and kid, helped the homeless, donated money for his daughter's dead teacher's funeral—a woman, as it turned out, he had killed. He was a man everybody had thought was safe. No one had suspected what was really going on in his head.

Zachary pushed these thoughts out of the way. He knew that Dougan was a good cop. He was looking into Jose's death and hadn't had a stroke when Zachary had given him all of the information about the missing men. If he had not been what he appeared, it would have been easy enough for him to set up a meeting with Zachary in some remote location and then to make *him* disappear. He wouldn't have shown up at Mr. Peterson's house when he heard about the rock through the window.

"Where do you want to start? Do you want me to tell you about my most recent interviews?"

Dougan sat back, putting his notepad on his knee, one leg crossed over the other. "It's as good a place to start as any. Tell me about who you talked to."

Zachary told him about Naylor and his shop and finding clothes there that Jose had worn. Pat leaned forward as he listened, his eyes wide.

"Eric Naylor and Jose were seeing each other?"

Dougan's eyes flicked over to him. "You didn't know?"

"No. They never acted like it when we were out as a group. I had no idea that they had a relationship outside of what we all did together."

"How much do you know about Naylor's relationships?"

"Well, nothing… he comes to our group as a bachelor. He's never brought a date. I assumed that he saw people, but never anyone in our group."

"And you didn't know that Jose's clothes came from Naylor's shop?"

"No. I suppose… I should have wondered where Jose got his clothes. He couldn't have been making much mowing lawns and moving bricks for A.L. He sent whatever he could home. He was always nicely presented. I never even thought…"

Dougan chewed on the end of his pencil. "It would be a jump to assume he was keeping clothes as trophies, especially if he has them out on the sales floor. But I would like to get my hands on that one outfit, just to make sure there is no blood spatter or anything suspicious on it."

Zachary nodded. "Do you have enough to get a warrant?"

"Don't need one if I can just walk in there and buy it off the rack."

"Oh. I guess not."

"Describe to me where it was and what it looked like."

Zachary did the best he could, and Dougan took down the details.

"And is that it? No, you went on to La Rouge after that."

"Yes. One of the men that Naylor had mentioned was seeing Jose was there and agreed to see me. Honore Santiago."

Dougan looked at Pat questioningly. Pat shook his head. "Not part of our group. I know who he is, but he didn't hang out with us."

"And you?" Dougan looked at Mr. Peterson.

"He doesn't see anyone else—" Zachary protested.

"Zachary," Mr. Peterson said quietly. "Hush. I can answer for myself."

"But you don't—" Zachary forced himself to stop. He looked down at his feet, waiting for Mr. Peterson to answer.

"I don't know him well either," Mr. Peterson confirmed. "As Zachary will no doubt tell you, Honore has a long string of dalliances, and while we might run into him occasionally at La Rouge or other venues, he's far too… capricious for our tastes."

"Does he date the type of men who are missing?"

Loren and Pat looked at each other.

"Yes," Pat confirmed. "Younger men, usually of color. That same sort of body type." He indicated Zachary. "Smaller, wiry… Zach would be very much his type, aside from his white skin."

Remembering how flirty Santiago had acted with him, Zachary felt his cheeks heat. He hoped that at least the bruises covered his embarrassment. Mr. Peterson chuckled.

"I wouldn't recommend you take up with Honore, Zachary."

"You think he's dangerous?" Dougan asked.

"I don't think he's a serial killer. But he's not… stable."

"If Jose was unfaithful, do you think Santiago would have reacted violently?"

"Well… it's hard to be unfaithful if there's no expectation of being faithful," Mr. Peterson explained.

"They were both seeing other people," Zachary said. "Santiago said so."

Dougan nodded. "Doesn't mean he couldn't have changed his mind and decided he didn't like Jose seeing other people. I've seen it happen before. People start with grand ideas of how an open relationship works for everyone, and then they find out they actually have feelings and want the person all for themselves."

Zachary hesitated. "Do you know what he does?"

Dougan looked at the notes he had made. "What he does? No. What does he do?"

"He owns a funeral home and cemetery."

Dougan frowned. His mind obviously followed the same scenarios as Zachary had already considered. He nodded slowly. "It's something to think about. But we won't be able to get a warrant, and I don't think he's going to invite us over to dig up any graves and troll for extra bodies."

"He admits that he knew a lot of the men who disappeared, and was involved with some of them. It's possible that he was responsible for *those* disappearances, and the others were just men who disappeared on purpose, like you thought to begin with," Zachary said.

"Why would he admit to being involved with them, though?" Mr. Peterson challenged. "Wouldn't he deny it?"

"Some serial killers like to brag and point out how smart they are. Some almost seem to get caught on purpose so they can tell how many people they killed without getting caught."

Dougan flipped a page over in his notepad. "Besides, we would have found him out if he lied. People would have seen them together. Did your Mr. Santiago know Philippe?"

"I don't know… he didn't mention him, but I would guess so. If he liked younger immigrant men. He and Philippe were both seeing Jose. Even if they didn't date each other, they must have known about each other."

"I went over to see Philippe to ask him a few questions."

Zachary nodded. Maybe that was why Philippe hadn't called him back. He was talking to Dougan or he was irritated with Zachary for pointing Dougan in his direction. He didn't want to talk to the police.

"I wasn't able to make contact with him," Dougan said.

"He was probably working."

"I checked with his work. He didn't show up today."

"And he wasn't at home?"

Dougan studied Zachary, his eyes sharp. "No, he wasn't at home. Nobody was at home."

Zachary thought about the number of men who were living there and was surprised. He would have expected there to be at least one person there at all times. They wouldn't all have the same shifts. Someone would always be around.

"Nobody?" he repeated, thinking that maybe Dougan just meant Philippe wasn't home. Or Philippe and Nando.

"It had been cleared out," Dougan said. "Not a matchstick left in the place."

Zachary sat there with this mouth open. They had all moved out in the middle of the month. They'd packed up all of their stuff and abandoned the apartment.

"There were a lot of people living there. I can't believe they're all gone."

"When was the last time you talked to Philippe?"

"Tuesday. He called me when he couldn't get John on the phone. Before I called you. I tried to get him, but his phone just kept going to voicemail."

"You don't think anything has happened to him?"

"I'm hoping it's just that he's mad at me, so he's rejecting the calls. With everything that was in the papers, Nando might have figured out about Philippe and Jose seeing each other."

"Why is that significant?"

"Nando is Philippe's uncle. Phillipe is living with him so that Nando can make sure he doesn't get into any trouble. I don't suppose he'll be too happy to find out that Philippe was seeing a man who is now missing. That doesn't sound safe to me."

"I would guess not. And you think that they've all just gone underground. To avoid having to talk to me and you."

Zachary nodded. But what if the killer were Santiago, or someone else in the same circles? What if one of them had known about Philippe and decided that he knew too much or had seen something he shouldn't have?

"If it was the serial killer, then they wouldn't *all* be gone. Just Philippe. He couldn't make that many men disappear that fast."

"No, probably not. That would be quite an undertaking. But if Philippe disappeared, what would Nando and the others do? Go to the police?" Dougan directed the question at Mr. Peterson.

"No. Definitely not. I guess they'd disappear."

Dougan nodded. "Any indication that someone was watching them or investigating them, and they would disappear."

Zachary looked through his notepad, thinking about it. It made perfect sense that the men had all disappeared, but Zachary didn't like it. Why hadn't Philippe called? Why didn't he at least called to tell Zachary not to look for them? If he wanted to find Jose's killer, why didn't he answer Zachary's calls?

"I'll keep calling. He'll answer sooner or later."

Dougan shook his head, but didn't speak his doubt out loud. "If you manage to reach him, let me know. I need to talk with him. It's pretty hard to put a case together if the witnesses keep disappearing. He's the one person we know John Mwangi talked to about the missing men. He may know things that were not in the papers. If Mwangi had suspicions about who was involved, he might not have written it down, but he might have talked to a sympathetic listener."

Zachary nodded. "I'll let you know."

He tried to push down the growing dread that something had happened to Philippe, that the killer had reached him.

It made sense that Philippe and the others had just gone underground because of the publicity.

That had to be why.

CHAPTER TWENTY-SEVEN

ZACHARY, YOU'RE LOOKING PRETTY rough," Pat observed. "Is it time for you to take another painkiller?"

Zachary's head pounded and every part of his body throbbed or protested when he moved. "Yeah." Zachary blinked his eyes. His lids were getting heavy and the pages in his notebook were starting to blur. "And I think I'd better be heading to bed."

"The doctor told you to take it easy. This isn't exactly taking it easy," Pat chided. He got up and went into the kitchen, returning with a glass of juice and one of Zachary's pills.

"Have you had any more contact with Dimitri?" Dougan asked, ignoring the fact that Zachary had said he was ready to go to bed.

Zachary rubbed his temples. *Dimitri?* Then he remembered the younger man who had been with Teddy at The Night Scene. Teddy, the big teddy bear and Dimitri, his date, who had wanted to talk to Zachary about Jose. About their broken date and the cell phone that went to voicemail.

"Oh, yeah. Dimitri. With Teddy. No, I haven't heard anything else from him."

"He did have a number of phone exchanges with Jose's number before Jose's phone went offline."

"You got his phone logs." Zachary tried to smother a yawn. "So that helps pinpoint when he disappeared. Or when his phone stopped taking calls."

Dougan nodded. "It verifies what we already knew. So who is Teddy? Where does he fall into all of this?"

"I don't really know. Ran into him at The Night Scene. He was kind of hitting on me at the bar, but then he had a date there." Zachary shook his head. "I don't really understand the rules in a place like that. Or maybe I'm just seeing men's behavior from a different perspective than I ever have before."

"Teddy Archuro? He's been a fixture at The Night Scene for a long time," Pat contributed. "I know him from way back."

"You wouldn't have any concerns about him?"

"No." Pat looked at Mr. Peterson and they both shook their heads. "He's been around for a long time and I've never heard anyone complain about him.

Other than maybe to say that he's too friendly." Pat made a gesture to indicate Zachary and what he had just contributed. "But no, he's harmless."

"He's not harmless unless I say he is," Dougan said sharply. He closed his notepad and sat up. "If you have more contact with Dimitri, encourage him to talk to me. With half the witnesses disappearing and the other half refusing to make a statement, it's difficult to conduct an investigation."

Zachary nodded tiredly. "I'll do what I can."

Before going to bed, Zachary took one of the prescription painkillers and a sleeping pill. In spite of how exhausted he was, he knew that he wasn't going to be able to shut off his brain and stop analyzing the case and the discussion with Dougan if he didn't. Having a case debrief right before bed wasn't the best idea. But Dougan was there at his own initiative and Zachary couldn't very well brush him off.

He checked the security alarm settings before going to bed. Twice. There was no one visible outside when he looked out the window, other than one police car that had stayed to keep an eye on things for a few hours. Zachary knew what it was like to sit surveillance in a cold, dark car at night, and considered taking a cup of coffee out to the officer, but in the end he decided not to. To do so would mean disabling the door alarm and then re-enabling it when he returned to the house. Chances were, the cop already had a thermos of coffee in the car with him, which he would have to ration strictly to avoid inconvenient interruptions.

Zachary looked once more at the settings on the security system. There were footsteps in the hall and he looked up to see Mr. Peterson taking a last run to the bathroom before bed. When he returned, he gave Zachary a knowing smile.

"Everything is properly armed. Between you and Pat, it's probably been checked a dozen times. You want a warm milk before bed?"

"No. I'm fine."

"You need your sleep. You look like a zombie."

Zachary nodded and headed back to the guest bedroom. "I'm sorry to still be underfoot. Depending on what happens tomorrow, maybe I'll go home for a few days. Keep up by phone and email."

It was a good thing he had kept an emergency bag with clothes and necessities in the car, since he hadn't initially been planning to stay overnight, let alone for several days. But he needed to get fresh clothes or launder what he had, and he longed for his own space.

"It sounds like Dougan and his men are talking to people. You probably don't want to get in his way. But don't feel like you have to go home on our accounts. We're happy to have you here."

"You guys don't need me kicking around here. If I can get the rest of the interviews done that I want to tomorrow… I'll leave it to Dougan to check out these other places where Jose might have hung out. I wish Philippe would respond. I know he's just gone quiet because he and the others don't want any attention, but it still bothers me." Zachary sighed. He knew his attention was bouncing from one piece of the case to another, and if he let himself, he would just keep babbling on.

"Maybe he'll call you tomorrow. Or maybe by the weekend, he'll decide that they're safe and he can respond to calls. I'm sure the media attention just has him spooked. But that will die down as they don't find anything new to report on."

"Yeah. Okay, I'm going to bed for real now."

"Get a good rest. You won't make any progress on the case if you're too tired to think straight. You'll do better after a solid night's sleep."

Zachary nodded. He went back to his room, swallowed a couple of pills, one for anxiety and one to help him sleep. He stripped down and slid into bed, waiting for sleep to come.

CHAPTER TWENTY-EIGHT

H E WAS GROGGY WHEN he awoke. Someone was shaking him by the arm and he didn't know why. He just wanted to return to the darkness and sleep. His body needed rest. His sleep was often restless and disrupted, but he was so deep in the well that he couldn't open his eyes.

The shaking persisted. Zachary tried to push the hand away. A foster mom or group home worker trying to get him up for school? He was too tired. He was sick or it was too early in the morning. The middle of the night. Why would they try to get him up in the middle of the night?

"Zachary. Come on. Talk to me."

Zachary groaned, trying to protest.

"Try to sit him up. See if that helps."

Zachary tried to fight back against the manhandling, but that just woke him up further, when he wanted to return to the darkness.

"Zachary. Wake up."

He hurt all over. He felt bruised down to his bones and his head was thudding, feeling huge and ungainly like a lead balloon. He tried to hold it still, as it was making him nauseated whenever it flopped one direction or the other. He put his hands up to his face to brace it and help hold it still.

"Are you awake? Zach?"

"Why?" Zachary groaned. "Why won't you let me sleep?"

"It's late. You're always an early riser."

He was aware of fingers on his wrist, pressing over the pulse point. He tried to remember. Was he in the hospital? Had he been in an accident? That would explain why his body hurt so much, but not why they were trying to wake him up. At the hospital, they let him sleep, unless there was some test or procedure they had to do.

Zachary managed to get his eyes open a crack. At first, he couldn't comprehend his surroundings and figure out where he was. He frowned and blinked and tried to clear the blurriness from his eyes and sort out the inputs.

"Lorne?"

"Yes. Are you okay?"

Zachary tried to rub away the pain in his head, but his face and head were too tender.

"What's wrong?" Zachary asked, trying to focus. "Did something happen?"

"You scared the hell out of us, Zach." Pat's voice was nearby, but Zachary didn't want to turn his head to look at him, still too woozy. "How many pills did you take?"

How many pills? Zachary rubbed his tender eyes and looked around, at the side table and at Pat, then all the way back to Mr. Peterson, studying him closely.

There were several pill bottles beside the bed. Pills he always took. He didn't remember being depressed the night before and trying to overdose. None of the bottles appeared to be empty, though his eyes still weren't focusing properly. He tried to remember. Painkillers, anti-anxiety, sleeping pills. He'd been feeling pretty rough before bed. The long day and his physical injuries must just have caught up with him. His body had just been more exhausted than usual, so he had slept heavily once his brain had let him.

"I was just really tired."

"It's almost eleven o'clock," Mr. Peterson said.

Eleven? For someone who was used to waking before six, that was very late. It was no wonder they had been concerned.

"I think… I just did too much yesterday. Can I get one of those pain pills? My head is killing me. And my side…" He tried to readjust the way he was sitting. It must have been Pat who had pulled him into a sitting position. Zachary's bruised ribs had flared up in protest.

Neither man answered him right away.

"I don't think that's a good idea," Pat said. "You were really deep under. You shouldn't be taking anything that could depress your system."

"Just a pain pill. Just one."

"I'll get you a Tylenol."

Zachary looked at the pill bottles on the table. He *would* just get one himself. But he would have to move, and they seemed very far away. He knew that Tylenol wasn't going to even begin to address the pain.

He let his eyes close again. "Then get me two Tylenol. The strongest you got."

Pat left the room and Mr. Peterson stayed there with him. He sat down on the edge of the mattress, rocking the bed and making Zachary seasick. Pat returned a couple of minutes later with two red pills and a glass of water. He helped Zachary take them, supporting the glass so he wouldn't drench himself.

"Are you okay?" Mr. Peterson asked.

"I'm just tired. I need more sleep."

"I knew you weren't getting enough rest. But this is more than being tired. Being tired doesn't depress your breathing."

Zachary didn't have an answer for that. He was listing to the side and tried to make himself comfortable, his consciousness already starting to drift.

"Gather up the pill bottles," Pat said. "We won't leave them in here. I'll call the pharmacist, go over the doses and the possible interactions. We'll make sure he doesn't take too many tonight."

Zachary remembered fleetingly that he was going to go back home, so they would have to give him his pills back. But then he was asleep again.

When the fog started to lighten and the pain broke through, Zachary tossed and turned for some time before finally waking up. He was curled up in a ball on top of his pillows in a distinctly uncomfortable position. Very slowly, he eased his body into a straight line and put his head on one of the pillows. But his restlessness was starting to assert itself, his brain working on the problem of the missing men. What he could remember of Mr. Peterson and Pat waking him earlier in the day niggled at the back of his brain.

He rolled slowly over, waited until his brain stopped sloshing around in his skull, and stretched his arm out until his fingers touched his phone. He pulled it toward himself. He held it in front of his face, squinting at the screen. It was mid-afternoon.

Zachary swore softly. He couldn't remember the last time he'd slept that late. Maybe never. Maybe when they'd been adjusting his meds, when he was off of his antidepressants and couldn't get out of bed. He'd been in the hospital, but he couldn't remember the details, his brain still refusing to work the way it was supposed to.

He pushed himself slowly up until he was sitting, hunched over and waiting for the world to stop spinning. He might have fallen asleep sitting there for a short time, but sitting up told his brain that he was supposed to be awake, and he gradually felt more alert.

Progress was slow, but he managed to pull his clothes on and start the long trek to the bathroom.

"Well, look who's up," Pat greeted. "Need a hand there, granny?"

Zachary grunted at him and continued his way down the hall.

He used the john, and splashed cold water on his face, and leaned with both hands on the counter, breathing and trying to work up the wherewithal to make it back to the bedroom again.

"Come to the kitchen," Mr. Peterson told him, when he opened the door.

Zachary knew that if he went back to the bedroom he was probably going to go back to sleep, so he followed Lorne into the kitchen, bright with afternoon sunshine.

Zachary squinted in the light and managed to make it into one of the kitchen chairs.

"Good to see you on your feet again."

"Yeah. Sorry about that. Guess I really crashed."

"That was more than just being tired."

Zachary cleared his throat. Mr. Peterson put a glass of water in front of him, along with one of the pain pills. Not Tylenol, but his prescription. Zachary took it gratefully with several long swallows of the cold water, thirsty after his long hibernation.

"I didn't overdose. I was just tired from doing so much."

"I believe you that you didn't *intentionally* overdose." Mr. Peterson waited until Zachary looked at him. He raised his eyebrows and spoke with emphasis. "But you *did* overdose. The pharmacist Pat talked to said that if you took a few of those pain pills along with a few sleeping pills, it could be very dangerous. Even if you're used to taking the sleeping pills."

Zachary shook his head. "I didn't. I just took one pain pill before bed and one sleeping pill. They said that was safe."

"Well, we're going to have to watch you closely to see how you react if you plan to do that again. You remember how when we first started you on meds, you had a couple of bad reactions."

It was a long time in the past. Zachary remembered throwing up at school from his day meds, and then Mr. Peterson having to take him to the hospital after his night meds. He'd started too many prescriptions at once and the ER doctor had been pretty annoyed that the Petersons hadn't introduced them individually to monitor for adverse reactions.

"Yeah… I remember that. But they didn't make me sleepy."

"You can have different reactions to different meds. I don't know if you've been on these painkillers before, or if you've combined them with this same cocktail."

Zachary wanted to protest, but he couldn't find a way to counter what Mr. Peterson was saying. He felt like a kid again, being lectured for a mistake that he'd made at school. Mr. Peterson wasn't saying it in a critical way, but it was almost worse for him to be so patient and understanding about it. Zachary didn't want any pity.

"Have you ever had a reaction like this? Where you couldn't wake up or were breathing so slowly?"

"I don't know." Zachary took another drink of the water. "Maybe." He had the shadow of a memory from long ago of the police trying to wake him up, back when he was eleven or twelve. But what would they have been trying to wake him up for? He couldn't pin the memory down properly. More clear was the outraged voice of Mrs. Pratt, his social worker in his head: *You were so doped up you couldn't keep your eyes open.*

He frowned, trying to remember, but he couldn't quite grasp it.

"Maybe once, in foster care. I can't remember."

Mr. Peterson put a cup of coffee and a slice of toast on a plate in front of Zachary. Being late in the afternoon, it wasn't really breakfast time, but it was Zachary's first meal of the day. He nibbled the toast without objecting.

He felt out of sorts getting started so late in the day. But once he'd had his coffee and the pain meds had started to work, he was at least feeling like himself again. He went through his notes from the day before, adding in other thoughts as they came to him, trying to work through everything he had learned from each person he had talked to, including Dougan.

He had promised Dougan that he would do what he could to encourage Dimitri to talk to the police, so he searched out Dimitri's number on his phone and called him. There was no answer. Zachary hung up when he got the voicemail message, thinking about it. It shouldn't surprise him that so many of the numbers he called just went through to voicemail. People had call display. They either ignored the unknown number or knew it was Zachary and didn't feel like having to talk to him. Dimitri was sure to know who he was now, after having seen all of the news coverage. He would know that Zachary wasn't a personal friend of Jose's, but had been asking his questions under cover. He wouldn't have the same motivation to talk to Zachary on the phone as he had to talk to him when he had viewed Zachary as the friend of a friend, and maybe a potential date.

He tapped his finger on the phone for a few minutes, then decided to text Dimitri, encouraging him to talk to Dougan to potentially help the police find the serial killer who had been running rampant in their community for years.

There was no immediate response. Zachary wasn't surprised. Even when texting with a friend or acquaintance, there often was not an immediate response. People were driving, in meetings, or doing other things. Dimitri would need time to review the message and decide whether he wanted to respond.

He checked his email and social media direct messages and put the phone down to continue to go through John's papers again, looking for patterns and how the players he had met so far fit into the picture. He was getting a better feeling for the shape of Jose's life. He stopped to text Philippe, again suggesting that they meet to discuss developments.

He shuffled through the papers, reassembling them in a different order.

His phone buzzed with a return text. Zachary picked it up.

Meet me tonight to talk. I have something to tell you.

Zachary started to compose a reply. His gaze strayed up to the top of the screen and he realized that the text had come from Dimitri, not Philippe.

"Well, well…"

What did Dimitri know? Had he only told Zachary half of the story when he'd thought him a curious friend? Did he know more, and wanted to share it now that he knew that Zachary and the police were trying to track down a serial killer? Things might have been different, now that he knew that Jose had not just hooked up with some other man, but was more than likely a victim of violence?

He texted back to Dimitri to arrange the time and place for their meeting. He remembered Dimitri's falsetto voice, his dramatic manner. Underneath that playfulness, he had real feelings for Jose. He wanted to know what had happened to his partner.

CHAPTER TWENTY-NINE

ZACHARY CALLED DETECTIVE DOUGAN once he had things set up with Dimitri.

"Goldman," Dougan acknowledged when he picked up the phone. "What's up?"

"You asked if I could do anything to get Dimitri to talk to you."

"Yes." Dougan's voice was brusque, as if he had other, more important cases to deal with.

"I called and texted him to encourage him to talk to you, and he texted me back. He wants to meet with me to tell me something about Jose's case."

"He does. Did he say what?"

"No. But I have a time and place set up, if you want to come along."

The was a silent pause. "Did you tell him I would be coming?"

"No, I thought it would be easier to explain and convince him to tell you about it once we saw him in person."

"Yeah, you're probably right. What are the details?"

Zachary relayed them to him.

"Alright. I'll see you then. I'll hang back to begin with, let him see you and get comfortable. Then I'll move in and we'll get him to spill what he knows."

"Okay." Zachary's heart was pounding faster as he thought about the meeting with Dimitri. It would be his job to keep Dimitri calm and on track so they could find out what he knew. It wouldn't be easy to do; Dimitri was obviously a highly-excitable person.

But it could be just the break they needed. If he could help break the serial killer case, it would be quite the feather in his cap. That would show the doubters.

"Do you want us to come with you?" Pat asked as Zachary got ready to go to his meeting with Dimitri.

"No, it's fine. Dougan is going to meet me there. I don't really want to show up with a whole crew for this meeting."

"He knows us, though. It wouldn't be like we were all strangers ganging up on him. I just don't like the idea of you meeting him alone at night."

"I won't be alone. Couldn't be much more safe than having a policeman along with me. You don't need to worry about it."

Pat sighed, nodding. "I'm sorry... I'm all nerves. You're very calm about the whole thing."

Zachary might have looked calm on the exterior, but inside he was just as on edge as Pat. His heart was going a mile a minute and his stomach was tied in knots. He didn't know whether Dimitri would be the break in the case that they needed, or if it was just a ruse to see Zachary again. He did not look forward to Dougan finding out that it had all been a line, if Dimitri didn't come up with anything.

He made sure that all of his papers were put away properly. He left his nearly-full notepad and took a new one with him instead. He needed to be sure that all of his records were kept safe. He should have been taking pictures of his notepad to upload to the cloud so that he had a backup, but it was too late to worry about doing it before the meeting.

He had one more cup of coffee and put on his jacket. "I don't know how long I'll be," he told Mr. Peterson. "Don't wait up. If Dougan ends up taking Dimitri in for questioning, I could be most of the night."

"Well then, it's a good thing you got in a good sleep last night," Lorne said lightly. "We'll see you tomorrow."

Zachary slowed and looked around. He had arrived early, wanting to be able to scope out the unfamiliar area before Dimitri arrived. He didn't want to be taken off-guard by an ambush, however unlikely that might seem. Whoever was killing the men must be feeling the pressure of the investigation and the media attention. It wasn't easy to work in the dark when a spotlight was being shone on you.

The streets were deserted. It was a residential area with some light commercial development; strip malls, convenience stores, coffee shops, and schools. There might be a few people out walking their dogs, but after dinner things were pretty quiet in the neighborhood.

Zachary drove in widening circles, looking for anything out of place. Why had Dimitri chosen the area? Was it his own neighborhood? Or maybe he worked close by? People didn't choose places they were unfamiliar with for meetings.

His phone buzzed in his pocket. Zachary pulled over and fished it out. On the screen was another message from Dimitri.

Are you alone?

Zachary hesitated, uneasy. Of course Dimitri expected him to be alone, but asking if he was implied that Dimitri had something to hide. Eventually, Zachary texted back confirmation that he was by himself.

Good. You can't trust that cop Dougan.

Zachary stared down at the screen. *Dougan?* Dougan had done all of the appropriate things. He'd made inquiries into Jose's disappearance, though he hadn't done any more than he had to, glossing over with routine inquiries only. He had asked for John's files in order to review the possibility of a serial killer, though he hadn't yet opened a file on the serial killer or organized a task force. He had ordered the logs on Jose's phone when Zachary provided it to him and cross-referenced Dimitri's phone number. He hadn't asked Zachary for anyone else's numbers, but it was possible that he already had access to a database of all of the numbers he needed. He had even gone back to Philippe's apartment when the young man had not answered his phone.

Zachary shifted, his brain working through the possibilities. Remembering the cop in Russia. Seventy dead women. Seventy that he had admitted to and described, more that he had lost track of. A loving father and husband. A decorated cop. And one of the worst serial killers the world had ever known.

Why can't I trust Dougan?

His text back went unanswered. Had that been enough to scare Dimitri off? Was he sure now that Zachary was in league with Dougan, sitting in the dark, waiting to ambush him when he showed up for the meeting?

Zachary wasn't sure where Dougan was. He had said that he would wait until Zachary had met with Dimitri before moving in. Zachary hadn't seen him during his reconnaissance of the neighborhood, so as far as he knew, Dougan wasn't there yet. But he could be sitting in a darkened car somewhere, watching Zachary drive by and waiting for Dimitri to make an appearance.

Zachary waited, but there was no further text. It was still early for the meeting with Dimitri. Zachary put his phone back in his pocket and pulled the car out onto the street to continue familiarizing himself with the area. If Dimitri decided not to show, then he wouldn't show. Zachary had to assume he would, and he'd be ready.

There was a wooded area up ahead. Zachary squinted at it through the darkness. A park? It seemed like a strange place for one. He drove closer and saw a decorated archway leading into the park, the name of the park inlaid within the wrought iron frame: "Peaceful Retreat Cemetery."

Zachary stared at it, making the connection to Honore Santiago. He was sure it was the name of Santiago's cemetery. But why would Dimitri want to meet Zachary there?

CHAPTER THIRTY

S ANTIAGO WAS ONE OF Jose's partners. So was Dimitri. They had to know each other, to know about each other. Were they somehow acting together? Were they involved with each other as well?

He wanted to contact Dougan, to give him a heads-up that it might be an ambush. They might be dealing with two men rather than just one. There might be something going on that Zachary hadn't yet been able to wrap his mind around.

But the seeds of doubt that Dimitri had sown about Dougan were sprouting and twining around his brain and he couldn't be one hundred percent sure that the cop was clean. Dimitri could be right. He might be the one who held all of the answers, and he said that Dougan couldn't be trusted.

Zachary sat in the car, looking at the words in the arch over the entrance. Eventually, he had to satisfy himself that there was no one lurking in the cemetery, and he drove in.

He turned his brights on, casting long, dark shadows of tombstones and trees over the smooth, even turf. He watched for any movement, fresh graves, equipment out of place, or anything else that might be suspicious. He saw movement through the trees and dimmed his lights. He drove the rest of the way around a loop in the other direction and drove out of the cemetery.

If he were lucky, then whoever was in the cemetery would think that he was just someone who had made a wrong turn. He drove far enough away that anyone inside the cemetery would not be able to see the vehicle, parked it, and got out. He hesitated, weighing his options.

He took out his phone and texted Dougan.

Zachary walked back into the cemetery, slowly and as quietly as possible. He didn't use his flashlight, but let his eyes adjust to the dark. He could hear the man before he could see him, the sound of heavy equipment.

Looking through the trees, Zachary could see a small excavator at work. He probably didn't need to be tiptoeing around with the racket the engine was making. He kept behind trees as much as possible as he approached, not wanting to attract attention with his movement.

He couldn't see the operator of the excavator. The headlights and the lights that would normally have been lighting up the cab had been turned off so that he had to rely on the moonlight for illumination. He could only vaguely see the shape in the operator's seat, not well enough to discern if it was Santiago.

He was pretty sure that gravediggers didn't normally work at night, even if it were still early evening. If there were an interment in the morning, they would have been sure to get the work done earlier in the day. The man was working without lights for a reason. He didn't want people calling in the unusual nighttime activity to the police.

Thinking about the police, Zachary looked over his shoulder the way he had come, but still didn't see anyone else. If Dougan were there, he was keeping carefully hidden, like Zachary.

The excavator backed up and clattered to a stop. Zachary froze where he was and watched the figure climb out of the equipment. He had on a bulky coat so it was still impossible to make him out.

The man walked away from the excavator and the hole he had been digging, his footsteps crunching through the gravel. Zachary watched him until he was out of sight and his footsteps were no longer audible.

He crept closer. He decided he really didn't like cemeteries in the dark. It was one thing during the day when the sun was shining and there were people around, but night was another thing altogether. There was good cover most of the way to the freshly-dug grave. Zachary looked around, checking for any sign of the shadowy figure, but he seemed to be alone.

He stood there for a few more minutes, his own skin dimly illuminated by the moonlight. There wasn't really anything to see. A rectangular hole in the ground. The excavator, its engine ticking as it cooled down. A tarp and some hand tools beside the grave; shovel and pick for finishing off the edges of the grave. He supposed that the man had gone to get the other equipment needed to stage the grave. The rails and strap system that Zachary had seen used at graveside ceremonies to hold the casket and then lower it into the grave when everything was done. Maybe it was just a worker who had not managed to get everything done that he was supposed to during the day. Maybe Zachary had jumped to conclusions, spooked by the idea of tracking a serial killer.

He blinked a few times, focusing in on the smaller details of the gravesite. There was a headstone moved to the side, which suggested that the grave being dug was previously occupied. Zachary knew that sometimes a grave was used for a second body, perhaps a spouse. So it wasn't that unusual. If somebody were disposing of a body illegally, then they surely would have picked a more isolated spot, not an existing grave that had been dug up again. A visitor might notice that and find it suspicious. Zachary stepped closer to have a peek at the tombstone.

He knew he was stepping out from the cover of the trees, but he would hear anyone coming down the gravel path again, and no one would be able to see him unless they were past the break in the trees.

It was too dark to see the name and dates on the stone. He didn't know whether it was just the dark or whether the stone was older and worn, the letters blurred in the dim moonlight. His toe bumped against the tarp. Just a little nudge, not hard enough to dislodge it. He looked down at it, his brain registering the fact that it wasn't just a rolled-up tarp, but had some heft to it. It hadn't been weighted down with tools or rocks, but had something wrapped up inside. And of course he knew what it was going to be without looking.

He bent down anyway and touched the tarp. It was cold to the touch as if it had been outside for a long time. It hadn't just been pulled from a warm vehicle.

The smell that Zachary detected wasn't just the newly-turned earth from the grave. And it wasn't whoever was in that grave, probably buried years before and contained in a sealed casket. The stink of decomposition so close to the tarp was almost overwhelming. Zachary felt for the edge of the tarp. It was rolled neatly, with the seam on the underside.

He could wait. He could go back and hide in the trees and let the police deal with it when they arrived. He knew that was what he should do. But if Dougan were not on his way, or worse, if he were involved in the crime, then Zachary needed to find out everything he could before the return of the man trying to conceal the evidence. Breathing through his mouth instead of his nose, Zachary tried to get a purchase on the bundle to roll it over.

His body protested, his muscles and his bruised ribs throbbing with the pain of the effort to roll the heavy burden over. He closed his eyes, held his breath, and heaved. He managed to roll it one hundred and eighty degrees, revealing the edge of the tarp so that he could begin the unwrapping process.

Zachary had his winter gloves on already so, sure he wasn't going to leave any evidence behind, he started to work the edge free and pull it up. It wasn't a quick process. He didn't want to destroy any evidence the killer might have left behind or to spread the already-nauseating smell. If he were on a detective show on TV, the reveal would have been almost instant, with the fictional private eye or cop pulling back a corner of the tarp, which would be directly over the victim's face, to reveal his identity.

The wind had picked up, rattling the now-loose half of the tarp noisily, making it whip into Zachary's face. He was sure it wasn't clean and didn't want any fluids or pathogens, however microscopic, being sprayed into his face. He held his breath again, hoping that the next flip of the bundle would be the last.

He pulled back the tarp again, finally freeing it from the dark shape that had pinned it down. Though his eyes had adjusted to the moonlight, he still couldn't get a clear view of what was now undeniably a body, lying face down on the tarp.

His brain worked through the different possibilities. Jose? Philippe? He knew it wasn't John, who had been burned and was at the medical examiner's office or somewhere further along in his journey. He wore a suit. So probably not Philippe. Zachary swallowed hard and moved up to the head, holding his breath one more time and bending down to peer into the face of the badly-bloated corpse.

It wasn't Jose or Philippe.

It was Dimitri.

CHAPTER THIRTY-ONE

ZACHARY JUMPED BACK, SHOCKED.

How could it be Dimitri? They had just been texting each other.

He scrabbled for his phone, not sure what he was going to do with it when he pulled it out. Call Dougan again? Take a picture? Re-read the texts he had exchanged with Dimitri?

He managed to work it out of his pants pocket before a heavy blow landed on the back of his head and neck, dropping him onto the corpse.

CHAPTER THIRTY-TWO

I T WAS ANOTHER GROGGY awakening, and at first Zachary thought he was still asleep at Mr. Peterson's house. His head throbbed. He needed another pain pill. It was dark, not light, so they had been wrong about him sleeping in. It was still night time. If he could force himself to move, he could take another pain pill, and maybe another sleeping pill, and go back to sleep until he was feeling better.

But he wasn't in Mr. Peterson's house. Wherever he was, it was dark and cold. He wasn't in a nice, soft bed. Zachary groaned and tried to move. He couldn't remember everything that had happened, but it was like there was another self in the back of his brain, yelling at him that Dimitri was dead and Zachary was in danger. He couldn't remember how he knew that, but it was the truth. He tried again to get up, fighting against the throbbing pain and vertigo. He couldn't move his hands to get them beneath him.

"Zachary Goldman."

He froze at the whisper. The room was dark, but the whisper gave him something to focus on and, staring into the black space, he thought he could make out the outline of the man.

There was a flare of light, and then a glow. An old-fashioned oil lamp, the wick lit by a match. Zachary swallowed and tried to lick his lips, but his mouth was so dry it didn't help.

The lamp was bright after the blackness of the night. The room around him was rustic. A cabin or shack, crudely furnished. The large shape put down the lamp and moved toward him.

Teddy.

Zachary immediately remembered Pat's reassurance that Teddy was safe. They'd known him for years.

And the serial killer had been operating for years, right under their noses, suspected by no one.

Teddy was a big man. Looming up in the darkness, he was even bigger than Zachary remembered, tall and broad, casting his shadow all the way across the room.

Zachary tried to move. He thrashed to escape, but it was no use. His hands were cuffed in front of him. He was on the floor and his leg was shackled to the iron frame of the bed beside him.

"Thought you were smart, didn't you, Zachary? You thought you could just waltz in and catch yourself a killer. Well, it isn't that easy, is it? Not when the killer is smarter than you are, always a couple of steps ahead."

The noise of the tarp had covered the footsteps of the returning killer, Zachary realized, his mind shooting off on a tangent instead of staying focused on the man standing before him. Teddy had probably returned walking through the grass rather than on the gravel pathway, and the wind and the flapping tarp had kept Zachary from hearing his approach. He should have been more aware. He should have been looking around, keeping a better lookout.

He should have waited for Dougan's arrival.

Zachary looked around the room, trying to figure out where he was. Was he still in the cemetery, in a crypt or an equipment shed? Had Teddy hauled him off somewhere even more remote?

He was trying not to focus on the fact that Teddy was getting closer to him. He denied the possibility that he could be in even worse danger, that Teddy was there to kill him.

Why hadn't Teddy just rolled Zachary and Dimitri both into the grave and covered them up?

Zachary looked at the bed. At least Teddy hadn't brought Dimitri's corpse back with him. How much time had passed, then? If he had stopped to bury Dimitri, that must have taken at least half an hour. Where was Dougan? Had he decided not to show up after all? Were he and Teddy partners in crime? Or had Teddy done him in too?

Teddy reached down for Zachary's leg and Zachary felt a sharp pain jab into his thigh. He let out a hoarse shout and his heart raced. He was sure that Teddy had neatly nicked an artery and Zachary was about to bleed out. He tried to reach for the wound, but the combination of the handcuffs and his woozy head prevented him from being able to sit up and put pressure on it.

"There now," Teddy crooned. "Just relax for a few minutes and let that take effect. Nothing to be concerned about. You'll feel much better."

"No…"

Teddy tousled Zachary's head like he was a little boy, then gripped him under the chin, holding him tightly to prevent him from turning away. "You're not a bad-looking boy. At least, you weren't before they messed your face up like that."

Zachary tried to pull away, but his muscle responses were sluggish and he was starting to feel light-headed. Not light-headed, exactly, but removed. As if he weren't the one in control of his body anymore. Whatever drug Teddy had injected him with was taking effect swiftly.

He stopped trying to pull away from Teddy.

Teddy smiled. The expression was ghoulish in the lamplight. "You see how much better this is? Why don't we get you more comfortable?"

He ran his hand slowly down Zachary's leg to the shackle. Producing a key, he unlocked it. Zachary thought he should take the opportunity to kick Teddy. A well-aimed kick to the temple or crushing his nose would disable him, and then Zachary could make his escape.

But he didn't kick Teddy. Teddy bent over and picked Zachary up with one arm under his knees and one under his neck, like a sleeping child. He lay Zachary down on the bed.

Zachary tried to protest. "No…"

"Don't you worry. I've never had anyone complain, when it was all over." Teddy chuckled to himself.

CHAPTER THIRTY-THREE

ZACHARY WAS FAR AWAY when the cavalry finally rolled in.

Without any warning to Teddy, the cops came crashing in through the door of the shack, flashbangs tossed in ahead of them to stun their quarry. Teddy didn't have a gun. He froze with the knife in his hand, too startled to do anything but turn toward the door with his mouth open.

In the seemingly chaotic entry, Teddy was disarmed and thrown to the ground. He clearly had nowhere to hide any additional weapons. They handcuffed him, shouting charges and a Miranda warning. They wrapped a blanket around him and hauled him out of the shack, Teddy grinning like he was having the time of his life.

It was Dougan who bent over Zachary on the bed, feeling his pulse and calling his name, but Zachary himself was far from the scene, watching it all from a distance, time and space morphing into shapes he hadn't known existed. He remembered Santiago's words, 'I've never really felt like I move linearly through time…' It hadn't made sense to him before, but now he understood.

He watched without emotion as Dougan took a series of pictures and then pulled the single sheet of the bed over Zachary's body.

"Need paramedics in here!" Dougan barked. "Where are they?"

They must have arrived and assembled with the cops before the breach, because they were right on hand, pushing their way in the door as soon as Dougan called for them.

"Preserve all the evidence you can," Dougan ordered. "Make sure they take blood as soon as he gets to the hospital. Swabs of everything. Full forensic kit. Act as if this is the one and only thing we can get Mr. Archuro for. I want it to be ironclad. Is that understood?"

"Not our first rodeo," one of the paramedics growled, bending over Zachary's body to shine a light in his eyes and check his pulse.

"I don't care about your hurt feelings. This monster needs to be locked up."

"We'll take care of it," the other paramedic, a woman, reassured Dougan.

The drugs were wearing off and Zachary was more in control of his faculties a few hours later when he heard Mr. Peterson and Pat arrive. The ordeal of the forensic examination was finally over. He could hear the doctor talking to them before they were allowed to see him.

"Is he alright?" Pat demanded. "I want to know what that bastard did to him."

"Under patient privacy laws, I really can't give you any specifics. I'm sorry. If Mr. Goldman wishes that information to be shared, I can talk with you later. But right now, I have to assume that he wishes it to be kept private."

"Is he awake?" Mr. Peterson asked.

"He may be in and out. And he may appear to be conscious of what's going on around him and be able to answer questions, but then later wake up and have no recollection of it. His memories of the past few hours and the next few may be patchy or even totally lost. Don't worry if he asks you the same questions over and over. It will probably be a while before he's really back with us."

"He was drugged, then."

"I can't answer that. Let's see how he feels about sharing that information once he's feeling like himself again."

There were a few more murmurs, and then the two men were escorted to Zachary's gurney. There were curtains pulled around the bed. Zachary knew by the noise on the other side that he wasn't in a private room yet. He was still in the emergency room examination area.

"Zachary." Mr. Peterson was the first to his side, reaching out to touch him and reassure him. "Zach, how are you?"

Zachary shied away from his hand, his body convulsing with sudden panic.

"Whoa." Mr. Peterson pulled back slowly. "It's okay. I'm sorry. Too fast."

Zachary let his body melt back into the mattress again, breathing through his open mouth and watching the two of them uneasily.

Mr. Peterson leaned in slightly, trying to meet Zachary's eyes and evaluate his state. "Pretty rough night, huh?"

Zachary breathed in and out a couple of times and nodded. "Yeah."

"Oh, Zach," Pat's face was lined with grief. "I'm so sorry this happened to you. All because I had to involve you in Jose's disappearance."

"No. Not your fault. I shouldn't have gone on without Dougan."

"Why did you?" Mr. Peterson asked. "You said you weren't going to meet with Dimitri alone. Why didn't you wait?"

"I wanted to make sure... I was afraid of losing the evidence. That by the time Dougan got there, it would be gone and he wouldn't be able to get a warrant. And I wasn't sure... I didn't even know, at first, if what was going on in the cemetery was related. It could have just been a coincidence, someone in the cemetery right before I was supposed to be meeting Dimitri. I didn't know if it was anything related, I just wanted to check."

"You took a real risk."

Zachary nodded. "Poor impulse control," he reminded Mr. Peterson with an embarrassed shrug. "It's always been at the top of my psychological profile."

"Yes, it has. Of course, we had hoped you would outgrow it."

"Not yet."

Mr. Peterson gave him a warm smile. "I think you turned out pretty good. I just worry about you. If the police hadn't gotten there when they did..."

Zachary swallowed. He had no doubt whatsoever how it would have ended. Teddy had been explicit in his descriptions of what he planned to do, and he hadn't planned for Zachary to be found when it was all over. Teddy had plenty of places close at hand in which to hide a dead body, where he could continue to visit it for years to come.

"The police got there," he said. "I'm okay."

"Are you?" Mr. Peterson's eyes moved down Zachary's body and back up again. With Zachary wearing a hospital johnny and a sheet pulled up over him, Mr. Peterson couldn't see the things Teddy had done. The most he could do was guess. Zachary wasn't going to divulge any details.

"I'm just sore," he said. "Nothing a few pain pills won't cure." He closed his eyes, resting, thinking about sleep. As removed as he still felt from himself, he wondered whether he would ever sleep again. Maybe he would always float above himself, watching his sleeping body from a safe distance. "You won't have to worry about me taking my pills tonight," he said, nodding toward the IV bag.

Mr. Peterson lowered himself into a chair. He kept his hand near Zachary's head, as if wanting to comfort him, but worried about Zachary's reaction. "I'd rather be worrying about your pills tonight."

There were strange lights and colors behind Zachary's lids when he closed his eyes. He opened them again. "I'm sorry about that. About taking too many. I'm usually very careful."

"I know you are. I think that's one of the reasons it scared us so much. You're more likely to not take something you ought to than you are to take too much. When you weren't up and I went into your room and found you so pale and your breathing so shallow... I was afraid at first..." He didn't finish the thought.

Zachary knew what he'd been afraid of. Mr. Peterson knew that Zachary had attempted suicide in the past. That he might not have made it past the previous Christmas if he had been left alone.

"I'm sorry," he said again.

Some time passed without any of them saying anything.

"Where's Dougan? Did he come to the hospital?" Zachary asked.

"He's got his hands full right now," Mr. Peterson advised. "He said he would check in when he could, but he's got a body and a serial killer on his hands, and that's way above his pay grade. He will be passing everything on to whoever is heading up the investigation into Teddy Archuro."

"Teddy," Pat repeated, putting his hands over his eyes and shaking his head. "Can you believe it? I can't. He never seemed... he was normal, just like anyone else. I never saw anything weird..."

Zachary thought about how Teddy had zeroed in on him at The Night Scene. Zachary had attracted Teddy's interest as someone new. He remembered how Teddy had suggested a shorter, more intense relationship. Just how short and intense, Zachary had not guessed. Teddy had been a predator, on the prowl for fresh meat.

"I think I'll go to sleep now," he said. "I want to be awake when Dougan gets here later."

Both men nodded. Mr. Peterson touched Zachary's shoulder very lightly, the weight of a butterfly. "Do you want someone to stay with you? In case you wake up and don't know where you are or need someone to talk to?"

"No."

Zachary was too enervated to explain. He wanted them to just go home and leave him alone.

CHAPTER THIRTY-FOUR

HE KNEW THAT DOUGAN would come when he was able, to discuss the case and tell Zachary what their findings had been so far. He lay awake into the morning, staring at the tiles on the ceiling, knowing that despite what the doctor had said, he wasn't going to fall asleep.

Nurses checked on him periodically, usually expressing surprise at finding him wide awake. An orderly showed up to take him to the room he'd been assigned. He entertained Zachary with a Caribbean-accented monologue as he wheeled Zachary's gurney through the hallways and elevators to find his new home.

Zachary couldn't help evaluating the orderly as he'd been evaluating everyone the last few days. An immigrant, obviously. But not an illegal or he wouldn't be working in the hospital. He didn't match the body type of the immigrants who had disappeared. He had a big, well-padded body rather than the small, wiry frame Teddy seemed to prefer. That meant that Zachary could relax. The orderly was just the man taking Zachary to his room, away from the constant din of the emergency room, where he would be able to sleep.

Except he knew he wouldn't.

Eventually, Dougan did come see him. His face was tired and drawn. He looked like he had aged ten years since Zachary had first met him. But he gave Zachary an encouraging smile and nod.

"We've got him. We've got him wrapped up nice and tight. He'll never see the outside of a cell again."

Zachary waited for the relief, but it didn't come. The world went on, whether Teddy was in jail or out. He was hardly a blip on most people's radar. Others like him would continue to operate in the dark long after Dougan and Zachary had shuffled off their mortal frames.

"How did you find him?" After the words were out, Zachary knew he should have said 'me' or 'us.' But he didn't correct himself. Dougan flopped into a chair and leaned back, arms and head draped over the sides and back like a long-legged spider.

"You led us to the cemetery, where, as you probably guessed, we found Dimitri's body. It was obvious by the state of the body that he'd been dead for some time. Not just an hour or two, but probably since you first talked to him. That threw suspicion squarely onto Teddy. We put all of our resources into finding him. APB out on him and his vehicles, warrants to track his phone, Dimitri's, and yours, searched title records for any properties he owned, got dogs to try to track his vehicle where it had been parked at the cemetery, everything we could think of."

Zachary nodded.

"The land titles got him. It wasn't just a place he had found, that shack in the woods. It was on land that he owned. There were fresh tire tracks on the road and we had a helicopter with thermal imaging fly over, which told us that there were, in fact, two men inside. With that, we went in hot on the basis of imminent danger."

Zachary stared at the tiles on the ceiling.

"He's talking," Dougan advised. "Just like you said, these guys love to talk once you catch them. They want to show you how clever they are and how they managed to avoid suspicion for years. All of the close calls that they had when a traffic cop pulled them over with a dead body in the trunk or some guy drugged and unconscious in the passenger seat." Dougan shook his head indignantly. "They're just so damn charming they get away with anything."

"When I met him at the bar..."

"What did you think? Did you suspect him?"

"I thought... he was *off*. He made me uncomfortable, but I thought it was just... because he was coming on to me. He thought I was gay, so he treated me like a possible conquest."

Dougan considered this, nodding. "I suppose it's lucky he was interested in you. If he'd been smart, he would have killed you and disposed of your body right away instead of just capturing you."

Zachary swallowed. "Did he say... why he didn't?"

Not that Zachary didn't know. That had been clear from the start. Zachary just wanted to know if *they* knew.

Dougan hesitated. "He's like a cat... likes to play with his food before he kills it. He didn't figure we were right on his tail. Thought he had plenty of time to stash you in the cabin and then go back to finish burying the body before anyone found it. Who would be tramping through the cemetery in the middle of the night?" Dougan cleared his throat. He didn't look at Zachary. "Then he could go back to the cabin and take his time. From what he's confessed, it takes him a few days to get through all of his usual rituals."

Zachary concentrated hard on the white tiled ceiling and the sounds and smells of the hospital around him. He would not acknowledge what had happened to him. He would simply deny the memories. They were not a part of him.

"What about Philippe? I didn't see any sign of him. If he wasn't at the cemetery and wasn't at the cabin… did Teddy have other places? Would he ever have several quarries at the same time?"

Dougan's head turned toward him, but Zachary continued to look at the ceiling, not responding to Dougan's attempt to make eye contact. Dougan shifted in his seat and looked back away from Zachary.

"He says he didn't have anything to do with Philippe's disappearance, and I'm inclined to believe him. He was skilled enough that he would have been able to take Philippe without tipping the others off. But Philippe and Nando Gonzalez and all of the rest of them? He couldn't be responsible for all of them disappearing."

"Unless Nando was freaked out when Philippe disappeared and got everyone out of there before the police could come looking for another missing man."

"Could be," Dougan allowed, "but I'm inclined to believe what Teddy Archuro says. I think if he'd taken Philippe, he would have been happy to admit it. That seems to be his response on all of his other accomplishments."

Zachary breathed a sigh of relief. That was one thing, anyway. He hadn't pushed Teddy into eliminating Philippe. He didn't know how he would forgive himself if his investigation had caused the boy's death.

CHAPTER THIRTY-FIVE

WANT TO GO HOME."
Mr. Peterson had been surprised to find Zachary sitting up, waiting for the clothes that he had requested, eager to get out of the hospital.

"I don't know if that's a good idea. You need some recovery time."

"Not here. I don't want to be here; I want to go home."

"Well, I suppose we can keep an eye on you there…"

"No. Back to my apartment."

He saw the hurt in his former foster father's face and knew that he'd said the wrong thing, or said it the wrong way.

"It's not because of you," he assured Lorne, "I just want… the reason I was here was to find Jose, or to find out what had happened to him. I've done that. I need to go back to my other work. I don't want… everything that has happened here. I don't want to be reminded about it every time I turn around."

"I can understand that. But I'm concerned. You're still hurt. A lot has happened. I think you need some support."

"I have a therapist and friends, and I can still call you. Pat can set up Skype and we can talk face-to-face, just like if I was still there."

"That would be nice. I'd like to hear from you more than I do." Mr. Peterson's mouth thinned into a straight line. "Zach… do you want to talk about it? I don't think we should… pretend that nothing happened."

"No."

"You should talk to someone. It doesn't have to be me, if that would be uncomfortable. But you need to work it out. Get some counseling, a support group."

"I will."

He saw that he had answered too quickly. Mr. Peterson didn't believe it. Zachary motioned to Mr. Peterson's bag.

"I need to get changed."

Without a word, his old friend handed the bag over. Zachary couldn't help flinching when Mr. Peterson's hand moved toward him with it. An alarmed tightening of all of his muscles. He swallowed and took the bag.

"Thanks. Be right back."

In the small hospital bathroom, he leaned for a minute on the sink, taking long, even breaths and pushing the panic away. There was no reason to be anxious. He was going home, where he could be alone and relax. He could catch up on the routine investigative work that he had let slide while he had been looking into Jose's disappearance.

Zachary made himself move. He pulled on the clothes, relieved to have his body properly covered again. The loose, thin hospital johnny had made him feel too much like he was still naked. He felt more secure dressed like a real person. Like he could go back to his former life without a hitch.

CHAPTER THIRTY-SIX

HIS PHONE WAS RINGING yet again. Zachary had been turning it off for a couple of hours at a time in order to give himself time to focus on work, but he didn't want to miss calls from new clients, who weren't likely to leave messages.

The number was unfamiliar. Not one of the reporters who had been calling him repeatedly, wheedling and cajoling for the inside story. But he was getting a lot of calls from kooks too. It was getting easier to pick up the phone and just terminate the call when it wasn't someone he wanted to talk to. He no longer felt bad about hanging up on people. So much for the phone etiquette lessons painstakingly instilled by a series of foster mothers and group homes. They hadn't anticipated a situation like the one Zachary was in.

He tapped the speaker button without picking up the phone. "Goldman Investigations. Zachary."

A few seconds of staticky silence ticked by.

"Hello?" Zachary prompted, finger above the red 'end' button.

"Zachary?"

It wasn't a good line, static and background traffic noise making the voice difficult to recognize.

"This is Zachary."

"It's Philippe."

Zachary turned off the speaker and put the phone to his ear, relief flooding through him. "Philippe! You're okay."

"Yes, I am fine."

"When you wouldn't answer any calls and then disappeared... I was worried. I didn't know if *he* had gotten to you."

"Teddy Archuro," Philippe said in a voice that was still stunned. "I knew him."

"He didn't—you didn't date him?"

"I hung out with him a couple of times. Not a date, just casual... getting to know him."

Zachary drew in his breath in a whistle. Philippe could have been Teddy's next victim. In spite of what Zachary had been through, he could take comfort in the fact that he had prevented Philippe from being tortured and murdered.

"The news reports said that the police were looking for remains. Do you know…?"

"They haven't released anything official, but they have recovered some… I think they probably found Jose, but the medical examiner hasn't confirmed identities yet."

"Where?"

"He was using Honore Santiago's cemetery some of the time. And there are graves out at his property in the woods, where he had a cabin. I don't know if there was anywhere else; they're not giving me much information."

"Honore was not involved, though…?"

Zachary's heart gave an extra beat. Was Philippe involved with Santiago too? "No, I don't think so. If they have found any connection other than the cemetery, they haven't told me. But please… be careful."

"Honore is a nice man. Very generous."

"I'm sure he is. But he still had connections with a lot of the missing men. I just want you to be careful. Teddy wasn't the only predator out there."

At the knock on the door, Zachary got up and walked through the kitchen to look through the wide-view peephole. He opened the door, giving Kenzie a forced smile. "Hi, Kenz."

"How's it going, Zachary? I'm hoping you don't have too much going on tonight…"

"Come on in." He opened the door wider.

She walked in and looked around. Zachary gave the apartment a quick scan. He had been hard at work and hadn't had much time for cleaning or other chores. But he had picked up groceries and there wasn't a sink full of dirty dishes. He didn't think Kenzie would find anything of concern.

"I'm glad to have you home," she remarked. "Though you look like hell."

"No worse than most of the stiffs you work with," he teased.

"Actually, most of the remains look better than you do," Kenzie countered, hands on hips. "You could give most zombies a run for their money."

"That's just because it's healing. Bruises always look worse as they get older and change color."

Kenzie gave a nod of agreement. She opened the fridge and helped herself to a soft drink. "You want anything?"

"I'm good."

They both drifted into the living room. Zachary straightened up the papers he had been working on and piled them carefully in his tray. He closed his computer lid and sat down on the couch next to Kenzie. She looked at him for a minute, then leaned back and took a sip of her drink.

"I missed you."

"I was only gone for a few days."

She stretched her arm behind him. "But I still missed you. You hardly even called." She stroked the back of his neck.

Zachary jolted at her touch. He pulled back from her, feeling suddenly crowded.

"Wow." Kenzie stared at him. "What was that? I didn't hurt you…"

Zachary took several deep breaths. "No. Sorry. You just startled me."

She shifted her body a little closer to him, watching his face. Zachary couldn't help squirming, overwhelmed by her closeness.

"Seriously, are you okay?" Kenzie persisted.

"Yeah, fine."

She withdrew slightly and took several swallows of her soft drink. Zachary tried to calm down and relax his muscles.

"There weren't a lot of details in the news stories about how this Teddy guy was arrested," she observed.

"It was a good arrest. He's talking. He's never going to be out on the street again." He said it as much for his own sake as much as for hers. Reminding himself that Teddy would never be able to hurt anyone ever again.

"That's not what I meant," Kenzie said. "I'm not worried about whether it was a good arrest. I'm just wondering… about your part in it. They kind of glossed over the part about you being 'briefly captured' by this guy. Like it was just a few minutes… a standoff or something like that."

Zachary nodded.

"Is that what it was?"

He swallowed. "No."

"What happened?"

Zachary shook his head emphatically. "I'm not ready to talk about it."

"Okay…"

But he could see she was not ready to let it go. She was still looking at him analytically, trying to think of another way to get the story from him. Zachary picked up the TV remote and turned on the television. Not only did he not want to talk to her about it, he didn't even want to think about it. "You want to watch a movie?"

"If you want," Kenzie said. "I thought we'd visit."

"I just need time to unwind."

"Sure. You've had quite a week. Your body obviously needs healing time. Maybe your mind too."

He nodded. "It's been pretty taxing."

"I'm here. Whenever you're ready to talk…"

He nodded. "I know. But… I might not want to talk about it."

"I guess that's up to you."

He switched channels on the TV. Kenzie reached out, and he steeled himself not to react. She put her hand on his knee and he jerked it away. It was beyond his control, a reflex. His heart raced and he felt like he wasn't getting enough air.

"It's okay, Zachary."

"I'm fine," he assured her, even though it took everything he had to talk in a calm, even voice.

She offered her hand to him. Zachary took it in his. He held it between the two of them as he flipped channels with the other hand to find a movie they would both enjoy. He didn't cuddle up to her.

And he didn't pick a romance.

Did you enjoy this book? Reviews and recommendations are vital to making a book successful.
Please leave a review at your favorite book store or review site and share it with your friends.

Don't miss the following bonus material:
Sign up for mailing list to get a free ebook
Other books by P.D. Workman
Read a sneak preview chapter
Learn more about the author

AUTHOR'S NOTE

Serial killers are a fascinating subject. Despite their proliferation in fiction, both literary and TV/movies, they are a very small fraction of the criminal population. Of the US population of 327 million, with a prison population of 2.3 million, the number of serial killers in prison appears to be around 30 people. It is estimated that the number of serial killers operating in the US is between 25 and 50 people. As DNA testing continues to grow, I expect those numbers will change as serial killings which would previously have gone unrealized are identified, as has been the case with identifying serial rapists while processing cold case rape kits.

What makes a serial killer? While it is our nature to look for patterns and to identify them as somehow "sick" or "other" than we are, there is no one diagnosis or red flag to help us to identify serial killers before they strike or to explain their actions afterward. We think of serial killers as being psychopaths (not a DSM diagnosis) or having something like Antisocial Personality Disorder, but their diagnoses, if any, range from depression, to schizophrenia, to Narcissistic Personality Disorder. While TV would have us believe that they are geniuses, they range from borderline retardation to average intelligence, with only a few with greater than average intelligence. They're just good at not getting caught.

Again, we have been told that they usually (but not always) come from very abusive or traumatic backgrounds; but so do millions of others who have never killed even one person. And the "red flag" of cruelty to animals? It is estimated that 44% of children will abuse animals at some point. The older they are, the more of a red flag it becomes, but we can't use it to identify anything other than possible abuse or trauma in the home, particularly when it is part of the MacDonald Triad (animal abuse, fire setting, and bedwetting.) More resources on this and other issues mentioned in this book can be found in the Book Club Resources section for this book on my website.

Sign up for my mailing list at pdworkman.com and get Gluten-Free Murder for free!

PREVIEW OF HE WAS NOT THERE

Zachary was glad that Tyrrell had called. He had needed a reason to get away from Kenzie for a while. Their relationship, which had begun more than a year ago, had gotten more complicated since Zachary had been attacked, and he needed a reason to take a break from Kenzie's ministrations. He didn't want to tell her to leave him alone and give him some space, but he wasn't sure how else to get her out of his apartment when she came over for a visit.

But his brother Tyrrell's call had given him an excuse to say that he was busy and needed to deal with a family emergency.

Not that Tyrrell had said it was an emergency. He and Heather were perfectly willing to wait until a convenient time for Zachary, but for Zachary that was a good enough excuse to tell Kenzie that he needed to take care of family stuff and would have to see her later.

"Do you want me to drive you somewhere?" Kenzie offered, still happy to do whatever he needed her to.

"I'm fine to drive."

"I know, it's just that…" she trailed off, apparently unable to find an excuse for taking care of him. He hadn't been drinking. He hadn't been having a particularly upsetting evening. She just wanted to know that everything was okay. She wanted to keep an eye on him. Zachary appreciated it, but he didn't want the attention.

"I'm fine," he repeated, getting his jacket on to signal to her that it was time to go.

Kenzie reluctantly got her coat on as well. She pulled the hood on over her dark, short curls and gave him a brief kiss with her bright-red-lipsticked lips, holding onto him more tightly and longer than was necessary for a goodbye. He gave her a squeeze of acknowledgement and headed to the door. Kenzie walked out ahead of him and watched as he locked up.

"What's going on with Tyrrell?"

"I don't know. I need to see him to find out."

"Is something wrong? Is there anything I could help with?"

"No, I don't think so. I'll let you know."

Kenzie nodded. "Okay."

They took the elevator down together, and Zachary sketched a little wave as they separated in the parking lot. "We'll talk later," he said. "Thanks for coming by."

He would have suggested that the next time, he would come by her place, just so that he had some control over the timing, but she had never invited him to her apartment, so it was out of bounds. She needed her own space and privacy. He just wished that he could have some of his back too.

As he headed to the meeting with Tyrrell, he thought about his relationship with Kenzie, the medical examiner's assistant. Things had changed over the months that they had known each other, from a girl who was just interested in having some fun to a woman who was really interested in him and in taking their relationship further, to one who was in his space a little too often and felt like she needed to take care of him.

It had never been like that with Bridget. He had always felt warm and rewarded when she wanted to do something for him or showed her concern. His ex-wife had more often been angry and critical when he went through a crisis, upset with him for taking too much from the relationship.

He had tried to take care of Bridget too. He had tried not to let it be a one-sided relationship, to put as much into the marriage as he took out of it, but she had never seen it that way. She had only seen him sucking the energy out of her, taking time away from her parties and social events. He'd never felt smothered by Bridget. Like with his relationship with his mother before he was put into foster care, he'd felt like he had to earn every bit of attention and every smile and kindness she might bestow upon him.

It was good that his younger brother Tyrrell was back in his life. Zachary hadn't had any contact with biological family for thirty years and it felt good to see him again. And he was going to meet Heather. He hadn't seen any of the others since the fire. He could remember the scrappy little blond tomboy Heather had been. His second sister, a couple of years older than he was, she had been one of his little surrogate mothers. One of the two big sisters who tried to keep the younger children out of trouble and out from underfoot to avoid any unnecessary problems with their mother or father. To him, they had seemed so much older and more mature at the time. He had only been ten and they had almost seemed like adults to him.

He hadn't expected to meet any of the other kids. Even Tyrrell had said that he hadn't met Heather face-to-face since they had found each other. They talked on Skype or Facetime, but hadn't actually gotten together. What could have happened that had changed that? Was it just the natural progression of their relationship, or was there something wrong? Tyrrell had sounded concerned on the phone. Then relieved when Zachary said they could meet right away instead of trying to put it off and schedule something in the future. But maybe he was reading too much into it.

They had set up a time and place, allowing them both to meet halfway so that neither one had to drive halfway across Vermont to see each other. Zachary wasn't sure where Heather lived. Even though he was a private detective, he had never tried to find any of his siblings. They had a right to live their own lives without having to deal with him, especially since he was the reason that the family had been broken up.

Whatever reason Heather had for wanting to meet with him, Tyrrell had sounded pretty serious. Zachary pushed back the worry that it might be just to give him a piece of her mind about the problems he had caused in her life and the way he had ripped apart their family.

They had agreed to meet at a coffee shop. Clintock was a small town, so it didn't take long to find the little store. In a world that seemed to have been taken over by Starbucks, it was nice to see some independent shops were still alive and well. Zachary sat in his parked car for a few minutes, suddenly anxious about going inside. He knew Tyrrell didn't hold any resentments about what had happened to their family. But Heather was an unknown. Zachary had tried hard to please his big sisters when he was young. With his ADHD and their family problems, it had been an impossible proposition. One of them would go off on him for some stupid, impulsive mistake he had made, and he would get that knot in his stomach, that feeling that he had again come up short. And the worry that he always would.

Now she wanted him back in her life again. Why? What if he couldn't meet her expectations? He spent too much of his life with that lump in his stomach, worrying that he would never measure up to expectations. His clients', Bridget's, Kenzie's, the police officers that he worked with, his doctor and therapist, his surrogate fathers Lorne and Pat. They all had expectations, and he was only too aware of his failings.

The longer he stayed in the car, the harder it was going to be to actually break free of his fears and go in there and see what Tyrrell and Heather wanted, so in spite of his anxiety, he forced his body to climb out of the car, lock the doors, and walk toward the coffee shop. He clicked the lock button on his key remote a couple more times just to be sure, then stood at the door of the coffee shop, staring inside.

He saw them before they saw him. They were sitting at a table in the back. The coffee shop tables were almost deserted. People lined up at the counter to order and pick up their drinks, but they didn't stay to consume them, taking them 'to go' and carrying on with their busy lives. Tyrrell looked much the same as Zachary, but his dark hair was cut longer and shaggier than Zachary's buzz-cut. They both had dark eyes and a narrow build. Tyrrell was taller than Zachary was, not having spent as many years in a home where the food was inadequate or on meds that stunted his growth. He didn't have the hollows in his cheek that Zachary attempted to hide with a few days' growth of beard.

Zachary always lost weight before Christmas, and he hadn't been able to get back to a healthy weight before the assault. Since that incident, he'd been lucky if he could keep his weight stable. He told himself it was just a side effect of the meds, not admitting how much of his day was spent thinking about what Teddy had done to him and of other assaults in the years before he aged out of foster care. He didn't want those experiences to be a part of his life. He wanted to forget them.

Heather's appearance was quite different than Zachary's and Tyrrell's. She was blond, with a full figure. Not overweight, but a look that suggested she was a mother, having borne and nourished a few children, giving her wider hips and a silhouette that was no longer girlish, but mature. Her face looked worn and a little sad. She talked to Tyrrell earnestly, but her manner was hesitant, not animated.

She didn't look angry. Yet.

As Zachary entered the coffee shop, a two-tone electronic chime sounded, and Heather and Tyrrell looked up and turned toward the door. Tyrrell said something to Heather, probably 'there he is,' and got up to greet Zachary.

Tyrrell was always cheerful and enthusiastic when he saw Zachary, as if he really were happy to see him. Zachary's doubts always built up when he hadn't seen Tyrrell for a while, thinking his brother wouldn't really want to see him. But when he saw Tyrrell's face wreathed in smiles, and the way he reached out his hand to shake Zachary's and then pulled him in for a hug, he couldn't doubt it. Tyrrell slapped Zachary on the back and then pulled back to look at him.

"How are you, Zach? Doing okay?"

It was the first time Tyrrell had seen Zachary face-to-face since the assault, so he looked Zachary over searchingly, wanting to verify for himself that Zachary wasn't horribly mutilated.

"I'm fine," Zachary assured him. He looked past Tyrrell to Heather, who had remained sitting and didn't rush forward to be reunited with Zachary. She watched the two of them, her expression pensive.

Tyrrell turned and looked toward Heather. "Come and meet her."

They walked over to the table. Heather gazed up at Zachary and still didn't stand up to hug him or shake his hand. He sat down and she nodded to him.

"Hi."

"Hi, Heather."

Her eyes moved over him, taking everything in and finally stopping on his face. "Wow. You know, you look just the same."

"Really?" He thought of himself as almost a completely different person than he had been before the fire. He'd only been ten years old; how could he look the same as an adult?

But he remembered recognizing Tyrrell's eyes. How they danced just the way they had when he was five. It didn't matter if the rest of him had grown up, Zachary had still seen his little brother in those eyes.

Heather nodded. Zachary fumbled for something to say. "You... grew up."

She gave a little smile. "Yeah. That's the way it works."

He didn't see it yet. He couldn't find the little girl's face he remembered in this grown-up woman.

"So, how are you? Tyrrell said that you are married with a couple of kids?"

"Yeah. They're grown up now, but I have a boy and a girl. And Grant."

"Grant is your husband?"

"Yeah."

"You're still married after the kids moved out? How many years is that?"

"Twenty-four."

"Wow. Coming up on the big one. That's really something. Not a lot of people make it that far anymore."

Of course, his perspective was slightly skewed, spending hours following unfaithful spouses during or before divorces. But lasting twenty-four years was still a big accomplishment.

"We've had our ups and downs," Heather said. "But... I never really considered leaving him over any of our issues. We just pressed on through them. You're not married?"

"No... divorced. We managed about two years. Doesn't measure up too well to your twenty-four years, does it?"

"Living with someone else can be hard." Heather's voice was toneless, she sounded as if she was far away. "If there are things that you can't come to terms with..."

Zachary nodded. "I guess... we were just too different. We wanted different things."

But it wasn't really their philosophical differences that had precipitated the divorce. The truth was far more painful than that. Zachary didn't see the need to bare his soul to Heather yet. They hardly knew each other. He had the feeling she had come to him in some kind of trouble. She needed him for something. There was no point in telling her all of his problems when she was looking for help.

Heather nodded and had a sip of her coffee. Zachary realized that he hadn't ordered, and probably should have. He had to decide whether it would make Heather more uncomfortable for him to be sitting there without a drink or for him to take a break to go get one. On balance, he thought it was probably better to stay where he was. Heather seemed like she would spook at the slightest provocation. He glanced at Tyrrell to see what he thought of the situation. Tyrrell gave him a quick nod of encouragement. But Zachary didn't know where to go with the conversation.

"So... are you in contact with any of the others? Other than Tyrrell, I mean?"

"Me and Joss have kept in touch pretty well. There were times when we couldn't, but as adults... we reconnected and have kept up with each other."

"You and Joss didn't stay together?"

"No. We were put in the same home to start out with, but... well, they said they couldn't handle both of us, and that it was interfering with their discipline to have us both there because we always got in the way. You know, if one person was getting crap, the other one was always jumping in. So they said that one of us had to go, and I was the troublemaker, so..."

"You were a troublemaker?" Zachary repeated. He could remember how Heather used to get after him when he had screwed up. He had always thought she was next to perfect. She and Joss were always trying to help their mother by taking care of the younger kids and whatever they could around the house. They were nearly adults, as far as Zachary was concerned. They couldn't have been more than twelve and fourteen when they were separated. That was awfully young to be taking care of all of the other kids. And Joss and Heather had been trying to drag up the rest of the children since they were much younger than that, probably nine or ten.

He couldn't believe that Heather would have been identified as a troublemaker. Zachary had always been a disciplinary problem, but not the girls.

"Sure," Heather gave him the corner of a grin, looking engaged for the first time. "You don't remember all the stuff I used to do? I was always getting in trouble for leading the rest of you into trouble. If everyone was into something, it was always me who had started it. I had brilliant ideas of fun things to do to entertain ourselves and they didn't always turn out well."

Zachary smiled. He did remember that Heather had been the more fun of his older sisters. She had been better at thinking up things to do and keeping the younger kids engaged and involved in a game or project. He didn't remember them ending badly because of Heather. He was so often in trouble himself, he just assumed that he had been to blame for whatever trouble they got into. "You used to make up great games. Imaginary zoos or trips. Going on an adventure. Cops and robbers."

"Yeah. We were all pretty good at pretending." Her expression grew distant again. "Maybe too good."

"What else were we going to do? It wasn't like we had electronics or the latest toys. We had ourselves, whatever we could find outside. Rocks, sticks, stuff we scavenged from other people's garbage. We had to do something."

"It was really different raising my children. They expected to have all of the things that their friends did. To be able to do all of the same things. I was always trying to get them involved in imaginary games, role playing, stuff like that, and they just wanted to watch TV or play video games. We never had that choice. We had to use our imaginations."

Zachary nodded his agreement. Tyrrell gave a bit of a nod, but he wouldn't remember much. He had only been five or six when they had been separated. He wouldn't have much memory of those lean times and how much they had lacked that other kids had. Not having the latest and greatest toys had not been their worry. They had been more concerned with getting enough to eat, and avoiding the back of one parent's hand or the other's. Or worse.

"So they moved you out how long after we were separated?" Zachary asked. "Was it right away? They never gave me an update on how either one of you was doing. I used to ask Mrs. Pratt, but she would just give me the brushoff, like she didn't even know. I knew she knew. She just didn't want to tell me."

"I don't know how long we were together. Maybe a few months or a year. Then they decided I needed to go somewhere else."

"Did you get moved a lot?"

"No, not too much. I was mostly with one family, the Astors. They weren't too bad."

Zachary nodded slowly. It was good if she'd managed to stay in one place. Not like him, jumping from one family to another so quickly that sometimes he couldn't remember where to go home after school. And institutions and group homes in between, when his behavior or anxiety was too much for a family to handle.

"I was there until I was sixteen, almost seventeen," Heather offered. "Then... mostly groups homes and shelters until I aged out. I figured I'd better get myself straightened out and either get a husband or a job, or I wasn't going to be able to last on the streets."

"Yeah." Zachary too had been driven to find a way to support himself right away. Mr. Peterson—Lorne—was the one who had suggested putting his photography skills to use in a way that would bring in some money. Art obviously didn't make anything, but private investigator work had brought in enough to pay the rent most of the time. "So what did you get into?"

"Into?" she repeated vaguely. "Oh... I didn't ever really find a job that would make me anything. I was in and out of a few relationships before I found Grant. Since then... he's a good supporter. I didn't have to work when the kids were little. Then once they were gone... he said there wasn't any reason for me to be rushing out to finding a job just because they were old enough to look after themselves. So... I didn't. I just stayed at home. Kept house. Kept myself busy."

"Yeah? Good for you. I bet you were a really good mom. You were so good with us when we were kids."

"I don't think I was too bad at it. But... I don't think I ever really excelled at anything, including being a mother." She shook her head and made a face, as if he'd tried to feed her something bitter. "I didn't come here to talk about small-talk and get caught up on each other's lives."

Her words were clipped and abrupt. Zachary blinked at her. He thought that he'd been putting her at ease so that she would be able to share whatever it was she had come to him about. If it wasn't about the family and reuniting, then what was it?

Heather opened her mouth, but she seemed uncertain of herself, no longer able to speak. She looked at Tyrrell as if he might help her.

Tyrrell hesitated for a moment before venturing, "Heather saw reports of what happened with Teddy Archuro."

So had everyone else in the country. Even on the international stage. Teddy Archuro had been big news. A serial killer who for so many years, had flown under the police radar, primarily because the men that he used and killed were illegal immigrants whose status as missing persons was never reported to the police department. No missing persons meant no investigation, and he was able to keep torturing and killing men until Zachary had investigated the missing Jose Flores. Then everything had changed.

"Uh-huh," Zachary waited for Tyrrell to finish the thought and explain why Heather wanted to contact him after the announcement of his involvement with the capture of serial killer Teddy Archuro.

Tyrrell looked at Heather to see if she would explain it to Zachary, but she said nothing, chewing on the inside of her lip.

"Heather wants to know if you would investigate an old case for her. Something that happened a long time ago."

Zachary looked at Heather. "What kind of case?"

She stared down at her coffee. Zachary again regretted that he hadn't gotten one for himself as soon as he walked into the coffee shop, but he seemed to have missed the opportunity. He waited, not pressing Heather to answer. She would get to it faster if he waited than if he tried to force her. He'd learned at least that much from his investigations and interrogations as a private detective. The hard-hitting style of the noir private eye didn't work. At least, not for him.

"It happened a long time ago," she said. "I don't know whether there is anything you can even do now. Cold cases are... I know a lot of them never get solved."

"Some of them do get solved," Zachary assured her. "Especially as new technologies come into existence. There are a lot of cases that have been solved recently solely on forensic evidence where the technology to use it just wasn't there ten or twenty years ago, but now they can go back and test the materials that they already have to find something."

Heather nodded. "I know... I think about that... whenever I see one of those cases..."

"You never know until you try it. What kind of case was it?" Most of his high-profile cases had been murder. With Heather approaching him due to his appearance on the national news scene, he was anxious about whether it was another murder case. What kind of murder could Heather have been involved in years before?

"I saw on the news, about that serial killer, how he would... *abuse* the men he kidnapped before he killed them."

"Yes," Zachary agreed. He focused on the pulse pounding in his head. He didn't want to go back there. He didn't need to replay what had happened to him. He had been rescued, and everything that had happened between being kidnapped and being rescued was like it had happened to someone else. He didn't need to integrate it as his own memory.

"Zachary?"

He didn't even hear Heather or Tyrrell trying to call him back to earth. He just saw and heard and felt the things that had been done to him. He was in the grip of the memory, trying to pull away from what happened to his body. Trying to separate from it. He didn't want to allow it to become part of his consciousness.

"Zachary." Tyrrell's hand on his arm made Zachary jerk back instantly. He looked at Tyrrell in panic, then looked at Heather, rising an inch or two off of his seat, before he realized that he wasn't in any danger and plopped back down.

"Sorry." He swallowed. He looked at Heather. "What happened?"

"I... I was just telling you... about how... I didn't know whether..." she looked back at Tyrrell for help. He didn't offer anything, just looking from her to Zachary. "They said that he had captured you. They said it like it was just a few minutes. Was it... just a few minutes?"

It might have been only a few minutes or it might have been hours. Zachary had no way to measure the time that had passed. Teddy had given Zachary drugs so that he could act without any resistance. Zachary had been so doped up, there had been no chance of escape from the sadist who worked him over, doing whatever his twisted little brain could come up with. And yet, he'd been conscious the whole time.

"I don't know," he told Heather honestly. "It seemed like a long time."

Heather nodded, and he saw understanding in her eyes. Not just a surface emotion, but something that told him that she too understood that disassociation and time distortion. As if she, too, had been through a similar experience. He looked at her, hesitating to ask.

"What happened to you?"

~ ~ ~

He Was Not There is available for order now!

ABOUT THE AUTHOR

Award-winning and USA Today bestselling author P.D. (Pamela) Workman writes riveting mystery/suspense and young adult books dealing with mental illness, addiction, abuse, and other real-life issues. For as long as she can remember, the blank page has held an incredible allure and from a very young age she was trying to write her own books.

Workman wrote her first complete novel at the age of twelve and continued to write as a hobby for many years. She started publishing in 2015. She has won several literary awards from Library Services for Youth in Custody for her young adult fiction. She currently has over 40 published titles and can be found at pdworkman.com.

Born and raised in Alberta, Workman has been married for over 25 years and has one son.

~ ~ ~

Please visit P.D. Workman at pdworkman.com to see what else she is working on, to join her mailing list, and to link to her social networks.

~ ~ ~

If you enjoyed this book, please take the time to recommend it to other purchasers with a review or star rating and share it with your friends!

Lightning Source UK Ltd.
Milton Keynes UK
UKHW022211060820
367830UK00013B/1397